Look for all three

First You Run
Then You Hide
Now You Die

A thrilling new trio of Bullet Catcher books
by Roxanne St. Claire, available now and
coming soon from Po~~~~ ~~~

The Cr
Roxanne

Take Me

"Sexy, smart, and suspenseful, *Take Me Tonight* is an absolute
must-read. . . . St. Claire really rocks."
—Mariah Stewart, *New York Times* bestselling author

"Roxanne St. Claire has outdone herself . . . you actually have
to put *Take Me Tonight* down every once in awhile just to catch
your breath."
—Romance Reviews Today

"Definitely one of St. Claire's best and not to be missed!"
—*Romantic Times*

"Five stars! This story will drag you in and not let you out!"
—A Romance Review

"Nonstop excitement. . . . Readers swoon from the first action-
packed kidnapping until the final take-down and resolution. . . .
St. Claire gives just the right amount of suspense and balances
that with hot romance that is well worth the read."
—romancedesigns.com

Thrill Me to Death

"Sizzles like a hot Miami night."
—Erica Spindler, *New York Times* bestselling author

"Sultry romance with enticing suspense."
—*Publishers Weekly*

"Fast-paced, sexy romantic suspense. . . . A book that will keep the reader engrossed in the story from cover to cover."
—*Booklist*

"Roxanne St. Claire's got the sexy bodyguard thing down to an art form. . . . [She] expertly entertains through the novel's emotional twists and sensual turns, rocketing us through a series of exciting events . . . one heck of a love story."
—Michelle Buonfiglio, Lifetime TV.com

"St. Claire doesn't just push the envelope, she folds it into an intricate piece of origami for the reader's pleasure!"
—*Winter Haven News Chief* (Florida)

Kill Me Twice

"When it comes to dishing up great romantic suspense, St. Claire is the author you want. Sexy and scintillating . . . an exciting new series."
—*Romantic Times*

"*Kill Me Twice* literally vibrates off the pages with action, danger, and palpable sexual tension. St. Claire is exceptionally talented."
—*Winter Haven News Chief* (Florida)

"Jam-packed with characters, situations, suspense, and danger. The reader will be dazzled. . . ."

—*Rendezvous*

Killer Curves

"A sleek, sexy, and very American romantic suspense novel."
—*Publishers Weekly*

"This book really grabbed me . . . refreshingly cool."
—*Orlando Sentinel* (Florida)

"A guaranteed powerful, sexy and provocative read."
—Carly Phillips, *New York Times* bestselling author

French Twist

"Great reading!"

—*Romantic Times*

"Intriguing suspense that crackles with sexual tension."
—*Winter Haven News Chief* (Florida)

Tropical Getaway

"Sizzling suspense and scorching sensuality!"
—Teresa Medeiros

"Romance, danger, and adventure . . . in just the right combination."

—*Booklist*

Also by Roxanne St. Claire

What You Can't See, with Allison Brennan et al.

Take Me Tonight

I'll Be Home for Christmas, with Linda Lael Miller et al.

Thrill Me to Death

Kill Me Twice

Killer Curves

French Twist

Tropical Getaway

Hit Reply

FIRST
YOU
RUN

Roxanne St. Claire

POCKET STAR BOOKS
New York   London   Toronto   Sydney

Pocket Star Books
A Division of Simon & Schuster, Inc.
1230 Avenue of the Americas
New York, NY 10020

This book is a work of fiction. Names, characters, places, and incidents either are products of the author's imagination or are used fictitiously. Any resemblance to actual events or locales or persons, living or dead, is entirely coincidental.

First Pocket Star Books paperback edition April 2008

POCKET STAR BOOKS and colophon are registered trademarks of Simon & Schuster, Inc.

For information about special discounts for bulk purchases, please contact Simon & Schuster Special Sales at 1-800-456-6798 or business@simonandschuster.com.

Designed by Carl Galtan

Manufactured in the United States of America

10 9 8 7 6 5 4 3 2 1

ISBN-13: 978–1–4165–4906–2
ISBN-10:   1–4165–4906–4

Acknowledgments

As always, a vast number of people offer time, talent, and advice to help me write books that are as realistic as fiction can be. My deepest appreciation goes to this team of experts:

Terry Irene Blain, writer, friend, and traveler who graciously took on the job of being my eyes, ears, fingers, and feet in Balboa Park, San Diego.

Dr. Tracy Arden, Department of Anthropology, University of Miami, who shared insights about academia and anthropology.

Marta Barber, President of the Institute of Maya Studies, who offered fact-checking assistance and guidance on glyphs, while across the country, the staff of San Diego's Museum of Man answered many questions about security that I'm certain they rarely get asked, and worry when they do.

My favorite Tassie and very first fan, Cheryl Mackey, who introduced me to the language, customs, and breathtaking men of the Tasmanian Special Ops Group. Fletch is for you!

Judy Watts of the *Charleston Post and Courier,* for the terrific insights into that city's history; to Nina Bruhns for the customized tour of Charleston; and to all of the generous romance writers in South Carolina who have shown me Southern hospitality at its finest

Poppy Reiffen and Kerensa Brougham, genuine California girls, for the detailed information about the neighborhoods of Oakland and the helpful e-tours of UC Berkeley.

My very own Bullet Catcher and "Glock Guy" Roger Cannon, who knows enough about weapons to keep me from taking a lousy shot.

A sweeping debt of gratitude to the entire team at Pocket Books, especially Micki Nuding for consistently excellent editorial skills, and my outstanding literary agent, Kim Whalen of Trident Media Group, who worries about everything I don't want to think about.

Last, but never, ever least, thank you to Rich, Dante, and Mia, who wait patiently while I spend hours with people who don't exist. I'm so proud to call you mine.

*In loving memory of Cecelia Feldmeier Zink,
my mother, my motivator, my number-one fan.
I miss you every day.*

PROLOGUE

Charleston, South Carolina, 1978

EILEEN STAFFORD FIGURED she had to be insane.

Why else would she be hovering in the shadows, waiting for the married man who'd wrecked her life, busted her heart, and made her give up the only thing that mattered to her? She sometimes thought that the trauma of that childbirth had ruined her ability to think straight.

Why else would she have agreed to meet him in an alley at one in the morning?

She rubbed her bare arms against the April chill.

It wasn't as if he wanted her back. But when he'd called, a glimmer of hope had flickered in her stomach. After all, they had a bond now—they were parents together. Regardless of the decisions she'd made.

Maybe he'd love her again. Maybe she could undo the mistake she'd made eight months ago, at that farmhouse on Sapphire Trail. If only he loved her.

She snorted softly. He'd never loved her. He'd *used* her. On the desk. In his car. On the floor. In his own home, on the nights his wife attended a DAR meeting. That's what powerful men did to their secretaries.

Revulsion rolled through her. He'd called her here for a reason. Money, so she'd never tell their secret? Fine. She'd take every dollar he offered, and he could save his precious reputation.

As she squinted to see her wristwatch, she heard a whisper of sound and the shuffle of a footstep, soft enough to tickle her neck with apprehension. Turning, she couldn't see anything but fingers of ivy cascading down the brick wall of the narrow passageway and a cement building with air-conditioning units and two trash cans on the other side of the alley.

Instinctively, she backed away, moving closer to the light, closer to the gate that guarded a church grave-yard. She wasn't superstitious, but hundred-year-old headstones and gnarled tree roots on a moonless night were just a little too spooky.

Is that why he picked this spot? Because he knew it scared her? Or did he remember the time they'd met in this alley before and made love against this very wall?

She closed her hands over the cool iron gate, and goose bumps rose when it opened. It squeaked an eerie note.

Footsteps pulled her attention back to the far end of the alley. She could barely make out the shadow of a man and a woman, walking quickly toward her. Her heart kicked up.

She inched the gate wider and slipped inside, stepping behind the wall. Had they seen her?

Their footsteps grew louder, followed by the woman's voice. Then the man's.

Eileen sucked in a breath. *Her* man's.

She flattened against the wall and listened. Why had he called her here, then showed up with another woman? And not his wife—that was clear from the slender silhouette. She slowly inched out from her hiding place, blinking into the darkness.

He had the woman against the wall, his grunt mixing with her moan. *Was* that him? She couldn't tell. He wore a long, dark coat, and the woman's hands were wrapped around his head, covering his hair.

It sounded like him—the panting, horny bastard. Is that why he'd summoned her here? To prove that it was over, that she was replaced? Fury shot through her, and she opened her mouth just as he backed away from the woman. The woman said something, he moved jerkily, and then an explosion cracked the night.

Jesus God in heaven. He shot her.

Over his shoulder, all Eileen could see was the face of the woman the instant she died.

Clamping her hand over her mouth to stifle a scream, Eileen dropped back behind the wall, sliding to the ground as shock and disbelief rocked her. Running footsteps—his footsteps, a *killer's* footsteps—scraped the stones, then disappeared onto Cumberland.

She couldn't breathe. A dead woman was ten feet away, shot by the man Eileen thought she once loved. A man who'd sent her here. Why? To witness it?

No. No—he'd set her up. It was so like him. He could do anything. Didn't he always say that, laughing and cocksure, when they lay tangled in sheets or half-undressed on top of his desk?

I can do anything, Leenie. I fucking own this town.

He could even commit cold-blooded murder . . . and set her up to get the blame.

With shaking hands, she pushed her hair off her face, her brain frantic for a way out.

Run. Before the gunshot brought the police and they found her here. She whipped open the gate and took one last look at the woman, blood oozing from her stomach, her eyes open and lifeless.

What had this beautiful blonde's sin been? Had she said the fateful words, too? *I'm going to have a baby.*

Swallowing bile, Eileen ran, her legs wobbling. She tripped on a cobblestone, stumbled, and gasped. If she could just get to her car without being seen, she could get home. The streets of Charleston were abandoned. No one knew she was here.

Trying to be calm, she forced herself to maintain a brisk walk, just in case someone was watching, all the way to her Dodge Dart. She opened the driver's door, slipped in, grabbed the keys from under the seat where she always hid them, and started the car.

She put the car in reverse, then placed a shaking

foot on the accelerator. She hit the pedal too hard, and the car jerked back, tapping the car behind her and yanking a grunt of despair from her chest.

I can do anything, Leenie.

She had to get home.

With each passing mile, her breathing slowed, her shaking stopped. Had she even seen that? Maybe she'd imagined it. Maybe this was just a bad dream.

She reached the Ashley River, the rickety old bridge the last barrier between her and home. Blowing out a breath, she glanced into her rearview mirror—and saw a flashing blue light behind her. How long had that cop been following her? Her heart slid around like the back end of the Dodge as she checked the speedometer and smashed the brakes. Thirty-five. Relief and worry all warred in her muddled brain, but she managed to pull over. Before she even touched the handle, the door was whipped open.

"Get out of the car."

She froze, blinking and shading her eyes, unable to see anything but the blinding light in her face. She pushed herself from the car and saw another policeman, aiming a gun.

"Was I speeding?" She sounded remarkably composed.

Wordlessly, the first cop moved his flashlight to the passenger seat. His eyes narrowed. She turned, following the beam, somehow knowing what she was about to see.

The gun. It had been right next to her all the way home.

"Eileen Stafford, you're under arrest for murder. You have the right to remain silent . . ."

And she would. He knew exactly how to keep her silent. He could do anything.

With a sob, she fell to the ground and let them take her away.

CHAPTER
ONE

Astor Cove, NY
The Hudson River Valley
Spring, 2008

ADRIEN FLETCHER WANTED something, and he wanted it bad enough to skip his beloved Sunday afternoon rugby game, remove his single hoop earring, cover his Aborigine axe blade tattoo with a long-sleeved shirt, and make small talk with his boss.

Amused and curious, Lucy Sharpe obliged.

"The client on the diamond drop sent me an e-mail last night," she told him, clicking through her BlackBerry for the message from the Dutch jewel trader. "He said you performed the job flawlessly and has requested you as his Bullet Catcher escort next month, when he plans to deliver another forty million dollars' worth of . . ." She smiled as she read the rest. "Useless overpriced carbon to the jewelers of the world."

Fletch chuckled, deepening a set of heartbreak dimples. "He's a good bloke, that Maurice Keizer."

"He's also one of our very best clients. I've already e-mailed him back that you will be assigned to him next month." She set the device on the desk. "I'm delighted with your work for him, and for the company, Fletch."

He tested the fortitude of Lucy's Louis XVI salon chair with a backward tilt of six-foot-one, two hundred pounds of sinew and muscle. "Then it's a perfect time to ask a favor."

She lifted her brows. "You can always ask me a favor."

"That's what I like about you, Luce, and that's why I'm here."

"Here in the United States working for the Bullet Catchers or here in my library on a fine spring day, when you'd rather be getting covered with mud and bruises?"

He glanced at his watch and shook his head, his honey-toned mane grazing his shoulders. "Game's long over. The boys are on their last pint of Four X by now. But it's the latter. I'm here for my next assignment."

"I thought you were taking a month off. I expected you to be headed to Tasmania to have that conversation with your father you've been putting off for most of your life."

He let the front legs of the chair thud back into place, tumbling one burnished lock toward a sharp cheekbone. "Don't you have some unwritten rule about not throwing confidences back in your men's faces?"

She purposely let the sincerity show in her expression. "I'm not throwing anything back in your face. I respect what you've shared with me. I'm simply giving you time to do what you need to do—for purely selfish reasons, of course. I like my team to be as fit emotionally as they are physically. You put your life on the line every day to protect principals, conduct investigations, and ensure the overall security of our clients. You can't do that with the perfection I demand if your personal affairs aren't in order."

He shooed that off with a wave. "The personal stuff is aces right now, Luce. I work hard, play harder, and rather like putting my life on the line. I'm here for a mate."

"A friend of yours needs to hire the Bullet Catchers?"

"Sort of. And I'd like to use the time between official assignments to take the job, which might require your resources and . . ." He paused and pinned her with a steady gaze. "Your support."

Her curiosity ratcheted up at his tone. He clearly wasn't expecting to get it easily. "What's the project?"

"I need to find a woman. I don't know who she is or where she is. And when I find her, chances are I'm going to get her naked, rock her world, and then make her wish I were dead."

A smile pulled at Lucy's mouth. "And how is this different from any other Saturday night for you?"

"Because this sheila might very well hold the key to solving a thirty-year-old murder."

She propped her elbows on her Victorian writing table, nestled her chin onto her knuckles, and met his level gaze. "Start from the beginning."

He took a breath, nodding. For a man whose personal hallmark—and occasional downfall—was impetuosity, this deliberation surprised and alerted her.

"My friend is working on a case to reunite a woman with a child she gave up at birth. A while back, he was digging up information for another client who was sold through a South Carolina black-market adoption ring back in the seventies. Evidently, a rural midwife ran a baby-selling operation from a farmhouse on a road known as Sapphire Trail. The whole deal was blown apart in a bust in 1982, and ever since, there's been an ongoing effort to reunite something like a thousand babies with their birth mothers."

Lucy nodded. "I've had some cases of black-market adoption searches, and I've heard about the Sapphire Trail babies. All the birth certs are falsified, and the leads are very, very hard to follow. But it can be done. How much documentation did they discover when they broke the ring?"

"Some." He stroked the shadow of whiskers that lined his jaw and the bit of golden hair under his lip. "My friend did locate the son of his client, and that case is closed. Now another Sapphire Trail mother has persuaded him to help her find her daughter, too."

"And you want to help him, and this other mother, find her child?" Why was this something she would object to?

"Yes. But it's a bit more complicated than that. This birth mother is serving life for murder one, and that sentence is about to end because she's been diagnosed with leukemia."

"So she wants to have this reunion with a lost child before she dies?"

"Yes. Especially since a bone-marrow transplant from a living relative might give her a few extra years. Years that might give her the time she needs to prove her innocence."

Her expression must have been skeptical, because Fletch leaned forward to plead his case. "My friend believes her. He really does. He's a bonzer investigator and thinks her case was botched from the beginning. So time is of the essence."

Time was always of the essence to innocent people in jail. Especially when they were dying. "Fletch, if you'd like to conduct a private investigation that could save someone's life and even lead to the release of someone wrongly accused, surely you know I'd have no problem with that. You are free for a month, until the Keizer diamond drop is scheduled. If you need to tap into our database or work with Sage Valentine's research and investigation team, by all means, you may. How much information do you have so far?"

He looked a bit relieved, but not completely. Did he really think she'd take a stand against a standard adoption search? Something wasn't right.

"I have a list of infants that were sold from the Sapphire Trail operation during the six-week period that this woman says she gave birth," he replied. "But the list only has the names they were given, not the names of their birth mothers. There are eight or nine female babies, who would be about thirty-one now. I'm going to track them down and interview them all."

"Why doesn't your friend do that himself, and how are you going to be sure you have the right woman? Some might not even know they were adopted, and their birth mothers' names might mean nothing to them."

"True," he agreed. "But evidently, this baby was marked with a tattoo."

Lucy gave him a look of pure incredulity. "Really."

"I believe my mate has the facts right," Fletch said, his strong jaw set in defiance. "He has very good instinct, and he's dependable and smart."

Had she said he wasn't? "Which brings me back to my first question. Why can't this man go interview these women himself?"

"Because he'd like to dig into the murder investigation files in Charleston while I find the daughter. Since the mother's sick, there might not be time for him to do both, so we thought we'd do the job simultaneously. Like I said, he's an ace investigator."

Lucy's fingers began to tingle, the way they used to when she was an operative for the CIA and she just *knew* that right around the corner, someone was waiting to take her down. That tingle had saved her life more than once. "Who is this friend of yours?"

Fletch shifted in his chair. He glanced down, then back at her.

The soft scuff of a footstep outside her library door broke the silence. Lucy looked over Fletch's shoulder, and suddenly all that hesitancy, that "you're going to hate this one" tone, was crystal-clear.

"Good afternoon, Ms. Sharpe."

Jack Culver leaned against the door jamb, his hands tucked into the pockets of khaki trousers, his thick, dark hair tousled as if he'd just rolled out of bed, his jaw stubbled.

She resisted the urge to swear and thanked God for the training not to move a single muscle in response to a man she'd stripped of responsibility and fired last year. Instead, she stood. "We're finished here."

"Aw, Luce, come on." Fletch shot up. "Just hear him out. Tell her the story, Jack."

She should have figured out what brought Fletch all the way up to the Hudson River Valley on a Sunday afternoon. He and Jack were as close as brothers.

She kept her gaze solidly on the Bullet Catcher she still respected. "What you do in your free time is your business, Adrien." He flinched at the use of his first name. "I don't mind, as long as you don't get yourself killed and you return to work when I need you. But this time . . ." She cut her glance to Jack. "I would counsel you to steer clear."

Jack kicked up one side of his mouth in a half-smile. A move that might weaken the resolve of most females, but not her. His sexy smile was wasted on her.

"I told you, Fletch." Jack's smile widened. "The woman has a heart of stone and a soul of steel."

She stabbed him with a glare that had buckled the knees of men far braver, stronger, and smarter than Jack Culver. "You are not welcome in this house or at any gathering of the Bullet Catchers. I don't give help to people who lie—"

"I did not lie."

"By omission," she volleyed.

"Lucy, listen to him," Fletch insisted.

"I don't want to hear—"

"Eileen Stafford did not commit murder," Jack said, straightening. "She's been rotting in jail for a crime she didn't commit for thirty years, and now she's going to die. I believe her in my gut, Lucy. She needs to stay alive long enough for me to prove it. To do that, we need her daughter. If we succeed, you get all the credit."

"I'm not interested in credit."

"Well, this job doesn't pay, so you might have to take kudos instead of your usual astronomical rates. That, plus the fact that you helped free yet another person unjustly imprisoned. You take those jobs pro bono all the time."

She crossed her arms. Of course, he would zero in on one of the things that really mattered to her; they all knew her pet projects. "There are a lot of wrongly accused people on Death Row, Jack. I can't save them all."

"You don't have to save them all. Just give me Fletch, and let him use your resources. I believe Eileen Stafford when she says she's innocent, and I also think there's just something noble about giving a dying woman a chance to live."

Lucy blew out a breath of pure disgust. "Oh, please."

"Come on, Luce." His voice dropped low. That New York City–tinged baritone of a jaded cop always snagged her. "Doesn't everyone deserve a second chance?" He had the audacity to wink. As if that could make her forget that he'd lied and it damn near cost the life of one of her best men.

"Not everyone," she said, pointing a red nail at the door. "You can wait downstairs, Jack. I'd like privacy with Adrien."

He nodded, his dark eyes giving nothing away. No hope, no gratitude, no glimmer of apology for the misery he'd caused a year ago.

When he was out of earshot, Lucy turned on Fletch. "Why are you doing this? You know that man is . . . dubious."

"I know that man is the best mate I ever had. I know that what happened a year ago almost killed Dan Gallagher, and I know how you feel about that. But bloody hell, Lucy, I wouldn't be *alive* if it weren't for Jack. He needs help, and I'm only doing what he'd do for me."

"He needs more help than you can give him."

"He's gotten his act together. He's got his own PI business now. And he's sober. He just wants a chance to prove he still has what it takes."

She held up her index finger. "You have one month. If you need my resources, let me know, and I'll decide on a case-by-case basis. After one month you will be on a plane to Antwerp, ready to escort one of my top, astronomical-rate-paying clients on another diamond drop. Do what you have to between now and then. But do not, under any circumstances, expect me to aid, abet, or otherwise enable Jack Culver."

"Ace by me, Luce."

She took a deep breath, surprised at how much seeing Jack again had spiked her blood pressure. "Just tell me one thing. I understand why this news might rock a woman's world and make her hate you, but why would you have to get her naked?"

He grinned. "How else am I going to find that tattoo?"

"Ladies and gentlemen, it is the great honor of Page Nine Bookstore to introduce Dr. Miranda Lang, assistant professor of linguistic anthropology at Berkeley, an expert in Maya studies, and the author of *The Cataclysn't: The End of the Myth, Not of the World*. Please join me in welcoming Dr. Lang, who will read a brief excerpt from her work, answer your questions, and sign copies of her book."

Miranda nodded her thanks to the store manager and started across the "Page Stage." She'd been at the university long enough to know this was a big deal. A camera flashed—probably one of her students—as she stood at the podium and looked out at the crowd of fifty or sixty people. A big turnout, especially considering that most of the anthro faculty would come only if they thought she'd fall flat on her face.

She smiled at the crowd. With her book finally published and her tour set up, that wasn't going to happen. Especially since Dr. Stuart Rosevich himself was in the front row, beaming at her. She beamed right back, hoping the head of Berkeley's impressive anthropology department knew of her gratitude for the chance he'd given a young Ph.D. Next to him, Adam DeWitt smiled more moderately, but it was sweet of him to show up tonight after their awkward conversation last week.

A few rows behind them were two low-level lecturers from the department and a few TAs. The rest were your basic anthro and linguistic nerds, some Maya enthusiasts, and the usual intellectuals who frequented readings at the Nine.

"Good evening." She aimed her gaze just above the last row, a speaker's trick that gave the appearance of eye contact. "The Long Count calendar," she read, "is the defining touchstone of the ancient Maya civilization, but that's all it is, not a prediction that the world is about to end. On the contrary studying the calendar can assure us that we will wake up on the morning of December 21, 2012, just as alive as we were on December 20. There will be no asteroid, no Armageddon, no astronomical conjunction in the heavens. There will be no cataclysm, no doomsday."

A pale-haired young man near the front started coughing, and she paused, waiting for him to finish.

"If you study their culture, their language, and their symbols as I have," she continued, "the Maya did not believe the world would end on December 21, 2012, despite the fact that their calendar and computations ended then."

She looked up to fake eye contact again, only to encounter some powerfully real eye contact. A tall, muscular man standing in the back burned her with a stare so intense it made her stumble over her words.

Wow—who let *him* into this mecca of geekdom?

She forced her attention back to the page. "Although some people believe this proves the end of the world is imminent, my research of the Maya hieroglyphics proves that is only a myth. There is no threat that something in the heavens will cause havoc on earth. There is no proof that December 21, 2012, will be the last day of human existence on earth."

She stole another glance at the man in the back. What was he doing here? Men who spent their days doing scholarly research didn't have bodies that belonged in the Temple of Warriors, or golden brown hair that curled over their collars and brushed their square, unshaven jaws. They wore glasses, not gold hoop earrings.

And they did *not* look at a woman the way he was looking at her.

She saw Dr. Rosevich, then Adam, follow her gaze. Oh, great. She'd been caught checking out the stud in the back.

There were people who didn't want her to go public with her theory, wackos who thought The End Was Near and her research was not just wrong, but harmful, who would love to see her book tank.

Maybe their plan was to infiltrate her book signings with a broad-chested, long-haired, magic-eyed decoy to make her lose her place and feel stupid.

Good strategy. It was working.

He shook back his honey-colored mane and the light caught the glint at his left ear. Lifting one side of his mouth, he cocked his head and melted her with a blistering stare of pure sex.

Unbelievable. He was *flirting* with her. And she . . . forgot what she was saying. Completely.

She covered with a sip of water. *No flirting with bronze-dipped gods.*

"Much has been made of the Maya Long Count and the arithmetic that arrived at the end date of December 21, 2012. Much has been made of the fact that the date corresponds astronomically with the date 0.0.00 in the Long Count calendar. But—"

"Much has been made because it's true!" the cougher yelled, leaping to his feet.

Behind him, a woman stood. "Of course it is! Millions of people think you are doing the world an enormous disservice by negating the astronomical impact of 2012 when something up there . . ." she pointed skyward. "Hits something down here."

"Then *millions* of people can stop worrying," Miranda said calmly and returned to the book. "The Maya calendar fixates on a particular point of time that modern scholars believe represented the creation of time according to complex Maya cosmology. However—"

"They knew the beginning, and they knew the end. How can you ignore that?" The pasty-skinned man pointed at her, wild blue eyes sparking like gas flames.

"Because if you understand how to read the Maya glyphs, as I do, the—"

"I can read Maya glyphs!" he declared. "And they say that the end of the world will happen during a cosmogenesis on December 21, 2012, and only a chosen group will survive!"

"That's right!" Another college student. "And people will die because of what you're spouting just to get rich!"

The man in the back moved slightly, his posture becoming alert as his attention shifted to the hecklers.

She gave a self-conscious smile to Dr. Rosevich and continued to read from memory, since the words danced around.

"So what if you're wrong?" the one with the wild eyes shouted, overriding her.

A girl, young enough to be a freshman in her Intro to Culture class, joined in. "People deserve to know the truth. You're playing with lives and human safety. The government needs to do something, and the first thing they can do is stop blind optimism and stupidity!"

A few more stood in the second row, sending prickly discomfort down Miranda's spine.

"That's what you're selling!" shouted another young woman. "A false sense of security!"

"You're burying the facts, just like they buried Maya history!"

"The facts are not changed or buried," Miranda replied, working to maintain her cool under the steamroller that had just moved through the room. A few audience members laughed nervously and two left. Dr. Rosevich stared at her as Adam shifted in his seat and glanced around.

In the back of the room, her long-haired bronze god was gone.

The one with the wild eyes lunged into the aisle,

opened a copy of her book, and read a line, his mocking tone changing the meaning of her words.

"That's not at all what I meant—"

He threw the book onto the ground and turned to another woman, seizing a paperback from her hands and waving it. Miranda recognized it as self-published trash warning of death and destruction in December 2012.

"This is the truth!" Wild Eyes announced, suddenly looking much older and more in control than the twenty-five-year-old she'd first thought he was. "This is the fact! This is the only truth!"

Suddenly he bounded toward the front of the room, and Miranda instinctively backed up. She hit a wall of man and spun around to come face to face with wide shoulders. Higher, she met amber eyes that had gone from flirtatious to dead serious.

He gripped her upper arm and in one move had her two feet from the podium. "Go. Now." He held her firmly, walking her to the railing that overlooked the first floor.

"Wait a second!" She tried to yank out of his grasp, but it didn't loosen.

He leaned close to her ear. "I'm going to help you. *Move*."

The store manager ran up the stairs, horror on her face at the chaos in the room. "What's going on?" she demanded, breathless.

The man steered around her. "Dr. Lang needs a safe place to go. Now."

Without questioning, the young woman thrust out

a huge ring of keys. "The silver one will get you into the stockroom downstairs. It's right past the—"

He seized the ring. "I'll find it." With a gentle push, he urged Miranda forward. "Move. Fast."

She managed to free her arm and glare at him. "Who are you?"

"At this moment, house security. You want to stay and be eaten by the natives or get somewhere safe?"

Her linguist's brain stalled. His voice was richly, beautifully accented with the distinct sheared sounds of Australia, and it matched him perfectly. A voice with purpose, with poetry in every vowel. She glanced over her shoulder, to where the instigator ranted on, standing on a chair and flipping flyers to the crowd.

"Go to this Web site," Wild Eyes called out. "Find out the truth. Find out how to avoid the inevitable." He paused to meet Miranda's gaze with one full of hate.

Holding on to her rescuer's powerful arm, she flew down the steps, turned a corner behind a stack of reference books, and hustled toward a door in the back. After stabbing the key into the lock, he threw open the door, stuck his head in, and checked it out.

"All right," he said, pushing her into the closet-sized room jammed floor to ceiling with cardboard boxes and the gluelike smell of freshly printed books. "In you go, luv."

Was he leaving her there? Locking her in? The wave of panic subsided as he stepped into the room and closed the door behind him.

"Are you all right?" he asked, the concern unmistakable in that lyrical voice.

She nodded. She would be as soon as her heart stopped pounding her ribs. "I'm fine. I just . . . didn't . . ." She blew out a breath and forced her shoulders to relax. "Thank you. I didn't see that coming."

He guided her to a cracked vinyl chair. "Quite a unique crowd you draw."

"I never dreamed the crazies would be here."

"The crazies? Who are they?"

She looked up at him—way up, since he had to be more than six feet tall—and searched his face. Who was this lifesaver who swooped in from nowhere? Was he one of them and this all a ploy to ruin her first event?

But she didn't see anything crazy about him, only intense whiskey-colored eyes framed in thick lashes the same shade as his too-long hair and the shadow of a soul patch on his chin. Dangerous, yes, but not crazy.

"Who are the crazies?" he repeated.

"A group of zealots who call themselves the Armageddon Movement. Who are *you?*"

He smiled, adding attention-grabbing dimples to his growing list of attributes. "Adrien Fletcher." He held out his hand, and she shook it. His palm was wide, strong, and masculine.

"Miranda Lang," she replied.

"The famous author." *Fie-mous oh-thah.* Oh, that was pretty. And just in case the accent weren't endearing enough, he added a little wink, as if they shared an inside joke.

"Not so famous." She released her hand. "No one's ever heard of me."

He pointed over his shoulder, in the general direction of the second-floor reading area. "Evidently those people have."

"Fans like that, I don't need." She frowned a little. "Why are you here? You don't look like a regular at readings."

"I just wandered in a bit ago. I saw there was an author reading, and I was curious. Didn't expect I'd have to work tonight."

"Work?"

"I'm a security specialist."

"Whoa." She drew back, a half-laugh caught in her throat. "Talk about serendipity."

"Talk about it," he agreed, unleashing another blast of dimples.

They made her heart beat even faster than the rough crowd. She stood and smoothed her skirt. "I think it's safe to go out now."

"Not entirely, but we'll check and then duck out."

Disappointment dropped her back onto the chair. "My first signing, totally ruined. I won't sell a single book."

"Don't be so sure." He reached for her hand and tugged her up. Despite Miranda's five-foot-six-plus-two-inch-heel height, they weren't eye to eye. More like eye to soul patch. "Controversy is usually good marketing."

Outside the stock room, only a few people meandered about, the commotion now over. Toward the front of the store she spied her table, the stack of books as tall as it had been when she'd walked in. A bottle of water sat in a ring of condensation, two pens next to it.

"Maybe I should just sign a few stock copies," she said wistfully.

He nudged her forward with a shake of his head. "Not a good idea. Anyone could be waiting to renew their heated debate."

"You're right." She walked with him to the front of the store. "Anyway, the night is spoiled, and over."

"It doesn't have to be over," he said, his voice rich with implication.

At the cash register, the clerk held out a plastic bag to him. "Here you go, sir. The book you purchased."

He nodded thanks, took the bag, and led her out to the dimly lit sidewalk. Then he opened the bag. "Would you sign it for me?"

"You bought my book? Before you heard me speak?"

"I thought they might run out."

"Yeah, *that* was likely." She found a pen in her purse and opened the cover, thinking of the right words to thank him and maybe impress him. She looked down at the open page, the pen poised. But all she saw was a piece of white paper with stark, dark letters across it.

Have dinner with me.

She stared at the boldly written words. All confidence, all flair and total command. And no question mark at the end.

"For an expert in the nuances of language, you sure are taking your time," he said.

She slowly lifted her gaze to meet his, drinking in

the smile, the dimples, the twinkle of invitation and attraction in his eyes. "When did you write this?"

"When I saw you walk into the store." He lifted one eyebrow. "C'mon, Miranda. At the very least, I can keep you out of harm's way for a few hours."

Under all that hair, an earring glinted. Under that tight T-shirt, a tattoo peeked. Under that lyrical voice, a man who had targeted her before she knew he existed.

He *was* harm's way.

And for some reason, that appealed to her. "Yes. I'll have dinner with you."

CHAPTER
TWO

"I HAVE A friend who calls this stuff truth serum." Miranda lifted the sake carafe and offered it across the low Japanese table.

"I've a friend who calls it vinegar." The ceramic container appeared tiny in Adrien Fletcher's large hands. He poured deftly, filling both cups and offering her one. "*Kampai*, Miranda."

"*Kampai*, Adrien." She tapped his cup, then sipped the warm, sweet rice wine, noticing he only let it touch his lips. The liquid burned her throat and moved through her whole body.

"Most of my mates call me Fletch." He stroked the sexy little triangle under his full lower lip. No doubt its only function was to tickle a woman when he kissed her.

"I'll stick with Adrien," she said.

"Suit yourself. So, have you ever been to Japan?"

he asked, continuing the casual, friendly conversation he'd started as they walked to the sushi restaurant on a quiet side street off College Avenue.

"Not yet. But I've never been to a lot of places that are best reached by air."

"You don't fly?" He looked perplexed and disbelieving. "At all? Ever?"

"Nope. Never."

"Why not?"

She shrugged. "If I knew why I have the phobia, I'd conquer it."

"But isn't an anthropologist, by nature, someone who likes to travel?"

"I travel by car and boat. I've been all over Central America for my studies, and I've sailed to Europe twice. Man saw the earth before there were planes. It doesn't stop me from living." She was rationalizing, dammit. "As a matter of fact, I'm going on a book tour tomorrow."

"By car?"

She nodded. "A cross-country tour that lasts six weeks."

"Six weeks?" He sounded genuinely disappointed. "Will you have some time off? Can you get back here at all?"

She picked up her sake and teasingly touched his cup. "We just met, Adrien. You want me to adjust my schedule for you already?"

He leaned forward, sending a zing of something earthy down to Miranda's toes. "I'll be gone in a month."

She managed a *que será* shrug. Jaw-droppingly sexy men who pursued her with secret notes and intimate dinners didn't land in her lap on a regular basis. Balding archeology professors who wanted to discuss the fine points of the hieroglyphics at Tikal and maybe get the name of her literary agent, yeah. Those guys were all over her. But this one . . .

"It's a shame that you don't fly," he said, his lovely clipped consonants ricocheting over the table as he casually shook his hair back. "You'll never see Tassie, then. Beautiful island, it is."

Byu-ee-ful ah-lind. Byu-ee-ful voice. Byu-ee-ful man. "I might see it," she said. "There are whole Web sites devoted to getting us aero-challenged folks around. It takes some time, money, and creativity, but there's a boat, train, or car to anywhere. Is that where you're from? Tasmania?"

"Yes, but please . . ." His dimples deepened to deadly. "No devil jokes. I've heard them all."

"I bet you have." She closed the menu. "The sushi boat is great here. So, are you visiting, or do you live here now?"

"I'm in the Bay Area on business, but I make my home in New York. I travel a lot, so it's not much more than an empty apartment and a place to crash after my Sunday ruggers match. Uh, rugby."

"What does someone in the security business do, exactly?"

"I work for a company that runs investigations and threat assessments, developing security plans for high-profile individuals. Sometimes I protect them or escort them to dangerous places. Sometimes I merely find them. Sometimes I just warn them when they are in danger."

"That's interesting," she said, cracking her chopsticks apart. "Who sends you off looking for these lost and endangered people?"

"Our clients"—he sipped his sake—"are confidential."

She couldn't help but smile. "How mysterious."

"Not really. I'm basically a ridgy-didge bodyguard, which isn't mysterious in the least."

"But it is handy. You certainly were tonight." She made a mock toast with her cup. "Thank you again for the rescue."

His eyes glinted just enough to make her feel as if she'd already downed the whole carafe of sake. "Tell me about your crazies. Have you dealt with them before?"

"From what I can gather, the Armageddon Movement is a small community—online, mostly. I don't know who runs it, but they fervently believe that the world is going to end in 2012, and the mission appears to be to recruiting members who buy into their dogma. They're opposed to anyone who tries to speak sensibly about the Long Count calendar, since they're hell-bent on convincing the world that it will end. As I said, crazy people. And they don't seem to be too well organized."

"That's where you're wrong," he said. "What happened in that bookstore was very well orchestrated. I had riot-control training in a former life, and that event was, in my professional opinion, choreographed to do exactly what it did."

"To stop me?"

"To scare you."

She straightened. "I wasn't scared. I was embarrassed and furious, but not scared."

"You should have been. Group threats like that have a tendency to escalate. A couple more of those people, one or two who get aggressive, and you've gone from a bit of heckling to seriously hostile in five seconds. You'd best watch your back on this book tour."

Her stomach dipped. "I really don't think they are a force to be reckoned with."

"Is your tour schedule public?"

"Of course. It's on my publisher's Web site and mine. It would be counterproductive to keep a book tour secret."

The waitress arrived, and he ordered sushi boats, then returned his full focus to her. "Is this the first time they've made physical contact?"

She thought about the question. Had someone actually made physical contact with her? "A few have approached me on campus, but I just don't think they're capable of . . ." Her voice trailed off.

"What?" he asked, leaning forward. "What is it?"

"There have been some bizarre problems with my book already."

"Like what?"

"A warehouse fire in New Jersey that burned thousands of books, and a derailed train that sent half my print run into a river in Tennessee."

"And you thought these events were coincidences?"

"I wondered, but my publisher was convinced it was just really bad luck, and I want to believe that," she admitted. "Although they didn't reprint the lost copies."

"You need protection."

She dropped her forehead onto the heel of her hand. "Oh, please. I really don't want to have this conversation."

"Why not?"

"Because I don't want to be afraid of them. Of *anything*." A man like this would never understand. A big, tough, fearless man who probably faced danger for fun? "I don't want to be paranoid."

He shook his head. "It's just plain insane not to have protection when someone is obviously sabotaging you. They'll only get more aggressive."

"Do me a favor," she said. "Change the subject."

"All right, then. Tell me, is your fear of flying why you stayed in Atlanta and did all your studies at Emory? So you didn't have to get on a plane?"

He *knew* that?

Her expression must have given away her question, because he tapped the Page Nine bag next to him. "Your biography on the cover flap." He leaned toward her and whispered, "You're being paranoid about the wrong things and the wrong people."

"Well, let's see. I just got verbally attacked, publicly mortified, and royally screwed by a bunch of wack jobs who are determined to stir up some kind of Y2K mania over 2012. The head of my department, who holds my future in his hands, witnessed the entire thing. A complete stranger shows up and saves me, then reveals that he'd been waiting to pounce on me with a dinner invitation. At which point, he tells me I should be scared. Very scared." She pointed a chopstick at him. "The list of things to be paranoid about just keeps growing."

"I didn't pounce," he said with a grin. "I was the essence of subtlety with that move."

The sushi arrived, and before she took her first bite, she asked the question she'd been wondering about. "You did 'orchestrate'—to use your word—our meeting, didn't you?"

"I did." He dipped a tuna roll in soy sauce, then looked right into her eyes. "The moment I saw you, I wanted to . . . get to know you."

Warmth that had nothing to do with the sake spread through her.

"And then I opened your book," he continued. "And heard you read. And I realized you were not only beautiful"—*byu-ee-ful*—"but intelligent as well." He tugged on the little gold hoop in his left ear. "I was immediately attracted."

She couldn't look away.

"And I still want to get to know you, Miranda." His gaze sharpened with raw, potent sensuality. "As well as possible in the time we have."

She'd never been seduced. Dated, kissed, and involved in sexual relationships, yes. But she'd never let anyone strip her guard, lay her down, and melt her bones for the sheer thrill of it.

Anticipation rolled from her head to her toes, along with something else. Desire?

"Then we'd better start getting to know each other, Adrien. I leave tomorrow morning at eight."

He curled long, strong fingers around hers. "You go first," he said quietly. "Tell me everything about you. Start with . . . where you were born."

She gave a bittersweet laugh that masked her reaction to the electrical current of his touch. "Well, I'm not sure. I was born on an airplane."

"Really." He let go of her hand, his expression interested as he filled her sake cup. "Tell me. I want to know everything about you. *Everything.*"

This was when it got squishy.

Fetch had attempted direct, with the sheila in St. Louis who slammed him with an original birth certificate and papers that proved she'd already located her real parents. He'd tried sly, with the dog trainer in Detroit who also had researched her parentage and knew plenty about the Sapphire Trail babies; she'd already found her birth mother in Pittsburgh. In Vegas, he thought he'd hit pay dirt with a sweet newlywed by the name of Noreen, but her own birth mother had found her via the Internet, and they'd had a tearful reunion on her wedding day. He'd already lost ten of his thirty days.

He strongly suspected that Miranda didn't have a clue she was adopted, since that tended to come up rather quickly in conversation. And given that she had buttercream for skin, smoke-blue eyes the color of a misty morning over Sydney Harbor, and mahogany hair wrapped in a knot thick enough to hint that it might be very long and quite fun to explore, all bets were off. And he had no intention of pulling out the guaranteed-to-cark-the-wine-buzz question: *Are you adopted?*

No. Tonight, he would do an investigation so heated by their undeniable chemistry that she wouldn't even realize how much of her past she'd revealed. Then, after a bit of heavy pashing in the darkest corner he could find, he'd root around in the sack with her until he spotted the ink.

Then he'd tell her why he was there, and not one minute before.

Worst case? He had the wrong girl and a good time. He'd be off in a day or so for the next name on the list. There were only five left.

"So how is it," he said, sliding into the easy opening she'd offered him. "that you were born on a plane?"

"My parents were flying home to Atlanta from Charleston."

Charleston? Too right. "When was that?"

"July 31, 1977."

Bingo! "So, what were they doing flying so close to Mum's delivery date?" How she answered that question would tell him exactly what she knew about her birth.

She merely shrugged. "I don't think they had strict rules about flying back then. People did all sorts of things when they were pregnant—including drink and smoke."

"So, does your birth certificate say you were born . . . in heaven?"

She smiled. "I don't think I ever noticed. Probably Atlanta. My parents have lived in the same house in a suburb called Marietta their whole lives."

If she'd never noticed something on her birth certificate, then she was definitely in the dark about the adoption. Yet Miranda Lang, daughter of Carl and Dee Lang of Marietta, Georgia, was a Sapphire Trail baby. That much he knew from his list.

"Do you have any sibs?" Had the Langs adopted more?

She shook her head. "You?"

"A half-brother I never met."

"You've never met him?"

"What can I say? My oldies are weird."

"Oldies? Parents?"

"Sorry, bad habit. Too much strine."

"Strine?" She waved a ginger slice on the end of her chopsticks. "Oh, I get it. Australyine. Strine. I like it."

"You do?"

"I'm a sucker for accents. Remember, a linguist?"

"Remind me to spew a string of strine, then, just to impress you." He winked, enjoying the flirtation.

She dabbed the corners of her mouth with a napkin but couldn't hide a smile. "How long have you been over here?"

"Uh-uh," he chided, tapping her knuckles as she reached for sushi. "Your life story is on the table now, not mine."

"Sorry, but mine makes for pretty dull dinner conversation." She finally shed her businesslike jacket and he stole a glance at the thin crepe blouse, the whisper of lace silhouetted under it, kissing a sleek collar bone and covering tiny breasts. She was bird-thin and narrow, and he wondered where the tattoo might be. He'd start where Aborigine babies were tattooed, on the bottom of her foot. And work his way up. Slowly. He took a deep drink of ice water, but it didn't cool anything down.

"Being born on a plane isn't dull," he said.

"It went downhill after that."

"The plane or your life?"

She laughed again, completely relaxed now. "Not downhill, exactly, but really not that interesting. I was raised in a suburb, home-schooled until I was sixteen, fast-tracked into Emory University, where I spent the next ten years amassing degree after degree, taking the occasional trip for postdocs and research, and finally getting an offer for an adjunct position at Berkeley. Last year, coinciding with the sale of my dissertation to a major publishing house, and much to my colleagues' dismay and disdain, I made assistant professor. End of story."

"I don't know much about the uni system in this country, but I guess a professor at a school like Berkeley is tall poppies in the field."

"Not such tall poppies." She imitated his accent nicely. "Assistant professor is pretty much the first floor of the ivory tower, and the way up is steep and crowded with competitors. Few of them are willing to make room for a thirty-one-year-old who hit the publishing lottery instead of toiling away in classrooms for decades."

He nodded, anxious to get back to where she was born and who gave birth to her. Or not. "So, does your mum tell you the story of how you were born on a plane? I imagine it's rather spiffy, as birth tales go."

"My 'mum' "—she grinned at the word—"does not. She says it traumatized her. But then, lots of stuff traumatizes my mother—like her baby moving to California. She's still not sure I can cross the street by myself, let alone the country."

"Overprotective, is she?" Wouldn't that be just like an adopted mother who doesn't want anything to happen to her illegally obtained daughter?

"If you look that word up in Webster's, you should find a nice picture of her."

"What's she protecting you from?"

She smiled slowly, reached across the table and lifted the sleeve of his T-shirt, revealing the spiky swirl of the black axe blade that decorated his bicep. Heat raced straight down to his gut—and below.

"From men like you." She let the shirt sleeve fall down.

He grinned and nodded enthusiastically. "Good call, Mum."

Some lovely electricity arced as they held eye contact. It would be so easy to ask her now. *What about you, Miranda? Got ink?*

But direct questions would put her off, and if she had no clue she was adopted, which she obviously didn't, she'd freak, and his plan to go tattoo hunting would end as fast as this dinner. Instead he moved closer, trailed a finger over her knuckles, and saw her eyes darken in response.

"And Dad?" He offered her the last piece of unagi, and she took it. "Does he protect you from the wrong kind of man?"

Her smile was wide and genuine and just too pretty. "My dad is amazing. He's the greatest guy. I always say that's why God gives you two parents."

Or four, as the case may be.

If he had the right woman, he was truly about to wreck what was probably an ideal childhood in Marietta, Georgia. But he had a job to do, and a friend to help.

Besides, a full-body inspection wouldn't hurt either of them, judging by the sparks crackling between them. If he didn't find the tattoo, he'd never mention what he knew about her real birth, and she would continue on her merry way with just a blissful memory.

"Miranda," he said softly, taking both her hands this time. "Let's get out of here."

He felt her pulse jump under his fingertips. "No more sushi and small talk?"

"You're leaving tomorrow morning. Do you really want to spend one more minute with a table between us?"

He watched her chest rise and fall in an unsteady breath. "Where are we going?"

"If you have to ask, maybe we're not going there after all."

She wet her lips and gave him a direct gaze. "I've never slept with a stranger."

He stood, placed a few twenties on the table, snagged the book, and then helped her out of the chair. "Then let's keep talking, so we won't be strangers anymore."

He wrapped his arm around her to guide her to the door, pulling her to his flank and settling his hand over a slender but nicely curved hip.

"Is it my turn to ask questions now?" she asked.

"Absolutely. What would you like me to tell you?"

She gave him a flirtatious smile. "Anything I should know before we walk out of this restaurant together."

"Fair enough. Let's see . . . I'm a former member of the Tasmanian Special Ops police, the best kicker on my rugby team, a stellar bodyguard, an exemplary employee, a trustworthy mate, a half-decent surfer, a lousy cook"—he pushed open the restaurant door, walked her around the corner, and pressed her against the brick wall—"and a helluva good kisser."

CHAPTER
THREE

HOT, POSSESSIVE LIPS covered Miranda's mouth with a kiss that blended skill and impatience and power. Jagged bricks scraped her silk blouse as she lifted her arms to pull him closer and give it right back to him.

She felt his heat, his muscles, his heartbeat . . . and, before that kiss had gone on thirty seconds, the outline of a stiff, sizable erection. He probed her mouth, his tongue seeking every corner, stroking and penetrating. Her book thunked to the concrete as he ran his hands down to her waist, her hips, her buttocks, rocking her slowly against him once, twice. The third time, she swore she'd have an orgasm right there against the wall.

Finally, he let her breathe. But only to nestle his lips against her throat, sucking gently and, just as she'd imagined, tickling her with that hint of beard that made every hair on the back of her neck dance with delight.

She nuzzled to get his mouth. "Kiss me again." Was that *her* voice begging a stranger for another taste of tongue?

He slid his hand up past her waist, caressing the side of her breast, then thumbing the nipple into a hard peak as he fulfilled her request.

When he broke the kiss, she eased far enough back to see the arousal that darkened his golden eyes. He played with her nipple, torturing her with two fingers, his erection pulsing against her stomach.

"How far do you live?" he asked.

A helpless breath escaped as her pelvis moved as if it had a mind of its own. Could she take this big, sexy animal to her sanctuary of a converted garage apartment? No man had spent the night there yet.

But *this* man, this night . . .

Miranda wanted him. She was young, single, free, and juiced up on sexual attraction to a man who made a living protecting people. A former police officer. What could be safer? She ran her palms down the planes of his chest, over the dips and cuts that showed he took tremendous care of his body, down, down, down, until her wrists grazed his belt.

"I'm about a mile from here. We can walk."

He grinned and pressed one of her hands against the huge tent in his pants. "*You* can walk. I might limp."

Blood drained from her head. She'd never felt

anything like that. Closing her eyes, she stroked the outline that outsized her hand by an inch or two.

"We could wait . . . until you, um, cool off."

"That won't be anytime soon." He took a step away, leaving her instantly chilled and bereft. "And you're shivering."

"Not from cold," she admitted, turning so he could help her into the jacket. He used the opportunity to plant a few more kisses on her neck, and she moaned softly, tilting her head in absolute delight.

"You like that?" he asked playfully, sliding hair pins from the knot she'd created.

"I love that."

"Ah, there you go." He sighed at the freedom of loose hair, then tickled his fingers on her scalp and planted more fiery kisses on her neck. "What do you call this color? Auburn? Russet? Umber?"

"Brown."

"Not hardly. It's gorgeous, like the rest of you. Just beautiful."

A hum of sexual anticipation vibrated every cell in her body. She nudged him impatiently. "Come on, Adrien. Let's go home."

He picked up the bag he'd dropped, then draped an arm around her to lead her out of the narrow street onto College Avenue.

"No one calls me Adrien," he said, "unless they're mad at me."

"Like your mother?"

"No. Not like my mum."

The dryness of his tone surprised her. "She doesn't call you Adrien?"

"She doesn't call me." He sidestepped them around group of college students.

"Ever?" Miranda asked as he tucked her firmly to his side again.

"If you really want me to cool off fast, just keep talking about my mum."

She pointed toward the tree-lined road of Hillegrass, the dark shadows so inviting now that she had a strong, sexy man at her side. "There's a shortcut to my house on Regent, up this street."

"Good on that, luv." He picked up their pace. "Now, why don't you give me your travel itinerary, and please tell me you are not seriously leaving town for the next six weeks."

Maybe this was a one-night stand, but at least he was making her feel as if it weren't, which touched her.

"Yep, six weeks. And I have to leave tomorrow because I've been invited to an event in Santa Barbara, which I'm slipping in before a TV interview and signing in LA."

"Cancel it," he said, the suggestion so quick and heartfelt she wasn't sure she understood. "I'm serious," he added at her look. "Stay an extra day."

"Sorry, nothing could make me miss seeing this place." Not even the hottest guy she'd ever met.

"Nothing?" He squeezed her flirtatiously. "You might change your mind by tomorrow."

She might. "I doubt it. I've been wanting to go to Canopy for a long time."

"What is Canopy?"

"An amazing real-life model of Maya ruins, on acres of private land near Santa Barbara. They have replicas of several famous temples completely re-created, right down to the last detail."

"Like Mayan Disney?"

"It's Maya; Mayan is the language. But this place isn't open to the public, and that's why I can't miss the event. Canopy is one man's home. Well, one woman's, really. Doña Taliña Vasquez-Marcesa Blake, a Mexican shaman married to a very rich American, who, she told me when we talked on the phone, was so worried she'd get homesick and leave that he built her a rain forest and ruins. That is Canopy."

"Like the tops of the trees in the rain forest."

"Precisely. She's evidently a fan of my book, and she's arranged a book party with all sorts of important people. So as flattering as your suggestion is, I'm going to Canopy."

"Then we'll have to make the most of this one night together."

They held tight to each other, like lovers on a mission to get horizontal, pausing periodically to kiss and whisper. As they walked past parked cars and overgrown shrubbery, they fell into a sweet silence, with just a cool spring breeze and a steady current of sexual electricity in the air.

"Here," Miranda said, pointing to the brown-shingled Craftsman that abutted the property she rented.

"You live there?" He sounded surprised.

"I live in a converted garage on the property behind it, but it's easier to get there this way. There are lots of reconverted houses in Berkeley. That's the charm of the place."

The Devlins' backyard was pitch-black, and no light spilled from her garage apartment on the other side of the shrubs dividing the properties. "At the end of the row, there's a break in the hedge. This is much faster than going all the way around the front."

"I'll remember that for next time," he said.

"Next time?" She raised her eyebrows. "You said you'd be gone before I get back."

"You never know what life's going to throw at you, Miranda. I certainly didn't expect to end my evening"—he watched her step into the narrow opening between the shrubs and an overgrown wisteria —"climbing through bushes with a beautiful woman." He followed her into the space, stopping to lock his arms around her and steady her feet on the twisted roots under them. "But I'm not complaining."

"Well, I sure didn't expect to get booed offstage and end up making out with an Australian bodyguard." The branches forced them into a tight squeeze, and she could feel he was still hard, and his heart was beating almost as fast as hers. "But I'm not complaining, either."

He lowered his head and kissed her gently, as though the desperation was gone now that the bedroom was no more than fifty steps away.

"As far as next time," she whispered in between

kisses, "I guess we'll just have to see how it goes tonight."

He groaned. "You want to know how it's going to go tonight?" He kissed her forehead, chastely. "First, we're going to have a wee spot of wine and conversation." He eased his hand inside her jacket, gliding over her breast in a slow circle. "Then we're going to help each other undress." He lowered his head and licked her bottom lip. "Then we're going to taste every single inch of each other's body." He nibbled. "With the light on, so I don't miss a thing."

Her legs were so weak she could have fallen backward into the trees and not cared. There was just moonlight and wisteria and the hottest, most seductive man she'd ever met. She closed her eyes, let him touch her and kiss her and sweet-talk her with his sexy accent.

"Then"—his hand tightened on her breast, his mighty erection against her—"we'll do this." He slipped his tongue between her lips, withdrew it, and slid it in again. "That's how it's going to go tonight, luv."

Dizzy, breathless, and aching with arousal, she nudged him out of the trees. "My front door is twenty feet away around that corner."

As they stepped forward, he suddenly froze, going taut, sharp, and alert. He pulled away and put one hand up to stop her from taking another step.

"What's wrong?" she asked.

"Do you smell that?"

She shook her head and sniffed. "Smell what? Fire? Smoke?"

"Blood."

"Blood?" She jerked away and blinked into the darkness. "You smell blood?"

"Right around there."

"That's my front door."

He went first, then stared and muttered something under his breath.

She closed the space between them and gasped, clutching her throat to keep from screaming.

It looked like black oil, slick and wet and *everywhere*. On her front door, over the steps, and drenching the stones surrounding her entrance. Blood smeared the garage door and stained the concrete driveway. The sickening odor wafted toward them.

At the doorstep lay the bright green feathers and long tail of a quetzal, its beak twisted at a freakish angle.

"Is that a bird?" he said, incredulous.

She stared, the message clear and horrifying. "It's a sacrifice to the Maya gods." And it warned of death.

CHAPTER
FOUR

HE WAS DEFINITELY not going to do the naughty with
Miranda Lang tonight, which left Fletch as frustrated
above the waist as below. Instead of the full-body
inspection he'd planned, he was sitting in her small
garage flat, listening to two Berkeley cops who didn't
have a full quid of smarts between them.

"Did you fail any students this last semester, Dr.
Lang?" Young Officer Solar seemed certain that the
symbolic mutilation of the national bird of Guatemala
was the work of an unhappy underclassman. He wasn't
the least bit interested in the melee that had taken
place at Miranda's signing. The other one, the more
seasoned McMurphy, took notes when Fletch offered
detailed descriptions of six or seven of the worst of-
fenders, but his notes were not very copious.

Solar continued to ask about students, which was
starting to piss Fletch off. Miranda's crazies were

well versed in this type of symbolism, and they'd
just demonstrated a pretty violent opposition to her
work. Why was this sook trying to pin it on a failing student?

And wouldn't an investigator worth a tinny of beer
ask who the hell he himself was and what he was
doing with the victim? They'd simply accepted that
the two had just met, dined, and come home, but no
one questioned him, let alone searched him. If they
had, they'd find a Glock 19 on his ankle, one that
he'd already revealed to Miranda when he secured the
property and the house. And in his wallet, they'd find
a bodyguard's license to carry concealed in the state of
California. And in his head, they'd find some brains
they might put to good use.

After an hour, they left, promising to follow up and
taking the quetzal in a plastic bag as evidence of what
they were calling "off-campus vandalism."

By then, all that fire he'd whipped up had turned
to ash. Seduction was out of the question tonight, but
he still needed to find out if she had the mark on her
body. Jack's friend in jail wouldn't reveal where it was,
if she even knew.

Since no tattoos were evident on any of Miranda's
visible flesh, he'd have to figure out some way to dis-
robe her. The nicely furnished flat had one thing in its
favor: it was minuscule, with one main room, a kitch-
enette, a bathroom, and a ladder that led to a sleeping
loft.

Although she was working hard to maintain her
composure, Miranda Lang was definitely scared right

now. That could either get him booted out the door or, if he played the game right, jones him an invitation to keep her company.

"Do you have any ratty old towels?" he asked, rising from the bar stool at the tiny kitchen counter.

Curled in a club chair, she looked at him as though she'd forgotten he was in the room. "Towels?"

"I thought I'd clean up the mess outside for you."

She gave him a grateful smile. "Thank you. I really appreciate you helping with the police; you obviously speak their language. But you were a policeman in Tasmania, right?"

"Sort of. Special Ops. It's a subset of the Tassie police, specially trained. Would your rags be in the kitchen?"

"No." She stood and indicated the bathroom door. "I'll get something for you."

He stayed where he was as she walked away, the angle not giving him a view into the little room where she'd disappeared. But after a few minutes, he followed. "You okay, Miranda?"

He found her leaning against the sink, a wicker cabinet open next to her, but she was gripping the porcelain and staring into the mirror. From behind, he caught her gaze in the glass and saw raw terror in her deep blue eyes. She took a slow, shallow breath, her jaw quivering and her skin the shade of goat's milk.

Instantly, he grasped her shoulders to turn her to him. "What's the matter?"

"I'm having a panic attack." She didn't turn, her body rigid. She put a hand to her breastbone, and he could see a pulse throbbing in her neck. Her breaths were so superficial and fast they couldn't possibly send any oxygen to her body.

"I haven't had . . ." Another ragged breath. "One . . . for a long . . ." And another. "Time."

"Okay, sweetheart. Relax." He folded her in his arms and tried to hold her, but she remained stiff, a completely different woman from the one who melted with one kiss and responded to his touch with spirit and sensuality. "Are you prone to panic attacks?"

"Not anymore." She ground the words out as though just by saying them, she could stop whatever had taken hold of her. "Not since I moved here."

He eased her out of the bathroom. "I'll get the cleanup work done later. Let's get you to bed."

Her eyes flashed with more panic, but then she nodded, seeing the sense of the suggestion. "I do need to lie down. Once I deep-breathe, it'll pass."

"Upstairs, right? Can you make it up the ladder? There you go." He guided her toward the steps. "I'll be right behind you."

He followed her up, holding her with one hand as she took the steep rungs one at a time. The tiny three-walled loft held only a full-size bed, a nightstand, and an armoire. Enough light seeped up from the room below that he didn't bother with a lamp. He would have, under Plan A. But even Adrien Fletcher wasn't enough of a larrikin to strip-search a panicked woman.

He laid her on the bed and sat next to her, shushing and cooing to quiet her jitters. Her breathing steadier, she stayed on her back, her eyes closed. He stroked her hair, her arm, and held her hand, brushing the knuckles.

Finally, she seemed at ease. "I can't believe my good fortune in finding you tonight."

"I found you," he said, hoping the truth would assuage the guilt that drop-kicked in his stomach. "And I'm happy to help you."

"You were right about not knowing what surprises life holds."

He threaded his fingers through hers. "That's what makes it interesting."

"Or terrifying." Her voice was rich with self-deprecation.

"What are you terrified of, Miranda?" He slid down next to her, and she inched over to make room for him.

"Before, everything. Now I've got it down to flying—though I'm no fan of small, dark spaces, either."

He propped himself on his elbow and studied her. "Why were you afraid of everything?

"I told you my mother was overprotective. Consider that an understatement. I love her dearly, but she's fragile and scared and did everything in her power to make me the same way. I was the little girl in a parka when it was sixty degrees out. I was the one not allowed to go to the amusement park for fear I'd fall off a roller coaster. I was the one who was home-schooled to keep me away from all the dangers that lurked in the locker room. She never wanted me to go anywhere or do anything or meet anyone."

"So you ran away to California." To escape parents who not only created fear but lied to their child about her birth.

Her smile was tight. "My dad, bless him, secretly pushed me from the nest. Quietly, and when Mom wasn't around, Dad urged me to apply for positions at schools far away."

"Have you had help? Professional counseling?"

She shook her head. "No. I just needed to be on my own for a while, and I've been here more than two years. I've made friends, had a few boyfriends, read a lot of self-help books, and attended seminars. I thought I'd beaten it. Then tonight, at that signing, it almost started again. When you showed up, I felt much better. But when I saw that bird . . ." She closed her eyes and visibly dug for control. "Once the police left, I couldn't fight off the panic any longer. It was a flat-out warning that someone wants to kill me."

He lifted his head from his hand. "What? You said it was a sacrifice to the gods or some such thing."

"It's ancient Maya symbolism, known to a very few experts in the field. The broken neck of the quetzal is a plea to Itzamna, a high-ranking god who is considered the inventor of writing and the patron of the sciences. To a purist Maya, he would be *my* god, for obvious reasons. That purist would believe that Itzamna has told someone that he doesn't approve of my writing or my science and that someone should sacrifice me to stop me."

Fletch scooted up a bit, squinting at her. "Do you believe that shonky nonsense?"

She didn't *not* believe. "I know that someone, somewhere, is warning me."

"One of the crazies?"

"Who else?"

He put his arm around her shoulder and turned her to him. "Listen to me, Miranda. Cancel your trip. Just jettison the whole thing. How many books are you going to sell signing in little mum-and-pop bookstores around the country or at some shindig at fake ruins? Is it worth it?"

She shot up, the fire suddenly back in her eyes. "I can't give in to them. Canceling my trip is the coward's way out, and I will *not* let fear win. I'm just going to be careful. I just need to . . . to . . ." Her expression brightened as an idea took hold. "Come with me."

"Pardon?"

She gripped him by the shoulder, her narrow fingers surprisingly strong. "You're a professional. You can protect me. Be my bodyguard."

"I have to . . ." *Find a woman, get her naked, and ruin her life.* "I have work to do."

"A job in the Bay Area, and then you're leaving in a month?"

"I . . . I . . ." How could he tell her? "I might leave even before that."

She sank back onto the pillow. "Sorry, I got carried away. I went from one-night stand to full-time job in less than ten minutes. I understand."

No, she didn't understand at all. He had twenty days left, and if she wasn't the sheila he was looking for, then he had five more women to track down and interview.

And if she was, then he had to persuade her to take a trip to South Carolina to meet a convicted prisoner who claimed to be her birth mum, take a DNA test, and possibly donate her marrow to the cause.

She wouldn't even get on a plane to South Carolina, let alone—

"Sorry, bad idea," she whispered, brushing his hair back.

He turned her hand that touched his cheek so he could kiss her palm. "It's just a work conflict, or I'd go in a heartbeat."

She nodded, clearly not believing him. "It's okay. I might not sleep with you now, but it's okay." She gave him a teasing smile, but he saw the sadness in her eyes.

"This wasn't about sex, Miranda."

"Oh, now I know you're lying." She poked him in the chest.

"I'm not," he insisted, his heart folding over at the way she was working to act as if his rejection hadn't hurt her pride. "And if I could . . ."

She quieted him with two fingers to his lips. "Don't say things to make me feel better. You've been wonderful. A lifesaver, literally. You can go anytime you like. I'm fine now."

"I don't want to go." He couldn't mean it more. "I'm not leaving you alone tonight."

"I'm not having sex with you," she reminded him.

"I don't expect you to. But I'd like to stay to be sure you're all right."

"I'm fine. In fact"—she pushed herself up and sat

on the side of the bed—"I'm going to spend the next few hours packing, so you might as well go." She reached to the nightstand and flipped on the light.

"How about if I sleep downstairs on the futon?"

She opened her mouth, clearly about to say no, then thought better of it. "All right." She shooed him away. "Now, go, I have to pack."

Downstairs, on a mattress meant for someone much smaller and lighter, he listened to Miranda move about, pull out suitcases, open drawers, zip the cases shut, and finally breathe softly in sleep. All the while, he considered his options.

Miranda did need protection, and he needed her. The problem was, if he got the proof that she was Eileen Stafford's long-lost baby, then he'd screw up her life. And if she wasn't, then he'd have to ditch her and go off for the next lady on the list.

The solution, when it presented itself, seemed like a doable compromise. He levered himself off the miserable mattress and climbed the ladder to her loft. Before he reached the top, he heard her sheets rustle.

"What do you want, Adrien?" she asked.

"I just want to ask you a question. Would you like a date for that party at Maya Land tomorrow? I don't have to work for a few days."

He waited four, five, six heartbeats, surprised at how much he wanted to hear the right answer.

"Yes," she finally said. "I would like a date."

"What happens the next day?"

"I'm driving to Los Angeles for the day, then to San Diego."

"I could go to LA and fly back on Monday." By then, he'd have managed to see every inch of her body, one way or another.

"You must really want to sleep with me." There was a smile in her voice.

"I told you, Miranda. It's not about sex."

"Right." She imitated his accent perfectly, making him grin as he went back down the ladder without a sound.

In the filthy bathroom of a Chevron gas station, K'inich Ahkal Mo' Nahb washed the blood from his noble hands. It stained under his fingernails, brown like the earth. The very earth that had buried him and suffocated him and cradled him for so many years.

He looked up from the sink, but the mirror was long ago stolen from the public bathroom. Graffiti marked the walls, along with chunks of peeling paint and filth. But Ahkal Mo' Nahb needed no man-made glass to see what he looked like. His image had been sculpted in stone for centuries. Leaning over the sink, he turned the faucet and began to wash his face.

Brilliant blue paint poured into the stained sink, blinding blue, royal blue. The color of kings. He'd painted his face for the sacrifice and enjoyed it. The act gave him power, immortality, and hardened him.

When he was clean, he turned out the yellow light, sat on the urine-stained concrete, and chanted, soft and low. It made him harder. He hung his head, staring at how his erection strained the cloth he wore, proud of his night's work.

"Put a move on it, for Christ's sake!" A heavy fist clobbered the metal door, then a solid kick. "You can't sleep in there, pal!"

He closed his eyes, finished his chant, and stood before whipping the door open.

The man jumped back, the fluorescent lights bathing his surprised face in yellow as Ahkal stepped out of the darkness. The other man blinked, sucked in a breath, and stared. "What the fuck . . ."

Ahkal ignored him and continued to walk to his car.

"Put some clothes on, man!"

Alone in the car, Ahkal took a cell phone from the glove box and dialed ten digits.

"Have you made the sacrifice, my lord?" a voice asked.

He smiled into the phone. "I have made the supreme sacrifice merely by walking this earth. Tonight, I left a message."

"Very good. But will she heed it?"

The smell of the dead quetzal on his hand made his head spin. He mustn't have cleaned it completely. "She will, or we will make the next message clearer. Miranda Lang must be stopped."

The thump of a fist on his window made Ahkal jump and drop the phone.

"Get out of here, you freakazoid! I'm callin' the cops!"

Without looking at him, Ahkal drove away.

Chapter
FIVE

"PLEASE DON'T WORRY, Mom." Miranda threw a rueful glance at Adrien, who flashed his deep, delicious dimple but kept his attention on the freeway traffic he navigated.

She hadn't put up much of a fight at the car-rental agency when he upgraded her Saturn to a chunky Range Rover that matched his personality and style and, evidently, budget. Once he flew back to San Francisco, she'd downsize to a car she could handle for the rest of the trip. But this was too much fun. They were way above the road—and most other cars. Though he drove fast, he was skilled, never once giving her a reason to second-guess her decision to let him drive her.

He was skilled at *everything,* she mused, while she listened to her mother drone on over the cell phone about how dangerous it was for Daddy to golf when there could be a lightning storm. "Men get killed that way, you know, Miranda."

"I know, Mom." Then she let her thoughts, and her gaze, slide right back to the man behind the wheel.

Who was a great conversationalist, a soothing presence, and, just as he'd promised, a helluva good kisser. Her tummy flipped at the memory, her fingers tingling to touch the bit of tattoo that inched out from today's T-shirt sleeve. Which, unlike last night's bad black, was white and tight enough to show every rip and cord in his body. And there were many. She especially liked that muscle that ran from his jaw down—

"You know that, don't you, Miranda?"

To his broad shoulder. "Of course I do. But Daddy knows what he's doing."

"That's not what I meant. Are you driving? You don't sound like you're paying attention. You're not on the phone and driving at the same time?"

"Hands free, I promise."

Adrien whispered, "Shame on you, lying to Mum."

She flicked him away, then came up with an excuse to end the call. "I see my exit now. I'll call you later, okay? Tell Daddy I love him. You, too. 'Bye."

"You failed to mention me to Mum."

"Can you imagine?" Miranda laughed. "By the way, Mom, I'm traveling with a long-haired, tattooed Australian security specialist I picked up at my book signing last night."

"Another lie," he said. "I picked *you* up."

"Either way, I just omitted the truth. It's not a lie when it's your mother; that's self-preservation."

"Has she ever omitted the truth to you?"

The question came from so far out in left field Miranda had to stop and think about it. "I guess I wouldn't know, would I?"

He shrugged, which drew her attention back to his arm. "You like my ink?" he asked, flexing his bicep.

"It's daunting. What is it?"

"An Aborigine axe blade."

"Lovely."

"It is, actually. I lived with a tribe when I was a teenager, and they gave me this as a welcoming present when I arrived." He put an easy hand on her leg, giving it a squeeze. "I've got more. I'll show you mine, if . . ."

She lifted his hand and returned it to the console. "Do I look like the kind of woman who would have a tattoo?"

"Do I look like the kind of man who would make snap judgments? You could have a tramp stamp, for all I know."

"A tramp stamp?"

He placed his hand on her neck, then traveled down her back, inching her forward in the seat until he burned the spot about a centimeter above her tailbone. "It goes right here, where no one can see it but your lover."

Heat burned where he touched, and her lower half melted.

"A very sexy tattoo," he said.

So was his. She arched her back to encourage him to pull his hand out, but he just glided up and pressed one finger into a muscle between her shoulder blades.

"This is another popular place for women to get tats." He continued north, tunneling into her nape. "Sometimes you find one here, too." He tapped the base of her skull. "Yes?" he asked teasingly.

He had to feel the goosebumps that rose all over her at that. "Drive, Adrien."

With a chuckle, he returned his hand to the wheel. He turned off the highway, and soon they were traveling through rolling hills, all crisp and dry and the color of toasted rye bread.

"Couldn't look much less like a rain forest," Fletch noted. "One match could turn this entire place into charcoal."

"California in the summer is dry as a bone. That's why I'm curious about how she managed to make a rain forest, of all things." She pulled a piece of paper from her handbag. "We want an unmarked road with a high white gate."

After a few minutes, they spotted an electronic gate in the middle of an eight-foot-high stucco wall with a simple brass plaque that said CANOPY. The gate was open, and when they drove in, it clanged closed behind them.

"They must have cameras or a sensor," he said.

The road curved sharply at first, then grew steeper until it leveled out under an umbrella of trees, the foliage growing thicker, darker, and greener with each passing mile. Just as the road narrowed to a single lane, it crested at a hillside.

"Oh, my God," Miranda said, leaning forward. "It's unbelievable."

Below them, a hundred acres of every imaginable shade of green rolled out like an endless emerald carpet, a shock of vitality in the middle of dried-up hills. Clusters of mini-forests dotted the landscape. Dropped in the midst were three massive orange clay structures shaped like stepped pyramids with giant open porticos on top, all adorned with brilliant turquoise and gold shimmering along the squared-off rooflines and columns.

"A bit like *Jurassic Park,* isn't it?" Adrien mused.

Only that was a movie. This was *real.* "It's a perfect reproduction of Palenque. The big building with a tower is the Palace, and over there is the Temple of the Inscriptions." She pointed to a smaller structure, farther away from the two. "And the Temple of the Sun. Some say it is the most perfect of all Maya architecture." She drank it all in, stunned by the imagination and breadth and splendor of it. "It's actually more beautiful than the ruins, because the colors and jewels are the way they were almost fifteen hundred years ago."

"Who *is* this guy?" Adrien asked. "This had to cost the earth to build."

"I have no idea who Victor Blake is," Miranda said. "But I can't wait to meet his wife. What vision this must have taken, and what knowledge of the Maya." She turned to him, excitement in her voice. "She's a shaman, did I tell you?"

"You mentioned it. I knew one once. An Ab, out in the bush."

"Was she a healer?"

"She was a he. Most shamans are, you know."

A few minutes later, Doña Taliña Vasquez-Marcesa Blake floated down the wide and noble steps of her sixty-five-foot pyramid-shaped home to greet her guests. She was every bit as breathtaking as the world she'd created as her backdrop.

She wore white linen slacks and a cool yellow tunic, her ebony hair slicked straight back into a smooth bun, with chunks of pounded silver around her neck. She moved with grace and focus, reminding Miranda of the animal that the Maya worshipped above all others: the jaguar.

Doña Taliña looked nothing like her plain Mesoamerican ancestors. From a flawless coffee complexion over striking cheekbones and piercing ink-black eyes right down to her delicate gold shoes, she was glorious, and surprisingly young. She couldn't have been forty, with a slender, toned body and a smile that emanated warmth.

When she reached out to greet Miranda, the warmth was a comforting, inviting, irresistible heat. They embraced as though they'd known each other forever.

"Dr. Lang! At last!" She cooed the words with a breathy Mexican accent, stroking Miranda's cheek with an affection that would be startling if it hadn't been so genuine. "I am so honored to have you at my home."

Her "home" was a replica of a fifteen-hundred-year-old vaulted stone palace, complete with reproductions of hieroglyphs and ornate carvings along the walls and enormous columns that supported a wrap-around portico, topped off by a four-story tower that loomed over everything. This replica was slightly smaller but no less impressive than the actual palace built by Pakal, arguably the greatest king of the Maya empire.

"Thank you so much for the invitation, Doña Taliña," Miranda replied, shifting her gaze from the beautiful woman to her home. "I'm the one who's honored."

At the sound of Adrien's door, Doña Taliña transferred her attention to him.

"This is Adrien Fletcher," Miranda said. "My . . . traveling companion."

Doña Taliña's eyes flashed surprise, but she covered it with another demonstrative greeting. Miranda hadn't said she was bringing a guest, since she only decided at three that morning, and she hoped her hostess would understand.

"Welcome to Canopy," Doña Taliña said. "I have some tea on the veranda ready for us. Someone will get your bags." She indicated for them to follow her up the stairs. "Will you need separate, adjoining, or a single room?"

"Separate," Miranda said.

"Adjoining," Adrien said at the same time.

Their hostess smiled knowingly. "We have an entire guest wing to guarantee your comfort," she said, curling her hand into Miranda's arm to lead her up the stairs. "Now, tell me about your travels and all the wonderful reception your book has been getting, my dear."

She continued small talk about the drive, the event that evening, and the weather, as they climbed three dozen stone stairs before reaching the shade of the portico, where lounge chairs surrounded a table spread with fruit and cold drinks.

At a single finger lifted in command, Doña Taliña's staff hustled to pour tea and serve food from silver and jade trays.

"My husband sends his apologies that he isn't here to greet you," she said. "He's been detained in a meeting in Los Angeles."

"What does your husband do?" Adrien asked.

Doña Taliña beamed with pride. "He is a brilliant entrepreneur, a man with vision and understanding. But he is humble and will simply tell you that he's a private investor. I'll tell you this, he is a natural salesman." She laughed softly. "He could persuade anyone to do anything. He persuaded me to leave the country I love to live in California."

"He's obviously worked hard to make you feel at home here," Miranda said. "Canopy is amazing."

"Thank you. It is home now." She turned to Adrien. "And it sounds as if you are far from home as well, Mr. Fletcher. How long ago did you leave Australia?"

"Nearly two years ago," he said.

"Do you plan to return?"

He glanced at Miranda before answering. "Eventually."

Doña Taliña still seemed amused. "Is your future tied to Miranda, then?"

"My future isn't tied to anyone, Doña," he replied.

Miranda stepped up to a mosaic mask mounted on a wall, seizing on a chance to change the subject. "This is absolutely gorgeous, Doña Taliña."

"Please, call me Taliña. We are not that formal at Canopy." She stepped closer to Miranda and reached up to touch the mask. "My husband commissioned this as a wedding present. That is *k'ahul ahaw,* but of course you know that."

"A holy lord," Miranda explained to Adrien. "And I assume that's pure jade."

"It is. He indulges me." Taliña tucked her arm around Miranda's waist, a whiff of musky perfume drifting from her. "And now you can see why I love your work. I love how you've captured the spirit of the Maya, demystifying without demolishing. I find it exhilarating to read."

Taliña's touch would be an invasion of personal space from anyone else, but the woman was so warm and authentic that Miranda didn't mind. "Thank you. I hope readers agree with you."

Dark eyes flashed. "They must. Anything else is just foolishness." She paused for a moment, surveying Miranda's face. "Tell me why you have such trouble in your spirit. This should be a time of strong happiness for you."

Could she really sense that? Or was Miranda's face giving away a sleepless night? "It was a long drive," she said. "And . . . a late night."

Taliña rubbed her hand over Miranda's back, frowning. "There's something else." Her fingers stilled. Right in that spot between her shoulder blades, the one Adrien had touched not an hour earlier. It tingled again, and Miranda drew in a surprised breath.

Adrien moved slightly, tensing up from his position against a carved relief of a warrior's shield, his eyes sharp on the two women. Taliña guided Miranda away from him.

"Sit here." Taliña gently pushed Miranda into a chair in the shadows, then took another next to her, closing fingers heavy with silver, jade, and a few choice diamonds over Miranda's unadorned ones. Wordlessly, she stared into Miranda's eyes for a long, uncomfortable minute, the pressure in her hands increasing with each second, along with the intensity of her midnight gaze.

"What did you dream last night?" Taliña asked.

"I don't remember." Had she even slept last night? She'd tossed, turned, sighed, relived kisses, and thought about the man sleeping on her futon.

"There was blood," Taliña said.

Miranda's jaw loosened in surprise, but she checked her reaction. Taliña released her hands and put fingertips on each of Miranda's temples. "There is worry here." She placed a light fingertip over Miranda's heart. "And alarm here. I can help you." Taliña stood and slipped through an arched doorway, into what Miranda assumed was the living area.

"Maybe she can help," she said, unable to meet Adrien's direct gaze. "Maybe she can simply divine who left that message for me last night."

"Maybe." But there was enough doubt in his tone to tell that he didn't believe.

Taliña returned through a different doorway, crisp linen brushing as she walked. She sat next to Miranda and held up a round hand mirror, encrusted with a rim of large, yellow topaz stones set in silver filigree.

"My *toli*," she explained. "It will allow me to see." She angled the mirror so they could both see the reflection. Miranda glanced at the glass and at her own face, seeing bluish circles under slightly puffy eyes, and the lone coat of mascara she'd applied at dawn had long ago flaked off. It didn't take a shaman to see the stress on that face.

Taliña stared at the reflection, frowning. "Someone wants to hurt you, my dear. Someone is going to hurt you very much."

Despite the heat, a chill lifted every hair on Miranda's body.

Taliña studied the mirror intently. For a moment, her eyes fluttered and rolled back, then she reached forward and embraced Miranda, lifting her from the chair. "There is a plan to inflict great pain on you." Slowly, mesmerized and still staring at the *toli*, Taliña stood, taking Miranda's hand. "Come with me," she urged, using her eyes to send a warning over her shoulder to Adrien. "You stay there."

His golden eyes narrowed, but he didn't move.

Deep in the cool shadow of the portico, Taliña placed her mouth so close to Miranda's ear that her hair moved. "Who is this man?" She tipped her head imperceptibly toward Adrien. "How well do you know him?"

'I don't . . . we've just . . . recently met."

Taliña's black eyes widened, and she shook her head, then looked at her mirror. "Be careful, my dear."

The warning chilled. "Of what?"

"Of those who say they want to protect you but have much different plans." She looked pointedly at Adrien, lowered the mirror, and took a step back. "Josefina will show you to your rooms, and I will see you in the courtyard for cocktails at seven. We're expecting more than four hundred people, so I'm sure you understand that I must leave you now." She nodded toward Adrien and the table. "Please feel free to make yourselves comfortable."

She disappeared under yet another archway, leaving Miranda worlds away from anything that resembled *comfortable*.

Could the shaman see something in Adrien Fletcher that Miranda hadn't?

She turned from the shadows to confront him, but he was gone.

CHAPTER
SIX

JACK CULVER SQUINTED into the thick foliage that rolled over the hills of the Dutch Fork area of Richland County, South Carolina, and pressed the cell phone tighter to his ear. "Canopy? What the hell is that?" he asked.

"Some bizarre California compound," Fletch replied. "Named for the trees."

"I'm in a pretty bizarre compound, too." Jack glanced at the fifteen-foot wall, the barbed wire that ran along it, and the huge iron gate that let women in but not out. "It's the Camille Griffin Graham Correctional Institute, and I'm on my way to see a killer of a woman."

"You said she's innocent."

Jack pulled off the road to finish this conversation with Fletch before he started the clearing process. Even when all a visitor wanted to do was stop in the infirmary and see a nearly dead woman, it could take the better part of an hour, a strip search, a discussion with some hard-edged correctional officers, a bit of banter with Warden McNally's just-past-her-prime assistant, and an endless wait to see Eileen Stafford.

And chances were she'd be asleep.

"My gut says she's innocent," Jack said.

"Your gut's been a bit natty lately."

"It probably wouldn't hold up in court," Jack agreed. "And still, I've been in Charleston digging into history, and my gut, natty as it is, says there's more to this than meets the eye." Much more. More than he could even tell Fletch.

"What did you find?"

"Mostly a big fat rug with a shitload of secrets swept under it. And no one willing to talk." The last ten days had been a series of blank faces and shrugged shoulders. Whatever went down behind the scenes in the Charleston PD and the ensuing murder trial thirty years ago, someone wanted it to go to Eileen Stafford's grave. "And why are you at a compound in . . . where is it again?"

"Santa Barbara. I'm here because I've got a live one."

"Reel her in, man. Eileen needs good news today. Which one is she?"

"Miranda Lang."

"Has she agreed to the bone-marrow transplant?"

Fletch snorted. "She doesn't even have a clue she was adopted. I'm trying to find the tattoo, but it isn't visible with clothes on."

"Get them off. You're good at that."

"Working on it, mate. Right now, she needs some protection services on a weekend of book promotion. I took that job, hoping it includes a tattoo hunt, but . . ."

Fletch's voice trailed off, and Jack frowned. "What is she? Blind? Gay? Married?"

"None of the above. In fact, she's gorgeous, smart, and quite available."

"What's the problem?"

"The problem is we just met up with a very astute and uncannily perceptive woman who might be on to me. She's already planting seeds in Miranda's head that I have ulterior motives."

"All men have ulterior motives. Strip her down and search, for God's sake, and in the meantime, I'll tell Eileen we're getting closer. Maybe she can give me something. Whoever she's covering for still has her believing he or she has the power to hurt her daughter. She wants me to help her, but she doesn't fully trust that I can."

"Listen, mate," Fletch said. "I like this woman, and I don't want to crap all over her life for no good reason. If she's not Stafford's daughter, then I'm not telling her she's adopted. But if she really can save her birth mother, I'll do it. Anything your friend can tell me—a name of who adopted her daughter, a location of the mark—is going to make things easier and faster."

"I'll get what I can."

"Good onya, then, Jack. Gotta run."

Fletch clicked off, and Jack headed into Camp Camille with resolve to get more out of Eileen Stafford, no matter what. That resolve evaporated an hour later, when he entered the infirmary to find the sick, bald, thin-skinned woman sleeping like the dead. For a second, he thought she *was* dead.

Then he saw the hole for the chemo port in her chest rise and fall in slow, steady rhythm.

Jack sat on the other bed and studied the face of a woman long ago lost in the system, seemingly a victim of a sloppy and impatient prosecutor, a lazy defense attorney, and a city so deep in poverty that no one cared about one legal secretary shooting another. And a victim, his instinct told him, of something even more nefarious than all that.

Of course, anything that came from his instinct was subject to doubt and scrutiny.

"Did you find her?" The voice, so tiny it could have been a child's, startled Jack.

"I thought you were asleep."

"The nice guard told me you were coming. The one who feeds me my yogurt."

Jack glanced at the open door, where a guard occasionally wandered by. Even though Camp Camille was high-security, no one expected a weak fifty-five-year-old cancer patient to try to escape.

"They told you I was coming?" he asked.

"They just said I had a visitor coming. I figured it was you." She opened her eyes and turned her head slowly to look at him. "Nobody else comes anymore."

"Did anyone used to visit?"

"Once in a while." She closed her eyes. He knew from the brief conversations they'd had, from the first time he'd come looking for a link to an entirely different case, that he couldn't push Eileen when she didn't want to be pushed. She'd just feign sleep.

"Let me ask you something, Eileen. Does the name Miranda Lang mean anything to you?"

She opened her eyes instantly, a little pulse throbbing under the fuzz of her nearly bald scalp. "Is that her? Miranda Lang?"

"Might be. This young lady doesn't seem to know she's adopted. Is that possible?"

"Of course. The mother might not have told her."

"But she'd have the mark you had put on her?"

"She would."

"Where?"

"I told you, I wasn't in the room. I just know that Rebecca did it. She was the nurse at Sapphire Trail."

Jack leaned his elbows on his knees at this new lead. "Rebecca who?"

"There were no last names at Sapphire Trail."

Of course not. That would be too easy.

"It doesn't make any difference now. What matters is finding . . . her . . . before I die. Then you'll know the truth. And the truth . . ." She shuddered.

"The truth is what, Eileen?"

"Just find her. Bring her to me. Then you'll understand."

Yeah, he'd understand that he'd been had by an old woman who would do and say anything to find the daughter who could save her life.

They'd been through this before, when she was stronger, more determined. But she was fading fast. "I need more to go on, Eileen. I've got friends working, and we're running out of time."

Lifting one hand, she touched the chemo port on her chest. "Don't I know it."

"Should I try to find Rebecca?"

She opened her eyes. "Be careful. He can do anything. You'll see."

"Who is he?" Jack asked softly. "You have to tell me."

"I can't. He'll kill you, too."

Jesus. He stabbed his hands through his hair and propped his elbows on his knees, leaning close to the metal rails of her hospital bed. "Give me something, Eileen. *Something.*"

"Talk to Willie Gilbert."

"Who's that?"

"He arrested me. He knows the truth."

"Where is he?"

"You're a former cop, right? You should be able to find each other."

The guard rapped hard on the doorjamb. "Time's up, Mr. Culver."

Eileen's blue-gray eyes widened slightly. "You told them your real name?"

"It's the only way into a maximum-security prison, Eileen."

"Be careful, Jack." She reached out a papery dry hand and whispered, "He can do anything. And it matters to a lot of people. A lot."

————————————

From a long balcony that connected his second-floor room with Miranda's, Fletch studied the impressive patio below, surrounded by a faux jungle, lit by rows of tiki torches, and peppered with well-dressed guests.

"I'm ready."

He turned to another vision, every bit as impressive.

Miranda stepped into the evening light, shimmering in silver metallic silk that draped over her slender body like liquid mercury. The dress stopped mid-thigh to reveal long, shapely legs in a pair of high heels designed with nothing but procreation of the species in mind.

He made no effort to hide his head-to-toe inspection. "Isn't going out in public looking that good illegal?"

She smiled at the compliment and nodded to the greenery behind him. "I know that using that much water *is* illegal," she said. "I wonder how Victor Blake gets away with it."

"I get the impression Doña Taliña calls the shots around here."

"She calls something," Miranda said. "I just haven't figured out what yet."

"Is that what you've done all afternoon?" he asked. "Tried to figure her out?"

She shrugged. "I rested in my room." He knew that, having kept a close watch on that door while he did a cursory security check of the home. "What about you?"

"I worked." In addition to the look-see of the house, he'd talked to Lucy. "I've asked for background checks on Victor and Taliña Blake, and my home office is trying to unearth some new data about the crazies for you."

"Why?" She looked hard at him, the same distrust in her eyes that he'd seen when she'd found him on the cell phone with Jack on the veranda. Seeds of distrust planted by their hostess.

"Information is power. If you know who these people are, they have less chance of terrorizing you."

"The crazies, yes. But why would you do a background check on Taliña and Victor Blake?"

"Because anyone who doesn't want you to be protected is a security red flag to me."

Miranda scowled at him. "She's merely . . . possessive. And I guess she questioned our friendship."

He lifted a brow. "You've got nothing to fear from me."

"Nothing?"

He raked her with a slow appraisal as he slipped into a sports jacket that hid his holstered weapon. "I admit I want to get naked with you, luv, but I don't want to hurt you."

For a moment, they eyed each other in a silent truce. Then she reached out to touch his tie. "You clean up pretty well, too."

He grinned, snagging her hand as she drew away and tucking her closer to him. "Let's go greet your adoring fans."

"That's a slight overstatement."

"Taliña adores you," he said. "She touches you a lot."

"That's her style," Miranda said. "She's very physical."

He slid an arm around her and dropped a kiss on her bare shoulder. "So am I."

She stiffened, then inclined her head, allowing him access to more skin. "What happened to 'this isn't about sex'?"

"This dress happened," he said, lowering his gaze to the material that dipped low enough to reveal the rise of her breasts. "And you knew it when you put it on to torture me."

"That wasn't my . . ." Her voice caught as he kissed her on the lips, so lightly it tickled them both.

"Yes, it was." He grazed a knuckle along the side of her breast.

A sharp rap on the balcony door surprised them apart. "Miranda, what's taking you so long?" Taliña Blake stepped out, obviously having come through Miranda's room. She wore all black, her hair tumbling in waves over her shoulders as she crossed the balcony. "I'm so anxious for you to come down." She slipped her arm around Miranda without so much as a glance at Fletch. "And Victor is dying to meet you."

"We were just on our way," Miranda said.

Fletch followed them down to the patio, where a short, barrel-chested older man with thinning hair and crystal-blue eyes waited at the bottom of the steps. The man's gaze flickered between Miranda and Taliña. He took Miranda's hand, offering a Euro bow and a handshake. "I'm delighted to meet you, Dr. Lang. I'm Victor Blake."

Miranda introduced Fletch as her companion, and Blake gave him a swift appraisal. "Mr. Fletcher. Welcome."

"Come and see the pyramid I've made from your books." Taliña said. "You will love this. So inventive!" Instantly, she spirited Miranda away from the men.

Fletch started after them, but Victor Blake blocked him. "Come to the bar with me. You'll never get five minutes of her time with Taliña around. I'm afraid the lady of the house is a bit starstruck."

"Starstruck? Miranda is a college professor who wrote a book." He allowed Blake to guide him to the bar, making sure he could see the two women from there.

Blake's odd laugh pulled his attention. "Who knows why that woman does anything?" he said, shaking his head like a doting husband. "I just do whatever I can to keep her happy."

"How long has she been a fan of Miranda's work?" Fletch asked. "The book hasn't been out that long."

He put a glass of red wine in Fletch's hand. "I have no idea. I really don't pay attention to that sort of thing. But I wouldn't question it, if I were you. Taliña is quite a handy benefactor for your girlfriend to have. She'll introduce hundreds of new readers to her work this evening alone." Blake held up his glass in a toast.

Fletch tapped the crystal and pretended to sip, then put the glass on the bar, scanning the crowd. Miranda stood in front of a flickering torch that offered a dead-on silhouette of her body through thin fabric.

"Nothing quite as intoxicating as watching a woman shine in her element, is there, Mr. Fletcher?"

Fletch slid him a sideways look but didn't respond.

"Taliña tells me you're a Taswegian."

He managed not to roll his eyes at the term. "True enough." As much as he'd like the little man to disappear, he was curious about to how the bloke made all this cash. "Have you been Down Under?"

"Many times on business."

"Which is what, exactly?"

"I owned a distribution company that serviced Hobart. It's a beautiful place. What brings you to the States?"

"The same," Fletch replied. "Business." He took another fake sip of wine. "What did you distribute?"

"Oh, I sold that business years ago. What line of work are you in, Mr. Fletcher?"

"Security." He glanced toward Miranda, but she must have stepped behind one of the massive sculptures that decorated the patio. "Executive protection, primarily. When were you in Hobart?"

"A while ago. So, that's why you're with Miranda? As her bodyguard?"

"No, I'm on my own time. Where did you stay?"

"Can't recall. Are you independent, or do you work for a firm?"

Fletch resisted the urge to smile. "I work for a firm." He paused and waited for Blake to make the next move.

"What's the name of the firm?"

"It's a private organization. Out of New York." He inched to the side when he lost sight of Miranda. "If you'll excuse me—"

Blake stepped in front of Fletch and blocked him. "The firm you work for? I bet I've used them."

For a moment, they stared at each other, Blake's eyes revealing that he was enjoying their verbal chess game. "I know you haven't, Mr. Blake. I've already checked."

The other man blinked in surprise, or in response to the ding of a fork against crystal.

"Ladies and gentlemen." Doña Taliña's soft voice was amplified by a tiny microphone and distributed by invisible speakers everywhere. "It is my honor and privilege to introduce you to a brilliant anthropologist, a talented writer, and a brave woman on a mission to rewrite history."

Rewrite history? Is that what Miranda was doing with her book? He nodded goodbye to Blake, then snaked through the crowd to get closer to her.

There was admiration in Taliña's voice as she spoke of Miranda's findings and her writing. Miranda appeared suitably humble and yet proud—and damn near edible in her slinky silver dress. He caught her gaze and held it, and attraction tightened his gut.

Attraction so strong and mutual, maybe she wouldn't hate him too much for what he was about to do. And he'd make the process fun.

"Please come forth," Taliña finished, "and have Miranda sign your book."

She wasn't going to have Miranda speak?

Miranda looked a little taken aback, but she covered it and graciously took a seat as guests began to approach her. She glowed while talking to each one, smiling and listening to their stories, handling the oversight so gracefully that no one could have realized her disappointment.

"As I said, nothing as sexy as a woman in her element." Victor Blake held a fresh goblet of wine as he neared Fletch but watched Miranda.

"I believe you said intoxicating."

"Sex is intoxicating," he shot back. "Don't you think?"

Fletch merely gave him a tight smile and returned his focus to Miranda, vigilant for any sudden movement or threat. But the only person who felt threatening was the man standing next to him, staring at her in a way that put Fletch on high alert. His study of Miranda wasn't sexual, nor was it fond, amused, or curious.

It was resentful.

Victor Blake was jealous of the attention his wife was showering on Miranda. As if on cue, Talíña put her hand on Miranda's shoulder, a move she'd done so many times that Fletch had stopped responding with a twitch toward his weapon. She was a toucher, and since he didn't sense hostility, he hadn't made an effort to stop her.

But hostility came off Blake in waves. His jaw clenched as he watched Talíña rub Miranda's shoulder, then stroke her hair in a way that was more proud than affectionate. Certainly not the kind of contact that would make a man jealous.

Was it?

Blake's body language suddenly changed, relaxing as he lifted his drink.

"Excuse me," he told Fletch. "I see a guest I've yet to greet."

Blake disappeared into the crowd as Fletch watched Miranda continue to sign books and chat with the endless stream of guests. Circling the perimeter of the vast patio, he checked for any familiar faces from the night before and noticed that Victor Blake had disappeared.

The last book signed, Miranda turned as she lifted a goblet of wine to her mouth and caught Fletch's gaze. He crossed the few feet that separated them, enjoying the flush that darkened her neck and throat as he neared her.

"So tell me, do you write the same thing in every book, or do you personalize?" he asked.

She took a sip of wine, then smiled. "I try to personalize." She shook her hand. "But my fingers ache."

He lifted her hand to his lips. "I can fix that." He kissed her knuckles and dipped closer. "You've done an awful lot of smiling and chatting, luv. Do your lips ache, too?"

She laughed. "Terribly."

Just as he leaned in for a kiss, Taliña interrupted. "You must see Pakal's Crypt." Her dark eyes blazed. "Almost everyone is gone, and I'm taking a small group on a private tour of my newest creation, my pride and joy."

"Pakal's Funerary Crypt?" Miranda asked. "It's one of the most amazing places on earth," she told Fletch. "Discovered in the 1950s. The carvings on the sarcophagus lid are some of the most beautiful ever found."

"Not to mention the stucco relief of the Nine Lords of the Night," Talíña added, scooping her arm through Miranda's.

"I did a graduate thesis on that relief," Miranda exclaimed, setting down her wine glass and not noticing Talíña's knowing expression. "I can't wait to see how you've replicated it."

"Then let's go," Fletch said. "I feel I haven't lived until I've seen this place."

Talíña shook her head. "I'm sorry. I would be delighted to take you tomorrow, but this viewing is for Miranda only."

"That's a very small group, indeed," he said smoothly. "Perhaps she'd rather wait until tomorrow, as well."

"Mr. Fletcher," Talíña said, "I'm delighted that you were able to accompany my guest to our home, but I'm sure you understand that we would like some private time together. I simply want to share the mystical, magical experience of seeing Pakal's Crypt with someone who deeply understands what it means in the scheme of Maya history."

He turned to Miranda, who'd been quiet during the exchange. "I'd like to go," he said simply, hoping she understood the silent message. *For your safety.*

"Adrien." She took his arm and gently guided him aside, as Taliña walked away, pretending to say good-bye to another guest. But he had no doubt she was listening. "I understand why she wants to spend some time alone with me. You weren't expected. There's no reason I can't go to this building with her."

"Except that someone threatened you with a dead quetzal last night."

She paled. "Not Taliña. I won't be gone even a half-hour. Then . . ." The unspoken promise hung between them. They would be together for the night. She squeezed his hand. "She's done so much for me. I don't want to insult her."

He relented with a nod. Though he wasn't about to let her trek into the jungle alone, she didn't have to know that. "Have fun, then." He planted a kiss on her hair.

Taliña was instantly at Miranda's side. "Let's start at the Temple of the Sun." She indicated one of the two smaller pyramid structures about a hundred yards away. "I have something to show you there first."

Fletch waited patiently as the two women climbed the huge set of stairs to the temple, by the light of Taliña's small flashlight. Then he started in the same direction.

"I wouldn't, if I were you." Victor Blake closed his hand on Fletch's arm, only to have it instantly shaken off. "Men are not welcome."

Fletch frowned. "Why is that?"

"Taliña runs an informal program to train women in shamanism." Blake said, his voice devoid of the jealousy Fletch had sensed earlier. "I'm certain she's showing some of her techniques to Miranda, and she really doesn't like it when men spoil the process. Don't worry. They'll be back."

"Then I'll just look around at some of the sights," Fletch replied, completely unconcerned if Blake knew he was lying.

"Trust me," Blake said with a lecherous gleam in his eye. "You'll reap the benefits later."

"Thanks for the advice."

"Have a drink and relax." Blake tried to force another goblet of wine into Fletch's hands. "This is standard procedure around here."

Not standard for me. He waved off the glass and darted toward the pyramid, swearing silently when he realized the women had disappeared.

They couldn't have gone far. He jogged up to the structure, a much smaller version of the palace house. At the top of the stairs, an area was empty but for three stone statues with classic Maya faces staring back at him.

He crossed the stone floor to see the property beyond, a black maze of shadows and foliage in the dark. None of the party lights illuminated that area, and no flashlight moved with the rhythm of someone walking. A very bad feeling settled in his chest.

He paused at the top of the back stairs, listening for sounds, for a familiar voice, but he heard only laughter and soft music from the few remaining guests in the courtyard. She said they'd start there. Had they gone to the other large temple a few hundred yards to the north?

He headed to the structure tucked even deeper into the thick shrubbery and trees. What had she called this one? The most perfect of all Maya buildings. He jogged up the wide stairs.

The flat top of the pyramid was one large, enclosed room, open only in the front, facing the steps. Turquoise, gold, and stone reliefs decorated every surface, along with more symbols and hieroglyphs on the walls. Pivoting to see every shadow and corner, he called Miranda's name. No response.

He glanced over his shoulder back at the courtyard, far enough away so that the party sounds barely drifted up. He moved to the centerpiece of the room, a massive stone sculpture of a jaguar, its jaws wide open, front paws reaching six feet in the air. Between the statue's back legs, a simple clay container held a lit candle.

Next to that lay the mirror trimmed in gaudy yellow jewels.

Fletch swore under his breath. She'd been here. Recently enough to light a candle that had hardly formed a pool of wax and to drop off her magic mirror. He headed back to the arched entrance, then stopped as the sound of his footsteps changed.

He went back. And forward. The ground under his feet was hollow. Curious, he walked the room, tapping his shoe and determining where the hollow points were. Was there an entrance to some sort of basement? In the shadows, he studied the base of the statue. It was wood and appeared to be bolted into the ground by four screws. Four loose screws.

With two hands, he pushed the statue. It moved easily to the left, revealing an opening under the base. In the darkness, he could make out a set of stairs descending into the hole.

Grabbing the candle, automatically drawing his Glock, he took the first few steps into the blackness. It was colder down there, and damp. When he reached the bottom, he held up the candle and peered into the darkness.

"Bloody hell," he whispered, his jaw loosening at the sight.

There had to be ten thousand copies of Miranda's book neatly stacked in ten-foot-high rows, towers and towers of glossy white with stylized red type.

This was not a fan. This was a fanatic.

This was *crazy*.

He returned up the steps and pulled himself through the opening. The room was still empty and dark. He grabbed the mirror and ran to find Miranda, his weapon still drawn, his every instinct on fire.

CHAPTER
SEVEN

Taliña kept the flashlight low so she could follow the path and guide Miranda deeper into the rain forest, but no one looking down from the temple could see them. Soon she would need no light at all, except the light she made from her own *kyopa*.

She shivered in anticipation. Miranda would understand. Miranda would help it happen. Miranda was a sister shaman; Taliña could feel the connection the moment they'd met. It thrilled her.

"I thought your paper on the Nine Lords was brilliant," Taliña said as they neared the turn to the crypt.

"You read it?" Miranda asked with surprise.

"It's on the Internet, and you incorporated some large chunks in the book. Of course I read it."

"That's . . . very flattering."

"I'm a student of the Maya, Miranda. You are a

teacher. It's natural that I would read your work in preparation for this visit." She put her hand on Miranda's back and led her around the eucalyptus tree that marked the spot where the path veered off. "And now I'd like to switch those roles and teach you some shamanism."

Miranda laughed softly. "I don't think I'd make much of a shaman, Taliña, but I'd love to see the—oh, look at that. It's *incredible*."

It was, indeed. The latest structure to be built on Canopy was truly a masterpiece. Taliña had supervised the laying of every stone, the master carving of the ten-foot-high walls and the fifteen-foot-long chamber inside. Unlike the ginger-colored clay of the rest of the structures on Canopy, the crypt was jade green and so full of that very polished stone that the energy inside was palpable.

"Come," she said, pulling Miranda toward the six stone steps that led to a narrow opening not even wide enough for them to pass side-by-side. "We wanted it to be a perfect replica, so you have to maneuver a bit to get in."

She shimmied into the opening and took Miranda's hand to lead her through. Inside, she shone her light directly on the gorgeous carved slab that covered most of the floor. Her gaze was on Miranda.

"Oh, Taliña," she exclaimed, dropping immediately to her knees to touch the work of art. "It's absolutely stunning."

"It is, I agree. And look." She shifted the beam of light to the walls. A five-foot-tall mosaic mask of pure jade, much bigger than the one in her home, hung on the flat wall at the opposite end of the long crypt.

Miranda crossed the sarcophagus slab on the floor to admire it. "Wonderful," she whispered, touching it and turning to Taliña. "You should give classes here. You should open this up to the public. It's such an incredible place to drink in the history and culture."

Taliña tilted her head in acknowledgment. "Then let me start now. Sit here, across from me." As Miranda sat, Taliña flicked off the flashlight. "I will teach you how to summon the *kyopa.*"

"Taliña." Miranda said suddenly. "Please turn the light back on."

She did. "What's the matter?"

Even in the dimness, she could see Miranda had paled as she rose to her knees. "I hate small, dark places. Please leave the flashlight on."

"That will defeat the purpose of creating our own light. You've heard of the energy light, haven't you? A light no bigger than your fist that hovers over the room, created by mystical energy?"

Miranda frowned. "Yes, but I thought it was folklore."

"You thought wrong." She managed to keep the insult out of her voice. Miranda sounded like Victor. "We'll leave the light on until we get closer. There, now. Sit back down."

As Miranda did, Taliña slipped the *toli* from the deep pocket in her tunic. "This one is smaller but just as effective," she said, angling it to capture Miranda's spirit in the glass. For a moment, she said nothing, studying the lovely face she saw, although she could see shadows under her eyes and the strain of worry.

"I see it again," she said quietly. "Someone wants to hurt you, my dear. Someone is going to hurt you very much."

A soft sigh was the only response.

Taliña closed her eyes, wanting to turn off the flashlight but not wanting to scare Miranda when what she had to say was so important. "Miranda," she whispered, "you must listen to me. He wants to take your soul."

"What? Who?"

"That Australian man. He wants to steal your soul. You must protect you soul," she hissed.

Miranda laughed, obviously not wanting to believe what was so clear and compelling. "He might want my body, Taliña, but he's not out for the soul. You're misreading something."

Fury rumbled through her, down to the cold slab under her. "Listen to me. He is not with you by chance or accident. I know that."

"He's with me because I asked him to be," Miranda said, a note of defensiveness in her voice. "I think you're seeing more into this than there is."

Taliña shook her head. "The *toli* is never wrong. He wants something you have. He will ruin your life. Ruin it." She spat out the last two words. "If you give him anything, be sure it is only your flesh and not your soul. Not your *life.*"

"Honestly, I just met him last night. He was at my book signing."

Taliña merely arched her brows. "And you think this was an accident?"

"I think it was"—she took long enough to answer that Taliña knew she'd sown doubt—"good fortune that I met him."

"It was fortune. I just don't know if it was good." She changed the angle of the mirror. "Let me show you the light now."

Miranda nodded slowly. "How?"

Taliña inhaled deeply, a cleansing, spiritual breath that allowed her to taste the wind and smell the bits of moss that grew inside the almost completely enclosed crypt. She sat very still, silent and calm, her eyes closed, her body ready.

She touched the flashlight, and darkness descended.

"Please, Taliña. The light."

"Do not fear," Taliña assured her. She looked into the darkness, willing the light, demanding it, moving closer to Miranda so that their crossed knees could touch.

"All right," Miranda said, resigned. "Just . . . make it fast."

She would make it however she liked. "You wear a coat of armor around your energy sources, Miranda. You have closed up access to your most vulnerable places." She tightened her grip on Miranda's knees, feeling the muscles tighten in response. "Relax. You are shielding yourself. Until you let that go, you cannot draw people to you and hold them. I'm going to teach you how."

Miranda took a slow, shuddering breath. "What are you going to do?"

"I'm going to take your shields away. You will spark with strength and confidence, inner beauty, and magnetism." She would spark with something else, too, but Taliña knew better than to warn her student of the aphrodisiac effects of the *kyopa*. "I will call the light and it will fill you with *jing* and *shen*. These are the most powerful of spiritual and sexual energy. When the light appears, you will feel the storm inside you."

"I'm going to feel some kind of storm if you don't turn on the light."

She ignored Miranda's tense joke, gently stroking the skin of her knees. Then Taliña began the chant. Time ceased. Heat rose. The storm slowly brewed.

"What will happen, my friend, is that you capture the lightning in a short and pleasurable trance. For one moment, Miranda, you will feel helpless. Don't fear that."

She felt Miranda stiffen ever so slightly.

"Breathe," Taliña ordered as she slowly slid her hands to Miranda's bare arms, the energy already emanating off her skin. "*Kyopa* is your most vital bodily force. It flows through you constantly, like your blood, and when you feel it shimmer and dance over and under your skin, you will feel the first bolt of sheet lightning in your body. Don't fear that," she repeated. "It doesn't last long, but it is unforgettable."

As her mother had taught her, and her grandmother, and her great grandmother, Taliña softly hummed, transferring power and energy as effectively as if she had been pouring her blood into Miranda's veins.

"This is known as the speaking of the blood," she said softly. "Your body's life source will begin to come alive, and all of your senses will be heightened, as vivid as if you had taken a mind-altering drug. But this is natural. This is beautiful. This is womanly."

Then it appeared. Blue and beautiful, but dim. The light shone over Miranda's shoulders, filling Taliña with joy. She knew she could do this.

"Look," she whispered, leaning closer. "The *kyopa* shimmers."

Miranda turned. "I don't see anything and . . ." She stood, breaking the contact like someone snapping a live wire. "I have to get out of the dark."

Taliña grabbed her leg. "Stay."

"No!" Miranda pushed by her to the opening. "I have to get out of here."

She whipped around and grabbed Miranda's leg. "No, don't leave yet."

Miranda fell, cried out, and tried to twist away.

The glimmer of blue was now faint and barely noticeable. "Look!" She grabbed Miranda's face and turned it to look at the light. "Look what I've done!"

"Rack off, woman!" A powerful hand slammed on Taliña's shoulder, yanking her back, ripping her from the trance.

She let out a hoot of surprise and jumped up as Miranda flipped on the flashlight and shone it on the threatening scowl of Adrien Fletcher. Frustration and impatience radiated from him. He wanted something from Miranda so fiercely that Taliña could practically taste it.

Something that would hurt Miranda, she *knew*. But she also knew his energy was unstoppable, and so was his sexual hold on Miranda.

"What the hell are you doing?" he demanded.

She closed her eyes. "You can leave now, Miranda. He'll help you find your way." Then she looked accusingly at him. "Won't you?"

"Damn right I will." He reached for Miranda, who threw an unsure look at Taliña. "Let's go."

They left her alone in the crypt, where the light had gone out completely.

Furious and punched by disappointment, Taliña picked up the *toli* and threw it against the angled wall of the crypt, watching the jewels crash to the lid of the sarcophagus.

He'd won this round. She'd win the next.

Maybe she was a total fake, and maybe she was as real as the dawn, but Taliña had done *something* in that crypt. Miranda felt bathed in energy, in a high-voltage arc of desire that made her whole body vibrate with need. She held tight to Adrien as he maneuvered them through branches and palm fronds, her body warring with her head.

Her body wanted to pull Adrien to her for a long, heated kiss the minute they were outside.

Her head wanted to know what the hell had just happened back in that crypt.

He stopped to let her get her breath, his hands

squeezing shoulders. "Don't ever do that again," he growled. "I mean it."

"Kiss me." The words were out before she even realized she'd spoken. "Kiss me." She yanked him closer. "Now."

He refused. "What is wrong with you?"

"I don't know." It was the God's truth. "I just . . . she just . . ." How could she explain that the force of her desire for him rocked her? All she could hear was the drum beat of her blood and her heart. She didn't want love or friendship or protection. She wanted *sex*. Now.

The kind of sex that shook a woman to her core. The kind that made you dizzy and desperate. The kind she'd never had in her life. The kind she knew she'd have with him.

She took his hand and tried to pull him, but he didn't move. "Where are you going?" he demanded.

"I don't care where. Somewhere private. Somewhere . . ." She grabbed his neck and crushed him to her, then kissed him.

Craving and hunger and need mixed with blood-boiling desire, jolting fiery impulses through Miranda's body, melting her brain, frying her flesh, hardening her nipples, and oozing sweet feminine moisture between her legs.

She could hear only her insane heartbeat, and the edgy, desperate, strangled breaths she managed to take in the milliseconds between kisses. Unwilling to break the contact, she pushed him deeper into the jungle, into the darkest place she could find, and dragged him down to the ground with all her strength.

She slid her tongue deeper into his mouth. He groaned her name in warning. She closed her hand over the tent in his pants. With a low moan of surrender, he blissfully, deliciously took control of the kiss, buried her breast in the palm of his hand, and pulled her against an erection so shockingly hard it could easily burst seams and zippers.

Which was exactly what she wanted it to do.

She sucked the tongue he offered as they knelt, then tumbled over the ground, locking one arm around his neck to control the position of his head and using her other hand to explore the incredible planes of muscle and sinew on his chest. She smelled wet earth mixed with hot man, and reason evaporated.

Desperate, she shoved her hand into his pants and grasped him, earning a helpless hiss from his mouth, the thrill of power surging within her.

"Miranda."

It did tickle her, that lovely tuft of hair under his lips. She licked it, stabbing her tongue into the coarse triangle while rolling her palm over the hard arousal that strained his pants.

He'd inched away, ended the kiss, moved his hand from her breast, leaving her bursting with need. She laid back on the ground, spread her legs, and gathered her dress to her waist.

Taking his hand, she guided it between her legs, pressing his fingers against her moist panties, and a scream welled in her throat. She opened her mouth, and he captured it with another fierce kiss, turning her scream into a soundless moan, sliding his fingers expertly over her, letting her ride and roll and ache, all the while sucking and stroking his delicious tongue.

He broke the kiss, but not the precious contact.

"Miranda." He kissed his way to her ear, struggling to speak, only able to whisper, "You're possessed."

"Yes." She barely got the word out, nodding and writhing against his hand. "I am. I *am*. And you can't stop. You *can't*. Take me there, please. Now."

She shook, she tensed, she vibrated with need. "Please," she begged again. "I'll die if you don't. I'll die."

She needed this, needed to take him in and squeeze the satisfaction from between her throbbing, aching, hypersensitive legs.

Sliding her panties to the side, he thrust a finger into her, then two, pushing and prodding and pulsing her flesh at precisely the right place. Three fingers plunged inside, and his thumb pressed the hood of her clitoris, circling, cajoling, teasing.

At the same time, he kissed her, their teeth clashing, their lips tearing at each other. His other hand glided up her dress, until his rough palm shocked her tender nipple, squeezed it with two fingers, and sent fire straight to the spot he owned with his thumb.

The lightning flashed again, blinding her even though her eyes were closed. The wind roared like a train, and her body sparked and whipped against him.

She was lost. Gone. Taken away and dropped into a black hole, where she swirled and folded and burst and dissolved into one long, endless, blissful euphoria that shook her body.

Again and again and again, until finally, blessedly, it stopped.

And she was free of the ache and the need, heavy with satisfaction, soaked with her own release.

The blackness lifted, her blood cooled, each breath hurt a little bit less.

Finally, she could open her eyes. How they had gotten from the crypt to the ground was hazy in her mind, but he was clear. Close and warm and sharply in focus.

Had she noticed how thick and long his lashes were or that his golden eyes had flecks of black in them? His hair, unkempt and wild, was pushed back, his temples soaked with sweat, his mouth reddened, swollen.

This had to be a trance. It was Taliña's magical, mystical shaman trance of ecstasy. She'd had no control, and he had . . .

Plenty of control.

Her fist was still closed over an enormous erection, and his fingers remained curled inside her body. She closed her eyes and let out one last, helpless sigh.

"I wasn't kidding. I *was* possessed."

"I believe you were." He eased his fingers out of her, and helped her sit up. "If I didn't satisfy you, you might have spontaneously combusted."

She *had* combusted, quite spontaneously. "I think she . . . made me . . . completely crazy."

"Someone did," he said with a teasing smile. "And while that is quite a lovely skill to have, it makes me wonder what else she is doing to make you crazy."

Miranda drew back, reality and common sense making their return as she finally let go of him. "What do you mean?"

"Your hostess has ten thousand copies of your book hidden in a basement of one of her fake temples."

"Ten thousand!" Miranda's sexual buzz totally evaporated. "Are you sure?"

"Give or take a couple thousand."

"Maybe she wants to give them as gifts to friends?"

"More than the four hundred who showed up tonight?"

"To her husband's business associates? As a Christmas gift?"

"That's an awful lot of associates."

Disbelief washed over her. "There has to be an explanation."

"Could she be one of your crazies? Maybe it's an attempt to hide all the copies of a book she doesn't want sold?"

"I don't think so. I don't get a dangerous vibe from her, and she's been so supportive."

"Supportive? She spirited you away to a dark crypt, juiced you up to a frenzy, and God knows what she'd have done to you next."

Why did she have ten thousand copies of Miranda's book were hidden in a basement?

"I want to see for myself," Miranda said, pushing up on her knees and straightening her dress.

"No need." He stood and offered a hand. "You can trust me."

But could she? What if Taliña's warnings were real? "If you don't take me there, I'll go find them myself."

"Miranda, I saw them. You don't need to go snooping around the basement of some temple."

"Yes, I do." She stood without his assistance. "Maybe they're just blank covers. Or maybe they're some kind of mistake print run. It's the Temple of the Cross, isn't it?"

"Fine. I'll take you there. But no matter what, don't leave me. You got that?"

"Yes."

To prove it, she held his hand tightly as they made their way through the rain forest. The trees were thick and plentiful, the tangy smell of cedar and spruce mixed with sweet orchids and wet earth. The only thing that gave away the real location was the utter lack of humidity in the air. No amount of irrigation could create the greenhouse of humidity Miranda had breathed in Mexico, Belize, and Guatemala.

Still, the smells, the trees, the leaves, and the canopy felt real. All that was missing was the shriek of a howler monkey or the squawk of a macaw. It was a wonder the shaman hadn't had her rich husband pipe in the music of the rain forest.

"What did she do in there, anyway?" Fletch asked.

"She was trying to get this light to shine. It's called *kyopa*. It's an energy of—"

He paused, holding her back as his gaze darted around the shadows. Then he reached his right hand to his waist, sliding his gun from under his jacket.

"What is it?" She barely mouthed the words, but he

gave his head a quick shake, quieting her without even looking at her.

With his left hand, he twisted her behind him, pulling her close against his back and locking her there with a solid grip. "No matter what I do," he whispered, "stay behind me. No matter how I move, stay on this side." He squeezed her closer, pressing her to his back.

Adrenaline rushed from the pit of her stomach to the tips of her fingers, and she moved closer to Adrien—a safe, solid man who'd take a bullet for her after knowing her for just twenty-four hours.

He held his weapon straight out, his index finger not along the barrel as it had been when he'd secured her apartment last night, but curled around the trigger, ready to kill with a touch.

Her pulse accelerated as she matched his stealthy footsteps, watching his head move from side to side. No one attacked, no sound slowed them, and Adrien followed his instinct and an impressive mental compass to get them back to Taliña and Victor Blake's Maya-inspired mansion.

"Where in the temple?" she asked. "Where were the book?"

"Underneath a statue of a jaguar." He pronounced it *jag-u-ar*.

"The jag-u-ar is the god of the underworld."

He snorted softly. "No wonder he was such a heavy bastard." He loosened his grip on her a tiny bit and eased her around to his side. Then he lowered the gun away from her, his finger off the trigger. "There's only one entrance, in the front. But there's hardly any light, so if you stay right in front of me, I'll block you, and we'll run up."

"Why do you think someone is going to attack us?"

"Years of training. Fear of error." He glanced around. "And the odd crack of a branch." The only people in the courtyard appeared to be the white-jacketed waiters and staff. "You ready?"

"I will be in a second." She reached down and slid her sandals off. "Let's go."

He gave her a tiny push, and they picked up their pace, staying deep in the shadows of the bushes and the foliage until they reached the foot of the structure.

Her heart pounding, she flew up the stairs into the darkness of the enclosed shrine at the top of the small pyramid.

As he'd said, the only thing in the cool stucco-walled room was a massive statue of a jaguar leaping in the air, its mouth wide. Ambient light filtered through the arched openings along the front, creating an eerie shadow of the beast against the back wall.

"The opening's under him," Fletch said. "Let me give it a burl."

He holstered the gun and braced his body against the hind quarter of the carved stone, a grimace pulling his expression as he pushed. It didn't move. He grunted and pushed again.

"Son of a bitch," he murmured, kneeling to the ground. "It's been bolted back in place."

Miranda turned slowly, examining the room. "There has to be another opening to the chamber below. I bet it's on the side, built into the wall, under the front stairs. That's how the original structure was built."

"Maybe not in this Disney version." He worked the bolts.

"I know where the downstairs opening could be. Come with me."

"All right. But if we don't find it, we're calling it quits."

She let him lead the way down the front steps. "Around the side," she said as they reached the bottom, her shoes hanging from her fingers.

"Wait!" He grabbed her hand, and his eyes flashed an alert. Then he pushed her against the wall. "I heard something over there." He indicated the left side of the building. "Go around to the right, stay low, and don't move," he whispered. "I'm going to see who's following us, and I don't want you in the line of fire."

She did as he said, sliding along the base of the square building, inching around the corner into the shadows.

As she pressed one hand against the cool stone, she felt it. The opening.

She dropped her shoes and jimmied the stone one way, then the other, until a door on cleverly hidden runners rumbled to the left.

She took a half-step into the darkness, blinking to adjust her eyes to the pitch black. Holding her hands straight out, she felt nothing, but on her right was a chilled stone wall, and a few steps to her left was another. But what was ahead of her? The chamber? Ten thousand books?

Discomfort slithered over her. She didn't want to go any further into the dark, away from the door. She ventured one more step, then a smack of stone against stone cracked behind her.

Oh, God, no! She spun around, smacking her hands on the wall that used to be a door and knowing, deep and certain, that she was trapped. She threw herself against one wall, then another, then another, then another.

There was no air. No space. No light.

Familiar, fierce, and suffocating, panic squeezed the life from her chest.

She threw all her weight wildly at the stone wall, but it didn't budge. She scraped her fingers down each side, trying to find a handle, a slot, a way out. There was none.

She tried to breathe but couldn't. She tried to call out, but her voice was strangled by fear. Sweat broke out everywhere. She sank to her knees, the only sound in her black grave her hopeless breaths.

Darkness and raw certainty engulfed her. She was going to die. Now.

CHAPTER
EIGHT

FLETCH BRACED HIS weapon with his left hand, peering into the thick foliage that brushed the orange stucco walls. Even a homemade jungle was a deep, dark, and dangerous place. He darted around the corner, ready to surprise whoever or whatever had been following them since they left the crypt.

But nothing moved. No predator's eyes gleamed in the dark. Had he imagined the rustling of trees? He walked along the side of the structure, scanning for the slightest movement, listening for the softest sound. Only a twig cracked under his foot, and in the distance, the tap of china and soft Spanish chatter drifted from the party cleanup.

He rounded the back, using his shoulder to skim the stone in case he found the opening to the underground chamber that Miranda thought would be there. Everything was still and quiet. At the last corner, he took one more check around him, then turned, expecting to see her where he'd sent her.

Bloody hell. Where did she go?

"Miranda?" He didn't shout, but she should have heard him. "Miranda!"

He sprinted toward the front of the pyramid, squinting into the brush and feeling the walls for that opening. Where was she? He called again, much louder this time.

His foot hit something, and his heart lurched at the sight of her shoes on the ground. Had someone taken her? Had she run?

Then he heard a whimper so soft that a man who hadn't spent months in hostage-rescue training would have missed it. A sound of desperation, a moan that came from . . . inside.

She was in there? He holstered his weapon and spread his hands on the walls. There was no opening, no crack he could see. "Miranda!"

He felt every inch of the rough stucco wall using his palms, his cheek, his whole body to sense, until he finally found the thin, hidden seam.

Dropping to his knees, he plastered his ear to the wall to hear her.

"Hold on!" he called. "I'll get you."

Stabbing his fingertips so furiously he broke the skin, he searched for the way in. Sweat ran down his temples, and every muscle strained with the frustrating effort. At her next muffled call, he kicked the damned wall.

She had to be trapped in the chamber under the

pyramid. Drawing his weapon again, he tore around the front corner and raced up the stairs, two at a time.

He shot at the bolts, the crack reverberating inside the enclosure, bullets and concrete and pieces of the wooden platform ricocheting around him. He threw his weight on the statue and powered it to the side.

"Miranda!" He rushed down the steps, moving from memory in the dark. "Are you in here?"

"I'm here!" Her cry was still muffled, but he could tell they were separated by something less dense than concrete.

He followed the sound to the mountain of books stacked floor to ceiling. She was behind them? How deep was this wall of books?

Deep.

He started flinging one after another over his shoulder, clearing the way to the other side. "Hang on!" he hollered as he whipped through another hundred books, the hard covers jabbing his hands, more sweat sliding down his face. There was no frigging air down here. How long would she last?

Behind the books, in a narrow opening he'd cleared, he reached a solid wall. He wanted to spit in frustration, mentally flipping through every possible option and coming up with zero.

"It's quite simple, really."

At the sound of a man's voice, Fletch automatically reached for his weapon.

"You just press this button."

With a low hum, the wall started to move to the right as if by magic. He dove for Miranda, pulling her out with one hand, positioning his gun to fire with the other. She gulped air, tumbling into him.

Then he turned his attention to Victor Blake's voice in the dark. "Thanks, mate. That handy switch work a light, by any chance?"

A match struck, flaring under the rounded jaw of their host. He looked at them, then at the mess, his expression pure confusion. "What the hell is all this?"

He didn't know what was in his own cellar? "This is a stockpile." Fletch dipped lower to support her, then guided her through the tossed books. "Of Miranda's books."

She'd held tight. Still getting her breath and bearings.

"Are you all right?" he asked, pulling her closer.

She half nodded, then shifted her attention to Blake, her expression changing as strength and oxygen started to surge through her again. "Why do you have all these?" she demanded. "Who trapped me in there? What's going on?"

Victor frowned, took the last step, and sighed. "I'm afraid Taliña's interests can sometimes border on obsession."

Miranda choked, her eyes burning Blake. "She *bought* these books? Why?"

"As I said . . ." He shook the match before it burned his fingers, cloaking them in darkness again, then lit another. "Please. Come upstairs. We can talk."

"You first, Blake." Fletch made sure the other man saw his weapon.

They followed him out into the air, Miranda's body trembling, but Fletch suspected it was as much with fury as fear.

"I'm afraid that this time, her obsession has gotten out of hand," Blake said. "She's fixated with everything that has anything to do with the Maya, and your work fascinates her."

"How did I get trapped in there?" Miranda asked.

"I'm certain that was an accident. There is a switch on the floor that closed that door behind you. It's simply another entrance to the underground of the pyramid. I use it as a safe room. I have several around the estate, for our protection."

The explanation made sense from a security standpoint but didn't begin to erase Fletch's unease. "Who rebolted the statue over the basement door?" he asked. "I left that wide open an hour or so ago."

"Probably one of the staff. Perhaps they came to replenish the supply of your books at the party."

"Why does she have so many of them?" Miranda demanded. "There were only a few hundred people here."

He drew in a long breath, lifted one shoulder. "You'd have to ask her."

"I will. Now."

"I'm afraid that's impossible," Blake said. "She's gone."

"Gone?" Miranda almost choked. "Where?"

"I don't know where she goes," he said, resignation and shame in his voice. "But periodically, she disappears into her jungle, where she . . ." He paused.

"She what?" Fletch prodded.

"She practices her craft." Blake's expression turned dark, his focus on Miranda. "I think it best you leave tonight, Dr. Lang."

Fletch couldn't agree more. "We're out of here."

"Absolutely not," Miranda shot back. "Not until I talk to her. When will she be back?"

"We never know." Blake turned to the rain forest he'd built. "But she always returns, eventually. And that's all that matters."

Miranda squared her shoulders. "I need to talk to her, and I will."

"No, Dr. Lang. You need to leave. Can I make it any clearer? Leave Canopy. Leave Taliña. Now."

Fletch's fingers twitched on the Glock. "We get the message, Blake." He put a bit of pressure on Miranda with his shoulder.

She didn't argue. But he knew she'd be back here—with or without him.

Eileen Stafford was right about one thing: it was easy for an ex-cop to find an ex-cop. Especially at dawn on a Sunday morning, when the ex-cop looking for information brings doughnuts to the overnight shift.

At the painfully precious clapboard building with the hand-painted ISLE OF PALMS POLICE DEPARTMENT badge hanging from a cornflower-blue railing, it cost Jack only a dozen Krispy Kremes to learn exactly where to find former Officer William L. Gilbert, who had left the Charleston PD just a few years after he'd arrested Eileen for murder and moved to this luxurious suburb to finish his years on the force. Now he could be found golfing.

And if he wasn't on the green at Seagrass, a ritzy strip of land that jutted into the ocean ten minutes from downtown Charleston, then sixty-year-old Willie could be found at his condo clubhouse, playing cards at the table overlooking the last fairway, drinking sweet tea with lemon with two of his cronies. They played every single day from eleven to two forty-five, when Willie had a massage, a haircut, or a visit from a lady friend.

Willie was a creature of habit, it seemed, and a very healthy and wealthy one at that.

It didn't take long to find the clubhouse at the Seagrass Condo and Resort complex and the casual game room and grille known as the Nineteenth Hole. There, among the ladies who lunched and the golfers who relived each stroke of the morning, was a table of three old men deep in a game of cutthroat pinochle.

Jack wandered over to the table, testing his observation skills to see if he could guess which one was Willie Gilbert. If not for the young lieutenant at the Isle of Palms PD who suggested that Willie's lady friend was a stripper and the former cop was a frequent user of a certain little blue pill, Jack would have picked the man with the alcohol-induced rosacea on his hollow cheeks. Or the slightly hunched fellow with thick-rimmed reading glasses and the bad comb-over.

So he went with the player who had no telltale signs of alcoholism, no deep crevices from smoking, no sad cop jowls or baggy eyes from sleepless nights at crime scenes.

"Willie Gilbert?"

The virile retiree looked up, and just for a flash, Jack could see the ready, defensive mask of a cop. It disappeared, replaced by an easy smile and a booming Southern drawl. "What can I do you for, son?"

"Name's Jack Culver." Jack reached out to shake Willie's hand. "I'm a private investigator. Can I talk to you when you have a break in the game?"

The other two men glanced at Willie, then at Jack.

Willie knocked the table, hard. "Bid or pass?" Then, to Jack, "What's the subject matter?"

"An old Charleston PD case."

The man to Willie's right slid his glasses lower and peered over the rims at Jack. "You play?" He jutted his chin to the empty chair.

"We don't play partners, Gabe." Willie's glare was easy to read. "Go sit on the patio, son. I'll be out in a spell."

"A spell could be two hours," Gabe said, flattening the few strands he had left over an egg-shaped dome. "Which case?"

Willie tossed his cards onto the table. "Son of a bitch, can't a man play a game of cutthroat in peace?"

"I can give you a call and set something up when it's more convenient," Jack offered. "Maybe around three today."

Sunday was Lady Friend Day.

Willie rolled his captain's chair back and gestured toward the French doors that led to an outdoor terrace. "Go."

Outside, they walked to a tile-topped table, still damp from morning dew.

"Those two old biddies don't need to hear everything," Willie said as he yanked out a chair. "What's on your mind?"

"Does the name Eileen Stafford mean anything to you?"

Jack saw the tiniest change in Willie Gilbert's hazel eyes.

"Of course it does." He waited a beat. Then another. "And?"

"You arrested her."

"I arrested a lot of people. Don't tell me she's weaseled her way out of jail."

"Not unless you consider dying of cancer weaselly."

Willie lifted his chin to scratch a clean-shaven face, the motion revealing a slight discoloration along his jaw, the work of an excellent plastic surgeon and his laser. "So, what do you want to know? The case is thirty years old."

"Do you remember it?"

He shrugged. "I remember that there was enough evidence to put her away for life. A gun that matched the murder weapon practically in her hands, her fingerprints all over the gate down in Philadelphia Alley where the victim was shot. No alibi and an eye witness who saw Stafford running from the scene of the crime." Willie leaned back, swiped his hands on his trousers. "What exactly are you working on?"

There were a number of different ways to go on this. The missteps in the trial, where Willie had testified. The fact that there was no gunpowder residue on her clothes or hands. The fact that her motive didn't hold water. The fact that Willie Gilbert lived well beyond the means of most retired cops. The old Jack, the one with unparalleled instinct, would have known exactly which route to choose.

"I'm trying to reunite Eileen with a child she gave up for adoption."

He saw an infinitesimal flinch before Willie shook his head. "News to me. 'Fraid I can't help you." He pushed back from the table.

"You ever hear of the Sapphire Trail babies?" Jack asked. "A black-market operation near Holly Hill up in Orangeburg County?"

Willie stared hard. "You want some free advice, Mr. Culver?"

"I don't know. Do I?"

Standing to his full six feet, Willie tucked his hands into the pockets of his dark green pants, his golf shirt pulling over gym-toned muscles. "Drop this case."

"Why would I do that?"

"Because Eileen Stafford is a pathological liar, a toxic, hate-spewing witch whose brain is so warped she probably gave herself leukemia." He made a mock salute. "I'm afraid I can't help you."

He headed toward the door, which opened before he got there. Gabe was on the other side, waiting. Over the thick rims of his glasses, he gave Jack an unreadable look.

"Willie," Jack called.

He stopped, waited, then turned. "What?"

"I never said it was leukemia."

Willie's tanned, unlined face paled slightly, though not so much someone else might notice.

"Whatever. I stand by my advice." Willie continued into the clubhouse.

A welcome shot of adrenaline spilled into Jack's veins,

as satisfying as a finger of Glenlivet. He still had it. He might not be able to fire a gun like he used to, but he could still smell a baddie. He headed down the outside stairs toward the parking lot, where the valet popped him his keys, and he caught them, left-handed.

Opening the car door, he couldn't fight a satisfied smile.

He still had it. And although Willie Gilbert hadn't told him much, he'd unknowingly told him something critical. The history here was important enough to matter. To someone. Still, thirty years later.

That's what no one knew but him. Well, someone knew. Eileen knew. And . . . a killer knew. His thoughts stopped when he slid into the driver's seat, frowning at the business card stuck in the steering wheel.

It was his own card, probably from the stash in the console of the rental, and a phone number was written on the back. He opened his cell phone and dialed. It clicked on the first ring.

"Back off, Jack," a male voice said. "Or she'll die."

"Who'll die?"

"The girl you're trying to find."

He turned back toward the patio, where Willie held a cell phone to his ear. He snapped it shut and disappeared into the clubhouse, never looking in the direction of the parking lot.

He still had it.

But the question now was, what the hell did he do with it?

Chapter
NINE

"Oh, my hearty, that was a party." Fletch belted his favorite drinking song as he soaped his body in the piss-poor stream of hot water offered by the overpriced beachfront hotel's shower. He'd left the door open a crack and could see the California morning sun streaming into the room, teasing him with fantasies of walking along the shore or spending the afternoon poolside with Miranda.

Not that they were there on holiday, but if she had a bathing suit in one of those suitcases he'd lugged into the suite in the dead of night, perhaps he'd find the tattoo with a simple suggestion that they take a dip.

It was definitely time for Plan B since the gods had once again smashed their sexual mojo. After fleeing Canopy, any chance of getting her undressed was put to rest with the firm latch of the bedroom door and the unspoken suggestion that he spend the night on the salon couch.

But she'd let him in a few minutes ago to use the bathroom, scrambling back into her bed without any greeting.

He turned the water to ice cold, faced it for a few minutes, and twisted the faucet off, hearing a low, long moan from the bedroom. Without hesitation, or a towel, he charged in.

She sat up in the bed, her back stick-straight, her eyes closed, her arms extended with her palms up, the low moan coming from her chest.

"Miranda?"

She didn't open her eyes. "Please. I need all my concentration."

"Meditating?"

"Oh!" She folded forward with the angry exclamation, burying herself in a mountain of fluffy bedding. "I can feel it start, and I'm trying like mad to ward it off."

"A panic attack?"

"Yes." The down muffled her response. "I. Can. Beat. This."

Water dripped onto the carpet as he reached the bed in four strides. "Of course you can. Here." He knelt next to the bed and lifted her shoulders, easing her back. "Close your eyes. Deep breaths. This worked for you the other night. What brought it on, anyway? You were fine when I walked in here." He hesitated, staying below the side of the bed but gently rubbing her shoulders as she sank into the pillow. "Me?"

"No." She exhaled. "I slept well, but when you woke me up to come in here, I just started reliving that . . . that . . . tomb." She punched the bed again, turning toward him. "Dammit! I was okay until I remembered . . . how dark it was."

He stroked her arm, stealing a quick look at the paper-thin cotton camisole top and sleep pants she wore. "I'm sure you were scared. You'd have every right to be, in that dark hole."

Her eyes flashed blue flints at him. "I don't want to be scared. More than anything in the world, I don't want to be scared." She closed her eyes. "But the fear's stronger than I am."

"No, it's not," he told her, continuing his soothing ministrations and stealing a few more glances at the way her breasts rose and fell with each calming breath. "You need to channel all that fear into something else. Anger. Action. Something you have control over."

"That's just it," she said. "I *don't* have control. I tried to find my way around that building, and *bam*, I was locked in. Trapped. Buried . . ."

"You're fine now. We got you out."

"What if you hadn't been there?" She hitched herself up on one elbow. "What happens when you're gone?"

Good freaking question. What *would* happen to her when he was gone?

He knelt lower, aware of his nakedness, the skimpy clothes she wore, and the great big bed that suddenly looked damned inviting.

"Does that help?" he asked, sliding his hand under

her hair to massage the tense muscles of her neck. "Do you feel better?

"Yeah." Chills rose on her skin, and her nipples hardened from the cool air of an overhead fan. Or maybe his touch caused her body to react. "That's . . . better."

Her skin! What was he doing admiring her breasts when he finally had the opportunity he'd wanted for two days? His gaze moved over the sweet, buttery skin of her arms and throat, her shoulders. He stroked the inside of her arm with a light, soothing, nonthreatening touch.

She inhaled again, definitely calmer. "Thank you," she murmured, turning to smile. "That helps."

"Turn over, luv," he suggested. "Let me give you a bit of a rub. You'll feel better."

She did, without any look of doubt regarding his motives. So trusting, so ready for a pair of hands to calm her down. He could do that. And he could examine her for a tattoo at the same time. "Just let me unwind you, then." He continued with soothing strokes, massaging her back, seeing nothing on the exposed skin. Under the top?

He lifted it and felt her tense. "No worries," he assured her. "I'm just relaxing you." He inched the T-shirt up her back, scanning every inch for even the smallest drop of permanent ink.

There was no ink, only deliciously soft, feminine skin. She shuddered under his fingertips, her soft sigh like a shot of arousal to his groin.

She arched slightly, almost giving him a glimpse of the side of her breast. Desire, sharp and hot, fired straight through him, and he burned to slide his fingers around to cup her delicate breast. To taste it. To taste *her*.

She wouldn't stop him. That knowledge just made him harder. He squeezed his eyes shut and lifted his fingers from her skin. It was wrong to take advantage of this willing woman; he was already on shaky ground. Seducing her and then running off if he had the wrong girl . . . Now that he knew her, *liked* her, that was sinking to the depths.

He forced himself to think like a mother instead of a man. Where might someone mark an infant? Aborigines did it on the bottoms of the feet and very high on the thigh, near the groin.

He ran his hands over the rise of her buttocks, her soft flannel pants offering very little barrier under his palms.

She rose again, a natural, feminine response, and, his cock went right up with her. Ignoring the drain of blood from his brain to his balls, he continued to stroke her thighs and her calves and finally reached her bare feet.

Massaging one, then the other, he checked the tender skin of the bottoms. He even separated her toes to check the delicate skin in between, and she wiggled them invitingly.

It would be so easy to lick that tender flesh and continue his inspection . . . with his mouth.

He shifted his weight on his knees. It had to be on the thigh. Or maybe under her breast, or on her stomach, or lower. He needed to see all of her.

And he needed to get his hands off her before he lost control.

"You should take a warm bath," he suggested. "That's very relaxing."

She turned her head to face him, her cheeks flushed, her eyes bright. "Alone?"

"I'll draw the water," he said, purposely not answering the question. "And you'd better turn the other way, unless you want to see all of my ink." And all of his body.

Her eyes widened. "Other than the ink on your arm?"

He rose a little, revealing the small black deer's head with stylized antlers slightly below his navel.

She stared at the drawing, and of course he just got harder, but he kept low enough so she couldn't see his full arousal.

"Is that a reindeer?"

"That's the emblem of my rugby club in Hobart, the Glenorchy Stags. A bunch of larrikins who hit the midnight tat parlor after we won the championship a few years back."

She smiled a little, her gaze hot on his flesh. "Any others?"

He knelt lower, and slid a finger in her waistband. "No fair. You've seen two of mine. What have you got?"

"None."

"You sure?"

She gave a soft laugh. "Of course I'm sure. And this is the second time you've asked."

He inched the elastic down, torturing himself with the sight of more creamy skin. "What if I don't believe you?"

"I'd say you're trying like hell to get me naked." She turned on her side, offering him another glimpse of the underside of her breast. "What do you want, Adrien?" The question was loaded with provocation.

"I want . . . to see you." It was the raw, honest truth.

"Right." She used his accent again, slathering sarcasm in the drawn-out syllable.

"It's true." He wanted much more, but balls to the wall, all he *had* to do was see her. "You've very beautiful."

Her smile widened. "Byu-ee-ful."

"You are," he said quietly.

She said nothing, but searched his face "Why don't you draw that bath?"

Why didn't he? "All right." His voice was husky as he forced himself to take his hands off her and twirl his finger. "Round you go, then. Unless you want to see my real stag."

She didn't move.

"Don't say you weren't warned." He pushed himself up, her gaze locked on his erect cock. He stood and turned to walk toward the bathroom.

"And that," he said, reaching back to tap the vivid red and blue design that covered his right shoulder blade, "is a bunyip."

"A whatyip?"

He imagined her staring at the beady eyes and sharp teeth of his favorite tattoo.

"The official monster of Australia."

"He's scary."

"That's why I got him." He closed the bathroom door behind him, and leaned against it, both hands closing over his aching hard-on. But he didn't stroke himself, even though release would have been instant and easy. It just wouldn't have been remotely satisfying.

Instead, he turned to the sink and flipped the cold water on.

The last thing he should do was mess this job up with sex. He cupped his hands and splashed his face. The *last* thing.

Miranda gave the door a solid push, one fist on the sheet she'd wrapped herself in the way they did in movies when no bathrobe was handy. Adrien stood in front of the mirror, a small electric razor buzzing in his hand, a towel around his waist. Behind him, the tub was nearly full.

"No bubbles?" she asked.

"I can't see you that way."

She dragged her gaze to his towel, adding a meaningful slant of her brow. "I can't see you, either."

"You've seen me," he said. "Get in while it's nice and warm."

She let the sheet fall and stepped in, sliding into the hot water.

"Feel better?" he asked, resuming the work on his face.

"Yes," she lied, dipping low enough for the water to cover her whole body, but angling her head against the tub so she could surreptitiously study the official monster of Australia. And his tattoo.

"How long have you had these panics?" he asked, adjusting the razor to a different setting. The tickle setting, no doubt.

"The first one I remember was around eleven. My mother said I used to have night terrors when I was a toddler, violent, wild nightmares with screaming that you don't remember."

"Do you still have nightmares?"

"Not since I moved to California—and rarely before that."

He nodded as though he was mulling that over. "Why do you think your mum was so over-protective?"

"My safety has always been her biggest worry."

"Why?"

She frowned at him. "Aren't all mothers that way?"

He snorted softly but didn't answer. *If you want me to cool off fast, ask about my mum.*

She didn't exactly want him to cool off, but there was no sign of the mighty erection she'd just seen, so maybe he'd cooled himself off. "So, what happened with your mother?"

The shaver stopped buzzing. "My mum racked off when I was about five years old." He tapped the side of the sink with his shaver, hard enough to send a little flurry of whiskers out of it. "She hated my dad with a passion. For good reason, too, since he was a stinking bludger who beat the crap out of her."

"And . . . she left a five-year-old behind?"

"Well, she was a stripper and a whore, so I didn't really fit into her lifestyle."

Stunned, she sat up at stared at him. "Are you serious?"

"As the dead." He turned, his caramel eyes hot and direct. "Not everyone has dreamy childhoods in suburbs with doting parents whose biggest concern is whether or not their baby gets a skinned knee."

"It's not my fault my mother was overprotective," she shot back.

He shrugged. "Think of the alternative. No fear . . . no family." His voice trailed off, and he looked back in the mirror at his reflection.

"I'm sorry," she said softly, drawing her legs up to hug them.

"Don't be. Wasn't your fault."

"Still . . ." She let out a little breath. The blinding sexual pull she'd felt in bed was diminished, replaced by a different ache. This one much higher, in her chest, as she imagined a tough little Adrien growing up like that. "No fear? Of anything?"

"Nothing."

"I don't believe you. You must be afraid of something."

He splashed water on his face, droplets flying everywhere, hitting the mirror, wetting his hair. "Not a freaking thing, luv."

"Not scared of dying? Of being alone? Of spiders? Nothing?"

He laughed a little, but it didn't reach his eyes. "I'm afraid of leaving you alone to fend for yourself against some creepy people who want to hurt you."

Then don't leave.

But she didn't say the words. He knew what she wanted. And if he didn't, there were more effective ways to tell him.

She stood slowly, letting the water slide down her body just as his gaze did, from her neck, over her breasts, down her stomach, to her thighs.

He stared at her, hard, relentless, and direct.

Then don't leave.

His towel tented, giving her a rush of satisfaction. His eyes moved like a steam iron over her skin, the heat of his gaze making her nipples ache and her stomach constrict.

"You said you wanted to see me," she whispered. "So look."

He did just that, the burn of his eyes as arousing as if he'd run his tongue along the same lines.

Heat pooled low in her, wet and warm and achy as his gaze settled there, so intense she felt her clitoris tingle and burn and throb.

Her fingers ached to rub it, to ask him to do the same.

"Turn around." His voice was husky and tight.

She did, sensing him come closer, feeling the fire of his scrutiny.

"Lift your hair," he said.

She scooped up her hair with two hands. He was right behind her now but still not touching.

She felt his breath trailing down her spine, then lower, and he dipped behind her. His breath warmed her skin, the heat of him just centimeters from the flesh of her bottom and thighs, intense, unrelenting, close.

And still he didn't touch her.

A single drop of feminine moisture rolled down the inside of her leg. She closed her eyes, tried to squeeze the wetness back, but the tightening muscles sent a sensation of sex right back inside her. The pull of an orgasm coiled up to her womb, shocking her with its force and the possibility.

He still hadn't touched her.

She put a hand over her mouth, closed her eyes, and squeezed again, astonishingly close to climax.

"I was right," he said, something odd in his tone.

She turned, her moist tuft eye level with him. He dipped his head to the side, and for a moment, she thought he was going to taste her. Heat clenched tighter, knowing she'd come the instant his tongue touched her.

She lifted shaky hands to take his shoulders and steady herself, ready for the onslaught of his mouth, but he stood so suddenly and fast that she almost stumbled back.

"You were right about what?" she asked in a strained voice.

"You're beautiful. Every . . . single . . . inch of you."

"Adrien. You don't . . . have to . . . leave." *Then touch me.*

He cupped her jaw, lifting her face toward his. The touch, so gentle after the scorch of his visual caress, surprised her. "I told you I wanted to go to Los Angeles with you. And I will. If I can help you find whoever is threatening you, I will."

"And then?"

He let out a frustrated sigh. "I have a job to do, and it can't be done in LA."

It was some consolation that he looked as pained as she felt.

"I understand," she said.

He shook his head. "Actually, you don't understand at all."

She stepped back as realization slammed her in the chest. "Do you have . . . is there another . . ."

"Another woman?"

She nodded.

His smile was wry. "In a manner of speaking."

Oh. She'd never considered that possibility. "Well, you get points for honesty. And fidelity."

He pulled another bath towel off the wrap, covering her. "I have been honest about how beautiful you are. And I've told you from day one that this little interlude was not just about sex."

Not even when she offered it and he wanted it. He tightened the towel across her chest and dropped a gentle kiss on her forehead. "Let's go to Los Angeles, luv."

When he left, Miranda looked in the mirror, at the face of a woman who'd just been royally rejected. Rejection hurt a lot. But it hurt less than fear, and for that reason alone, she'd let him come with her.

She got back into the lukewarm water and finished her bath. Alone.

CHAPTER
TEN

THE STREETS OF Westwood Village bustled with the beautiful people out to see and be seen on a Sunday night. The enclave of high-end boutiques, gourmet eateries, and red-carpet-ready movie theaters on the outskirts of UCLA was peppered with glamazons too perfect to be real, followed closely by packs of hot guys, stunning matched-set couples, and a few wide -eyed tourists. It seemed as if everyone was on a cell phone or talking to nearly invisible ear buds, and very few actually spoke English. Miranda heard Spanish, German, and quite a bit of Arabic from the glitzy crowd.

"I can't imagine any of these people coming to Westwood to go into a bookstore, let alone one featuring nonfiction about the Maya," Miranda said to Adrien, who maintained constant, maddening physical contact with her as they walked.

"Your book isn't about the Maya," he corrected. "It's about misperceptions and expectations. It's about the impact of the ancients on us."

She smiled up at him, delighted. "You've been reading."

He shrugged. "A few chapters here and there. Don't worry, luv, you'll have a crowd." He steered her around two teenage girls who might have been peeled from a spread in *Vogue*. "Especially after that masterful live interview on TV today."

She wished his compliments didn't make her so warm inside, but they did. Just like the strength of his arm around her, the smell of soap and shampoo, the sound of his ridiculously attractive accent.

She glanced at her watch. "It's only eight o'clock, and the reading doesn't start until nine. Let's get ice cream for dessert."

"Ice cream? Most folks need a pint of ale before a public appearance."

"I'll have a glass of wine when I'm done. Now I need comfort food."

He tucked her closer under his arm, a move so natural and affectionate that Miranda almost slid her own arm around his waist, until she noticed him glaring at someone who had his eye on her.

"You don't feel like you eat enough comfort food," he said as the man looked away. "But we have to go early to do a security check. I want to know where every exit and entrance are, and where you'll be standing and signing and how close I can be to you. And check out the customers and see if I'll have to convince any crazies to leave. So, the ice cream will have to wait."

"I really appreciate this . . . Fletch."

He cringed and punched his heart. "Buggers. I've been demoted."

"Not really," she said. "Think of it as a step forward in our friendship. Or whatever a bodyguard calls a person he's protecting."

"Principal. Tonight, you are my principal."

"And what do your principals call you?"

"The best in the business."

She laughed softly. "Then I'm in good hands."

He turned them off the boulevard to a side street and walked to the one-story brick building with a simple sign that read BRUIN BOOKS.

Miranda knew something was strange the minute they walked into the deserted bookstore. The cash register and a table stood empty, as did the tight rows of bookshelves beyond. There was no signing area. No podium, no chairs. No patrons. No copies of *Catclysn't* anywhere.

"Hello?" Miranda called, peering between the shelves. "Is anyone here?"

A door squeaked from the back. "Be right there," a female voice replied.

A few seconds later, a young Asian woman with a long ponytail ambled through the stacks, her arms full of books.

"Sorry about that," she said with a smile as she unloaded the pile onto a single stuffed chair in the front area. "Can I help you?"

Miranda checked out her name tag. "Hi, Ophelia. I'm Miranda Lang."

"Uh-huh." She gave a quick glance at Adrien, then back to Miranda. "Are you looking for something in particular?"

Adrien's expression matched the sinking sensation in her gut. Something wasn't right here. "I'm supposed to do a reading and signing. My book is *Cataclysn't*."

Ophelia's jaw dropped. "It was canceled."

Could she have the date wrong? The location? "My publisher set it up weeks ago. It's scheduled for tonight at nine o'clock."

"I know, I saw it on the calendar, but . . ." She frowned, and shook her head. "I was working when the call came in that said you couldn't make it. And my boss was pissed, because he had, like, two hundred copies of your book."

Had? "Who called? Was it Debbie Shervey at Calypso Publishing? She's the publicist arranging all this."

She shrugged. "I didn't get the name. I thought you were the chick who called."

Miranda's chest tightened. "When did this happen?"

"Like about three days ago?" she said in classic California up-talk. "The guy came and got the books yesterday."

"What guy?" Adrien asked.

She shrugged again. "I have no clue who he was. But he bought every one of the two hundred books, in their boxes, put them in a pickup truck, and left."

"How did he pay?" he asked. "Do you have a check number or credit card?"

"He paid in cash," she said. "All hundreds, and it was, like, four thousand bucks!"

"Would your publisher do that?" Adrien asked Miranda. "Would they cancel a signing and repurchase the books?"

"No. And if they did, for whatever bizarre reason, Debbie would call me." But it was too late to call anyone in New York now, especially on a Sunday night.

Why did this keep happening? Why was every event . . . sabotaged?

Disappointment and unease burned low in her belly. "All right, then," Miranda said softly. "I guess there's no reason for us to stay."

"I'm totally sorry," the young woman said. "Whoever called, um, said your whole trip was canceled, that you weren't doing any of the tour."

Miranda drew back. "Are you serious?"

"Yeah. She said the book was tanking big-time, and sales were really bad. My boss was kind of relieved when that guy came in here to buy all those books. He thought we'd be stuck with them or have to, like, remainder the whole lot."

What was going *on*? "Is your boss here? The owner or a manager?"

The kid shook her head. "I'm alone tonight. But I could call him. Do you want me to?"

She glanced at Adrien, who was staring up at the ceiling. "That a camera?" he asked.

"Oh, it doesn't work. It's just there for, like, show."

"And you have no record of the bloke who paid with all the hundreds? Didn't even issue him a receipt for the cash?"

"Just a sales receipt from the register. No name or anything. Sorry."

He pointed to a stack of boxes, none of them labeled. "And you're sure they're not in those cartons?"

"Positive," she said. "Those are a bunch of used textbooks some students just dropped off."

As soon as they got outside, Miranda said, "It's the crazies. They want this book to go away, and they're one step ahead of me."

"Someone is," he agreed, heading back toward Westwood Boulevard and the parking garage where they'd left the Range Rover. "I wonder if the ten thousand books up at Canopy are all of the books you were supposed to sign on this tour."

The possibility of that hit hard. "I won't let them do this to me," she ground out. "They can cancel my signings, but I'll just call and set them up again. They can buy all my books, but that will just force my publisher to print more. They can't do this."

"Good girl," he said, taking her hand as they crossed the intersection. "That's what you need to do. Get mad, not scared. But don't be"—his gaze, always scanning the area around them, suddenly stopped—"stupid, either."

She looked at the crowd. "What is it?"

"Nothing," he said, but the tone wasn't convincing. He put his left arm around her, tightly. "Come on. To the parking garage."

"What is it?" she repeated. "What did you see?"

"Let's get to the car." He pushed her faster, checking across the street as they broke into a near run.

"I have a right to know," she demanded, working to keep up with his long strides. "What or who is over there?"

"A familiar face," he said, hustling them faster, then turning into the street entrance for the covered parking garage.

"*Who?*" She wanted to look over her shoulder, but he didn't give her the chance.

He practically sprinted to the car, parked at street level. "Remember the guy who started all the problems at your signing up in Berkeley?" He clicked the keyless entry and pulled the passenger door open, urging her in.

"The one with the wild eyes who stood on his chair and raised hell?"

"You know him?"

"No, I never saw him before that reading at the Page Nine. I thought of him as Wild Eyes because he looked crazed when he started ranting."

"Interesting." He cocked his head in the direction of the street. " 'Cause he's down there, cruising Westwood Boulevard." He slammed her door shut.

Here? In LA? Why?

Adrien pulled himself into the driver's seat and turned the engine on. "He's your link."

"To the crazies?"

"I don't know," he said, backing out of the parking spot. "But he's in both places you are. There's got to be a reason."

"Let's find out."

He shot her a look. "In my line of work, we generally don't go driving into danger. We try to avoid it."

"I understand that for security, but I want to know who he is, what he's doing here, and why my book signing was mysteriously canceled. So let's follow him."

He shook his head. "It's not safe."

"If we can get some answers, maybe we can stop them. Get them arrested or something. I'd feel so much safer . . . when I'm alone."

He winced. "Foul play, Miranda."

"So is letting me go off across the country being followed by Wild Eyes, who wants to ruin every single one of my appearances. You can help me. Now." She squeezed his arm. "Hurry, Adrien, before he's gone."

"Oh, so now I'm Adrien again." He turned onto the main drag and hit the accelerator hard.

Fletch drove slowly past the outdoor restaurant, ignoring the bunyip in his head growling, *Don't*. Or was that Lucy's warning, reminding him how dangerous it was to act without thinking through the consequences?

Screw it—he owed Miranda this much. She had no identifying mark, and she wasn't Eileen Stafford's long-lost daughter. He'd start hunting down the next woman tomorrow. If they could root out the enemy tonight and scare the crap out of him, maybe she'd be safe to travel alone.

He scanned the street where he'd seen the guy.

"Any sign of him?" she asked. "All I can remember about him is that he had light hair, pale skin, and . . ."

"Wild blue eyes. There he is." Adrien pointed at a sidewalk café, where a half-dozen outdoor tables were filled with patrons in their mid-twenties with nylon packs and cups of designer coffee. "The third table from the right, near the building. In the navy shirt."

She threw an admiring glance at Adrien. "You're good. I never would have seen him."

"He was definitely the leader of the melee at your reading. All of the others looked at him before they talked, did you notice?" He slipped into a handicapped spot about twenty feet away. "Let's see where he goes from here."

The position gave them a direct shot of Wild Eyes, close enough to observe but not so close that he'd see them. He sipped his coffee and periodically answered or made a call on a cell phone, then pulled a handheld computer out of his backpack and fiddled with it. And then a book. But not just any book.

"Interesting choice of reading materials," Fletch said.

"Cataclysn't." She gave a half-laugh of incredulity. "I don't believe it."

Wild Eyes bit the cap off a Sharpie and started scratching all over the page. He flipped a few pages, wrote some more, then tore out a page, crumpled it into a ball, and shot it into a trash can three feet away.

"He's probably the guy who bought my books from Bruin Books, just to keep them off the market. Can you believe that?"

"No."

She whipped around. "You don't?"

"Listen, they buy into this whole imminent-end-of-the-world deal, right?"

"Right."

"So what the hell do they care if you don't? As far as they're concerned, it's all going to end whether you're right or you're wrong."

"True, but they want followers and support, so they see my findings as a direct conflict. I'm the voice of sanity they don't want to hear."

"But why do they want followers and support? For what? There has to be more to it." Fletch put his hand on her slender arm. "It's got to involve sex or money. When there's a coordinated effort like this, it's money. But sometimes its sex. Or both. That's what drives everyone and everything."

She narrowed her eyes in disbelief. "Not revenge? Jealousy? Hatred? Ambition?"

"All ancillary or somehow related to sex or money. People want more of both, no matter how much they have."

"Drugs?"

He shrugged. "The user isn't the baddie, the seller is. And he's doing it for money. So, whoever is bashing your books and buying them out, they want sex or money."

"You're missing a huge one. Religion is one of the biggest motivators of violence in history. Ask any suicide bomber. Oh, he's up." She pointed to their target.

Wild Eyes had stood suddenly, his phone pressed to

his ear. He threaded his way through the tables and to the street.

"Stay with him," Miranda said excitedly. "See where he's going."

Fletch pulled out of the parking spot into traffic, staying in the far right lane about twenty feet behind their target. When he suddenly jaywalked across the street, Fletch zipped across two lanes and followed him to one more corner.

"The bookstore," they said at the same time.

"It's nine o'clock now," Miranda added. "Maybe he has no idea it's canceled, and he intends to visit and make trouble like he did up in Berkeley."

"Maybe." Fletch stayed well behind, letting Wild Eyes hustle along, repositioning his heavy backpack as he headed to the store. The entire time, he kept a phone to his ear. When he reached Bruin Books, he went inside.

"Now what?" Miranda asked. "He's going to come out in five minutes when he finds out it's not happening. Damn, he's *not* the one who canceled it."

"There still has to be a reason he's following you from book signing to book signing," Fletch said, grabbing another illegal parking spot directly in front of the store. "Even if he's just here to heckle, I want to know why. And who sent him." He threw the car into Park, ignoring a mental warning not to leave his principal, not to seek out trouble, and not to act on impulse.

Miranda closed her hand over his arm and leaned closer. "I really appreciate this." She reached up and kissed his cheek. "And that other woman? She's damn lucky to have you."

He shut his eyes. "We'll see about that," he muttered.

"I think I should wait here."

"I agree. If he sees you, he might bolt. He might remember me from Berkeley, but he'll be looking for you, and I'll have the element of surprise on my side." He grazed his knuckle over her chin. "Keep the door locked, and do *not*, no matter what, leave this car. You understand?"

She nodded. "I promise."

"Here." He opened his door and stepped out, reaching across for her. "Get into my seat, in case you have to take off fast. The keys are in the ignition. If someone approaches this vehicle, drive away."

"Okay." She climbed into the driver's seat. "But if I do, how will I find you?"

"If we get separated, I'll find you at the hotel. Otherwise"—he kissed her mouth quickly—"I'll see you in a few."

She pulled him to her again, kissing him long and open-mouthed. "Thank you, Adrien."

He closed the door, waited to hear the click of the lock, and headed to the door of Bruin Books. Which was locked tight.

Bloody hell. The sign said it was open until eleven, and a customer had just walked in. He tried the door again and glanced toward the car where Miranda waited.

He could turn back and give up. He could talk

Miranda out of following this guy. He could . . . head down that alley and see if there was a back entrance.

One hand on his Glock, he jogged into a narrow passageway toward the back window, which he guessed was the office where the clerk had been when they'd entered.

When he reached it, he cupped his hands and squinted. The pane was white with dust and grime, almost impossible to see through. With his cuff, he brushed a spot clear. Cardboard boxes blocked the lower half of the view. He grabbed a crate from a pile of trash and climbed onto it to get a better look inside.

The room was dark and deserted. He rubbed the glass some more and blinked at the familiar red words on a white background. The boxes were full of Miranda's book.

The clerk had lied.

A door slammed around the back, and footsteps hit the pavement. Fletch leaped from the crate and vaulted toward the back of the building, inching out just enough to see who was running in the parking alley behind the building.

Even with a phone to her ear and her face distorted, he recognized the young sales girl from the bookstore. Ophelia. Fletch flattened himself against the building and hid in the shadows as she darted past, her voice bouncing off the bricks.

"He's fucking crazy, man. He's going to kill himself this time, and I don't care. Really. I just want out."

Out . . . from a bad relationship or the building?

Kill himself?

Ice ripped through Fletch's veins as realization and horror exploded in his head.

The backpack. The unmarked boxes. The conviction in that young man's voice when he stood on a chair and proclaimed, *This is the only truth!*

Miranda was right. Religion was a motivator for murder. To a zealot.

Fletch sprinted down the alley, back to Miranda. He dodged an oncoming car and threw himself in front of the SUV, diving for the passenger door, which she unlocked before he got there.

"Drive!" he ordered. "Fast! Now!"

Stunned but unquestioning, she turned the ignition.

"Hurry!" He reached across, whipped the wheel left, and smashed his foot on top of hers, gunning them out of the space.

"What's going on?"

They screeched down the street at full speed, turning the corner just as the bookstore detonated in a massive, deafening explosion that rained brick and fire and burned books down on Westwood Village.

CHAPTER
ELEVEN

TALIÑA STARED INTO the dancing, hypnotizing flames, mesmerized by what she'd done.

Twenty-seven tallow candles surrounded her, the light ricocheting off the five quartz crystals that formed a perfect cross on the altar of stone.

Carved cement and sharp pebbles dug into her knees. The cool air around the circular ritual slab chilled her bare skin. Electricity crackled in her hair, snapping sparks against her naked flesh.

It was time.

Bitter incense burned her nose as it mixed with the cloying smell of gardenia petals she'd broken and dispersed. Soon that smell would be replaced by the acrid odor of her séance, the pungent smell of sexual arousal that calling the *ajnawal mesa* always pulled from her sweat glands, and maybe the wet, delicious aroma of rain in her jungle.

She needed answers to her questions about Miranda, and there was only one way to get them: with the powerful shamanic witchcraft she'd learned as a child. A craft that could heal, save, and stimulate.

And kill.

But she'd take that risk, for Miranda.

She lay on her back, spread her legs wider than her hips, and positioned her palms flat on either side of her ears, jutting her elbows in the air. Then she whispered the age-old chant that soothed her soul and reached far beyond this world to another. She hummed in a low, monotonous minor key, the words so ancient they were meaningless but so familiar they comforted.

She imagined the voice of her mother, and her mother before. She imagined the voices of the midwives and apprentices, of the women warriors and prophets, diviners, dreamers, *dukuns*, spirits, and shamans. From womb to womb, the women connected and saved, they healed and gave birth, they screamed and painted and sang and performed rituals that protected souls and warned children and won wars and ruined men.

Women who ruled. *Women.*

Her love for the gender of her soul ran deep, allowing her to concentrate on one woman, and only one woman.

She understood why some would think Miranda was a threat, but Taliña didn't. Still, she wanted to know why Miranda had debilitating, hollow places in her heart.

The tallow grew low, the night cold. And her torso

began to rise. First her bottom, then her back, higher until she bent like a human bridge, rose to her toes, and formed a perfect arch, offering her nakedness, inside out, to the gods.

As her muscles tensed and pulled and strained, she began to sing, simple syllables floating on air. The pleasant, electric jolt started deep in the middle of her gut, the position forcing blood to slide to her head and to her feet, away from her midsection, away from her womanly core.

Her blood was shifting from her womb to fill her brain, to fill her feet, giving her the power to think and to run. A woman's best defenses: her brain and her feet.

Her arms shook with the effort, her legs wobbled. The smell intensified, so potent that she knew what she would see when she opened her eyes. She didn't know what color to expect, but the energy would be there. Her husband could strip her of many things but not this power.

Wasn't that why he married her?

She relaxed, opened her eyes, and saw it floating above the candles behind her. The energy was green, the color of fear, with a tinge of orange.

The pulsating ball, no bigger than a man's fist, floated over her, above her head, circling her, moving counterclockwise above the melting candles around the slab.

Satisfaction rolled through her. She'd succeeded! She'd called the energy, drawn it from the earth, the sky, the air, and the water. The ball of light paused over the altar, where Taliña's five questions were laid out.

She eased herself to the ground and rose to her knees, bowing in homage as she stared at the light in front of her.

What is Miranda's secret?

For a time, there was only silence in her head. Then, finally, the voice in her brain spoke.

Birth.

Birth? Miranda was pregnant? No, no, it was impossible. They'd exchanged energy; Taliña had felt her *kyopa*. If there was a child, the power of that spirit would be overwhelming.

It made no sense to her.

What is going to happen to Miranda?

The green light rose above the altar, flashed yellow, then red, then faded to black and disappeared.

Green for fear. Yellow for danger. Red for love. Black for death. A fast, unstoppable, and brutal ending for a beautiful, intelligent, sensual woman. Taliña lifted her head and stared at the blackness. There was no arguing with the energy of the séance.

A chill danced over her skin as the atmosphere changed. In the distance, thunder rumbled, almost drowning out the sound of a footstep. But she heard and braced herself for what was about to happen.

No, it wasn't thunder. That was his low, vicious, arrogant laughter.

"You fell for it, Doña Taliña."

Taliña closed her eyes, as trapped as Miranda had been in the underground tomb. She said nothing.

There were no words that could stop what was about to happen.

"I am working," she said quietly.

He laughed, blowing out candles as he circled her séance. "*I* did it, Taliña. Not you. Don't believe me? Watch."

She followed his gaze, and there was the energy ball.

"Want to see the red again?"

It changed colors.

Damn him. Damn, damn, damn him. She hadn't made that energy after all.

He held up his hand, and she saw what he held.

"You are very clever."

"We have a deal," he said, his voice gruff.

She bit her lip and cursed him, turning to take the position of a helpless female animal. That way, she didn't have to face him.

He was without mercy, more brutal than most nights, anger and jealousy and fear driving him as he stabbed into her body over and over and over.

Gritting her teeth and praying for the end, Taliña looked up and gasped when the ball of energy mysteriously reappeared. How could he do that? He was inside her, grunting like a pig.

This time, it was real, not one of his tricks.

The energy was bright, blinding crimson. The color of love. And blood. And . . . birth. Maybe she was doing that. Maybe this was really a message about Miranda's birth.

Everything went back to . . . the mother. Miranda's mother.

When he finished, Taliña crawled to the irrigation pond, washing off the filth of a man who took her almost every night—but certainly wasn't her husband.

CNN had aleady given it a logo and theme music. *The Westwood Bombing.* Hitting the mute button, Fletch glanced at the closed bathroom door where Miranda had disappeared for a shower as soon as they'd reached the hotel, whizzing up Wilshire Boulevard before police barricades were set up in a useless attempt to keep the bomber from escaping.

The news this hour: There were no apparent casualties except for a landmark bookstore in a bustling Los Angeles neighborhood.

But there was a casualty: the bomber. The need to identify Wild Eyes started to burn in Fletch's belly, along with the need to know why and who was behind it, calling the shots.

Since the shower was still running, he had time to make a phone call. He flipped his phone open to see four missed calls from Jack. His mate would have to wait, Fletch thought as he speed-dialed Lucy Sharpe.

"It's one-thirty A.M. in New York," she said before the first ring ended. "Do you know where your boss is?"

Fletch smiled. "In bed?"

"You know I never sleep. What's the matter?"

"Are you watching the news?"

She gave a soft groan of disgust, giving him the distinct impression that she did not appreciate this interruption. "No, I'm not watching the news."

"I'm really sorry, Luce, but you'd better put on the telly. I'm in the thick of it."

After a second, she asked, "Are you in LA?"

"Right-o. And that was a bookstore where, not moments before the blast, my principal was supposed to sign books."

"Your *principal?*"

"I know, I know. I'm not on the clock, and Jack's not our client, but she's—"

"Not your principal or my problem."

"Luce, please. Even if you can't consider helping Jack, I believe the woman I'm with was the target of that bombing."

"What happened?"

He kept his eye on the bathroom door. "That was a suicide bombing. I saw the bloke go into the place with a backpack. Miranda—that's the woman I'm with—was watching the front door, and I took the back. He didn't come out."

"What were you doing, exactly?"

Irritation skittered all over him. "My fucking job, Lucy. I was trying to figure out who is after this woman and why. I'd followed the man, and he blew up the building. I have a description of him, and his last known whereabouts was another bookstore in Berkeley. I saw him there. Don't we have someone up in the Bay Area who can get an ID on this guy? I don't know for certain if he was trying to kill Miranda or not, but thank God, he failed. If he works for someone who wants her dead, then whoever that is will surely—"

The water had stopped sometime during his impassioned plea. He heard nothing from the bathroom and reviewed what he'd said. Nothing that would have revealed the real reason he was there.

Before Lucy responded, he continued, "And could you run an ID on a clerk at the bookstore, too? She left just seconds before the bomb went off. An Asian girl wearing a name tag that read Ophelia."

"Tell me, is this woman the daughter of the woman in South Carolina?"

"No. Can you do the ID work for me?"

"So why are you still with her?"

Sometimes he wanted to kill the woman. "Because she's in danger."

"And this is your problem?"

"I'm making it my problem."

He heard Lucy let out a breath, her displeasure as clear as if she sat across from him, tapping her ruby red nails. *You're too impulsive, Fletch. That's going to cost you a life someday.*

His, probably.

He waited, watching the muted TV reporter, the bombed-out building in the background, and fire-fighters and police racing around like ants. Still no sound from the bathroom.

"Wade Cordell is just finishing a job in Silicon Valley," Lucy finally said. "He might be able to help with an investigation and get an ID."

He pictured the former Marine sniper who'd been working for Lucy as a consultant on special projects. So special that no one knew what the hell they were, but Fletch was pretty sure his expertise wasn't investigation. Unless that required shooting someone in the head from three kilometers away, which rumor had it was exactly what Cordell did as a consultant for some black ops deal before Lucy lured him into her company. "Is he qualified as an investigator?"

"I'll ignore the implication that I don't know how to choose the right man for the job, Fletch, just as I'll ignore your outburst and chalk it up to stress. Call Wade, give him the descriptions and details, and get some sleep, okay?"

"Right." Thats was why he liked this tough but fair sheila. "Thanks, Luce."

"I'm only doing this because innocent people could have been killed tonight."

In other words, it had nothing to do with the wild-goose chase he was on for Jack Culver. "Got it."

The bathroom door opened and Miranda stepped out, wearing a tank top and her sleep pants. Her hair was wet, combed over one shoulder, and her eyes looked weary.

"Talk to you tomorrow." He flipped the phone and reached for the remote, but Miranda grabbed it first.

"I want to watch."

"It's only going to upset you more," he warned her.

"Any casualties?" She switched to another channel.

"One person still in the hospital, several more released. It could have been much, much worse."

"No kidding. We could have been in the middle of my book signing." She pushed a strand of wet hair back. "Who were you talking to?"

"My boss." He reached for her hand. "C'mere, luv. Lie down and relax."

She sat on the edge of the bed. "So why'd you call your boss at this hour?"

"Because my company does investigations, and I want to find out who Wild Eyes is. And check out Ophelia, the clerk, to make sure she's legit."

"Good." Her back was straight, her shoulders square. "I assume the police will want to talk to me, as soon as they figure out that I was scheduled to speak that night."

"Maybe, but it could be a while before they make that connection. Maybe we'll be able to figure out why he did this, or who he worked for."

Considering that, she repositioned herself, propping the pillow behind her. "As much as I don't want to, I'm going to watch the news."

"Then I'll shower," he said. "But don't wallow in misery while you watch." He pushed himself off the bed and fought the urge to bend over and kiss her gently, to comfort her.

"I'm not wallowing in anything. I'm mad. Go take your shower."

He did, with no Aussie drinking songs echoing around the bathroom. He was about to turn the water off when she rapped at the door and called, "Your cell phone is ringing. Do you want it?"

He reached his arm out of the shower. "Can you hand it to me?"

When she did, he read Jack Culver's number on the ID. At this hour? He shut off the water and opened the shower curtain to be sure she'd left. She had, but the bathroom door was open. " 'Sup, Jack?"

"Where the hell have you been all day?"

"Santa Barbara. Los Angeles." He grabbed a towel to dry off with his free hand and checked the door. Was she listening? "Why?"

"Are you still with Miranda Lang? Did you find the tattoo? Is she our girl?"

Fletch snorted. "Yes. No. No."

Jack took a minute to process that. "She's not?" He sounded incredulous.

"Not according to my observations," Fletch said. "And they were careful."

"Are you sure the tattoo hasn't been lasered off?"

That left a scar, but he didn't want to say that out loud. "Relatively. More than ninety-nine percent. Is that enough?"

"I don't know. We have to find her, fast. *Really* fast."

"Why?"

"Because I have it on very good authority that someone knows we're looking for Eileen Stafford's daughter, and she could be in real danger because of it."

Fletch stifled a dark curse. The last freaking thing he needed was another woman in trouble. "Then maybe you ought to get on that job, mate." He wrapped the towel around his waist. "So it can happen faster."

"I would, but I can't leave Charleston. I have more work to do here. Plus, I could be followed. No one knows you're on this job, so I need you to get to the next adoptee on the list."

"I don't know how quickly—"

"Fletch. I know you like that woman. I'm sure she's hot and fun, and you're having a great time on your little road trip down the coast, but this is more important."

It was not fun. It was not a little road trip. And Jack was beginning to piss him off. In the next room, he heard sheets rustle, then a soft sigh.

But Jack was right about one thing: he *did* like this woman. She *was* hot and fun. And in trouble. Still, staying with her had nothing to do with the job he'd set out to accomplish.

"All right, mate. I'll call you later." He clicked off, stepped into the clean underwear he'd left on the counter, and dried his wet hair with a shake that would make a dog proud.

When he opened his eyes, Miranda was standing at the door. Her face was flushed, her eyes wide.

"He's not dead. I just saw Wild Eyes on TV. He walked right behind the camera."

Fletch folded her in his arms and pulled her hard against his chest. Damn Jack Culver and his search and his anonymous women in trouble. This one was real and scared, and also in trouble.

"It's okay, Miranda," he cooed into her ear, stroking her hair. "Don't let him scare you. That's what they're trying to do, these crazies. Don't let them."

She pulled away, her eyes full of determination and fear, the mix pulling at something deep inside him. He leaned his forehead against hers. "I won't leave you until you're safe, Miranda."

He felt her whole body relax into his arms, telling him she trusted him completely. And nothing—no mate, no timeline, no boss—would make him betray that trust.

CHAPTER
TWELVE

"TELL ME ABOUT your girlfriend." Miranda tried to make the request sound casual, considering they were pulling out of the hotel where they'd spent the night together. Although he'd slept on a sofa and she had taken the bed.

He snaked through the Century City traffic, glancing in the rearview mirror and maneuvering the big SUV with ease. "I don't have a steady woman in my life. I intentionally misled you, Miranda. I'm not involved with anyone but work."

"So you were referring to Lucy, your boss?"

"No, just work in general."

"What kind of—you just missed the entrance to the freeway."

"We're not taking the freeway."

"To San Diego? But surface streets will take all day. I thought you wanted to get there early to check security at the museuem."

"I have a quick stop to make," he said as his phone beeped softly. He glanced at the ID, then answered. "G'day, Mr. Cordell. Thanks for calling back."

She studied him as he described Wild Eyes' bird-like face, narrow lips, and platinum-blond hair and explained what they'd seen the night before.

A few days ago she'd been anticipating the solo trip, excited about seeing the country and having the time to think away from the pressures of the university. She wasn't that happy teaching, and she'd hoped to use the trip to think about how, or if, she should change her life.

Well, she'd certainly done that.

"Is there a database of student ID pictures?" Fletch asked Miranda.

"Yes, try the registrar's office. If they won't give it to you—"

"We know how to get it. I just needed to verify that it exists." He listened for a moment, then gave another detailed overview of what had happened at the Page Nine, the incident with the bird, and why they wanted to find Wild Eyes.

"Let me ask her," he said after a minute. "Miranda, who else in that audience did you know who might be able to make a positive ID on your behalf? Was there a friend or colleague astute enough to give a detailed description for a sketch artist?"

"Adam DeWitt," she said. "Another associate professor. He might help." Unless he still harbored a grudge because she wouldn't introduce him to her publisher.

"I don't know if he'll be in his office this week, but I have his address."

She reached for her bag, but Adrien stopped her. "We can get it."

Of course they could.

"Right, mate," he said into the phone. "Excellent. I owe you one." After he signed off, he turned to Miranda. "All righty, then. We've got a good man up in San Francisco, Wade Cordell, who'll do some snooping for us on Wild Eyes. Now, tell me why you think this Adam might not help you. Have some issues with him, then?"

Absolutely nothing got by Adrien Fletcher. She'd have to remember that. "We're competing for the same job. All faculty members in a department are, to some extent. He's a bit higher on the totem pole than I am, but with the book, I've surpassed him."

"Could he want to see you fail?"

She snorted softly. "Everybody wants to see everybody else fail. Welcome to ivory tower politics in academia."

"Bad enough for him to bomb a building?"

She almost laughed. "To be honest, he doesn't have what it takes to orchestrate something like that, although he'd probably like to think he does." She paused as he pulled into the right lane and put his signal on at Westwood Boulevard. "Are you going back to Westwood?"

"I hope we're not too late."

"For what?"

"Trash pickup."

A few minutes later, he was at the curb in front of the café where Wild Eyes had sat the night before. It was far enough from the bombed bookstore that the police hadn't cordoned off the place and early enough that few patrons were around. Media trucks filled the streets closer to the bookstore, but this area was relatively quiet.

"Wait here," he said, climbing out and heading toward the tables.

He went directly to the trash can that Wild Eyes had used for a basketball hoop the night before. Without even glancing around, he lifted the metal rim and set it on the ground, leaning over and peering in. Wouldn't the restaurant have emptied that last night?

He reached in, rooted around, looked up to her, and grinned. A second later, he pulled something out, replaced the lid, and strolled back to the curb.

In the car, he held a ball of paper gingerly by two fingers. "We can run a DNA test on this."

"I can't believe you found that." She shook her head, impressed. "Will you take it to the police?"

"I'll turn it over to Lucy's lab and see what we get."

"Can we open it? I'd like to see what he wrote all over it."

"Touch as little surface as possible."

He held one side, and with the very edges of her fingers, she drew the other side of the paper out, slowly opening to reveal the second page of the fourth chapter, a brief biography of Pakal, who ruled the

Maya for sixty-eight years and had a profound influence on the Long Count calendar.

All over the words, sharp blank ink had slashed a glyph.

"What's that?" Adrien asked, pointing toward the concentric circles above an oval with four "fingers" with a single thorn drawn into the palm.

"It's a symbol. It's actually quite accurate Maya writing."

"What does it mean?"

"It's the glyph for bloodletting. For asking the gods for a favor." Miranda swallowed as she slowly lowered the bottom half of the page. They'd be doodles to anyone else, swirls of shapes, dots, and roughly drawn pictures. But Miranda could read the Maya alphabet as well as she could read her own name.

Which was exactly what he'd written.

Under that, six numbers with decimal points. She pointed to those numbers and whispered, "That's yesterday's date. He planned to sacrifice me last night."

The editorial intern at the *Charleston Post and Courier* turned out to be quite a bit prettier and a little bit younger than Jack had figured when he started working her as a phone source. She'd taken his calls, answered his questions, and, as he'd hoped, arranged for him to get into the newspaper's library on a Monday, when it was closed to the public. She was a college student, majoring in journalism, but she'd told him during their first conversation that her backup career was as a PI.

He hated to tell her he wouldn't be hiring any interns soon, especially when she walked to the guard's station to greet him. She was all legs and hair and one seriously sweet smile in a too-short skirt and a breast man's paradise of a sweater.

"Mr. Culver?" She thrust out her hand and showed off her daddy's investment in orthodontics. "I'm Toni Hastings."

The newsroom was damn near deserted this early on a Monday morning, and Jack's presence barely merited a glance from the few reporters who sipped coffee, skimmed e-mail, and got settled for their week of work. Guiding him around the cubicle walls, Toni sparkled, flipped her hair, and gave him an animated tour all the way to the double glass doors of a darkened library, where she ended the trip.

"Like I said, there's no librarian here on Mondays," she apologized. "But I can help you out if you know exactly what you're looking for."

He did. Wanda Sloane's murder and the subsequent trial of Eileen Stafford hadn't been huge news, but surely there was some coverage in the local paper. Experience told him that police departments and courthouses might have the facts on a case like this, but the newspaper would have the slant.

"The photo files and physical clips are in there," she said, pointing to the electric rotating file. "The rest is every article and editorial ever written before we went to computers. Everything's on microfiche or in hard copy, but you might have to do some rooting around to find what you want."

He nodded, throwing his backpack onto a chair. "Rooting is my specialty."

"I'm extension six four five. You can use that phone."

"Thanks. I'll call you if I need help."

Three hours later, he stretched with a groan, then pushed a thirty-year-old editorial column aside.

The morning had produced nothing he didn't already know.

He'd read the court files, of course, and expected them to be bland and relatively useless. But the paper was worse. It was as if every word that had been written on this trial was whitewashed. Granted, this wasn't the trial of the century and didn't merit a lot of ink at a time when the city of Charleston was on the verge of bankruptcy.

But still, didn't some nosy reporter *somewhere* question the flimsy motive that Eileen felt threatened by a new gal who might take her job as a floating legal secretary at the courthouse? Didn't anyone question a prosecutor who relied on sloppy, compromised evidence, an eyewitness with proven night blindness, or the fact that the police had stored the clothing Eileen allegedly wore in the same bag as the victim's bloody dress, then claimed the barely there nitrite residue was proof she'd fired the gun?

It was as if . . . no one *cared*. Even the courtroom had looked oddly empty in newspaper photos. But someone had to care. Someone had to support Eileen.

He returned to the rotating file on the opposite wall, spinning through the contraption for more photos. Most of these were stored from the photographer's files, developed pictures that had never run in the paper. The captions were sporadic, faded, jotted in incomprehensible notes, and many of the pictures were out of focus or unidentifiable.

By now, though, he could easily identify Eileen, a sweet-faced brunette with curly hair and sharp eyes back then. The woman who showed up in court in a crisp herringbone suit and high heels bore no resemblance to the one who slept in a pale blue hospital gown at Camp Camille.

He flipped through the black-and-white snapshots. There were several of the state-appointed defense attorney, Ronald Wright, now dead. One of the stern-faced judge, now retired and living in Arizona. There was his good friend Willie Gilbert, looking self-important, and another of Eileen talking to a pretty young blond woman.

That woman, Jack noticed, sat behind Eileen on several occasions and was caught on film closing her eyes and covering her mouth as the guilty verdict was announced. A friend? A relative? He set aside every picture that had a caption and began slowly going through them. The newspaper photographer had been sloppy about getting names, though that was part of the job.

Jack went back to the first day of the trial. There she was again, just behind and to the right of Eileen's attorney, with an infant in her arms.

Jesus, could that be Eileen's baby? Jack peered at the picture, then flipped it over and let out a little grunt of success: "E.S., R.W., R.A., LTR."

Eileen Stafford, Ronald Wright, and . . . somebody . . . left to right.

R.A.

He sifted through the pile again, turning over every picture this time. And then he found it. No baby in this one, but the blonde was there. And a name. Rebecca Aubry.

He could hear Eileen's voice. *There were no last names at Sapphire Trail.* But there was someone named Rebecca.

He picked up the phone and dialed Toni's extension. She'd be able to get him into the *Post and Courier* database to find Rebecca Aubry's address. And it might cost him lunch, but he'd bet he could get her to let him take the picture out of the building for a few days.

Rebecca Aubry might give him some answers, but he might need something to convince her.

"You didn't mention the museum was located in the most famous building in San Diego." From across the expanse of Balboa Park, Adrien paused to study the vista of the Museum of Man bathed in Southern California sunshine and crowded even on a Monday afternoon.

Miranda had seen the California Tower several times, but the awe-inspiring white limestone tower stretching up into a cloudless blue sky and the glistening geometric patterns of the painted dome next to it never failed to impress her.

Adrien took her hand as they crossed a garden and

headed for the gabled front entrance. "It reminds me of a church."

"It's supposed to," she told him. "The façade is based on some of the most famous churches in Mexico and Spain."

As they rounded a large planter and climbed a half-dozen stairs, Adrien gestured toward a small poster at the door.

"There you are, luv. The event is on."

"So it is," she said, glancing at her image and the cover of her book on the small marquee. "Let's find Suzette, the coordinator, and get the lay of the land."

Just inside the entrance, Miranda approached a woman at a long welcome desk, getting a warm smile and outstretched handshake as soon as she said her name.

"Dr. Lang, we're so excited to have you here. We're expecting quite a crowd tonight."

"That's wonderful, thank you." Maybe the sabotage was over. Maybe Wild Eyes had made his point last night. "Is Suzette Kraemer here?"

"Let me call her." She phoned an extension, waited, tried another, then hung up. "Both her lines are busy, but go right ahead into the rotunda." She pointed to the left, into the museum. "That's where you'll be speaking tonight. You can see the stelae and the zoo-morphs. Whenever you're ready, go outside to the next building, where our admin offices are. Suzette's over there."

Miranda thanked her and turned to Adrien, who

had introduced himself to a young man dressed in black and wearing a security badge. She waited at the entrance to the rotunda, studying the wall-sized murals of a classic Mesoamerican Maya landscape that flanked each side.

"Looks a bit like your friend's house." Adrien came up behind her, putting a hand on her shoulder.

"Sort of. That's Quiriguá, in Guatemala—quite a beautiful ruin. Come on, I'm anxious to see the setup."

The room opened up into a spacious, sun-dappled area under a fifty-foot-high white dome. Along the back wall, the words "Heart of Sky, Heart of Earth" set an atmospheric tone of the ancients. While the architecture was impressive, the real focal points of the room were three towering stone stelae and two boulderlike zoomorphs.

Adrien craned his neck to the top of the tallest monument, giving a low whistle as he reached the top. "Is this the real deal?"

"No. These pieces are exact copies of classic Maya structures called stelae," Miranda explained. "They're casts of the originals, also in Quiriguá. Gorgeous, aren't they? And the smaller ones with the animal carvings are called zoomorphs."

He studied them, his hands locked behind him as he circled each. "What's the writing say?"

"It's mostly stories of the gods and their relationships with the kings. They're actually more beautiful than the originals, because the monuments of Quiriguá are eroded and aged."

She skimmed a finger along a few glyphs, remembering the hieroglyphic warning she'd seen that morning in Wild Eyes' writing.

"What do you think of the layout?" she asked, glancing at the small stage and podium that had been set up for her, then up to the wooden-railed balconies that overlooked the rotunda floor. "Other than the fact that someone could shoot me from up there."

"Someone could shoot you from anywhere," he said. "I'll have to get them to lock the second floor. And I'm going to arrange to get a metal detector at the door and increase the security on the floor tonight."

She gave him a grateful smile. "Thank you, Adrien."

"Thank me when it's over and all is well. Not that I want you to worry," he added quickly. "Just to be vigilant."

They continued around the room, their shoes echoing on the high-shine floor, speaking quietly in keeping with the atmosphere. Tourists and some staffers peppered the museum. Miranda stood at the podium, looked around to imagine a room full of people, and let her attention settle on Adrien. He was far less interested in the cases full of Maya pottery and much more interested in access to the room, the setup for speaking, and the various ways they could get out if they had to. He had his serious game face on, his body language all control and purpose. And so insanely . . . byu-ee-ful.

Desire punched her just as he turned and caught

her staring. He didn't move and didn't look away. No smile, no words. Just that purpose in his eyes that made her warm and . . . hungry. If he didn't think of sex when he looked at her that way, then what?

A man walked between them with a ladder, bringing her back to the present.

" 'Scuse me, Doctor," he mumbled, clunking the stepladder next to one of the stelae.

She gestured to Adrien. "Ready?"

They left the main building and walked across a side street to the small administration building, pausing to admire the blinding topaz and turquoise colors of the rotunda roof.

"It's a pretty place, isn't it?" she mused.

"Pretty wide open and not exactly high security," he replied grimly.

The reception area of the administrative offices was empty, but from the other side of a thin wall, a woman's voice rose in escalating dismay.

"This is totally unacceptable, Juan Carlos. Boxes of books just don't disappear."

Miranda closed her eyes. Oh, *no*.

"Hang tight, luv," Adrien said, dropping an arm around her shoulder. "She could be talking about any books."

"Right."

In the background, a phone receiver hit the cradle so hard it must have cracked the plastic.

"This is un-freaking-believable!" The woman sailed out from behind the wall, a willowy blonde who nearly stumbled from her own momentum when she saw them. She looked from one to the other and settled on Miranda.

"Dr. Lang?" Nothing in her voice said she was happy to see Miranda. "Oh, God, we have problems."

Air whooshed out of Miranda. "The books are gone." It was a statement, not a question.

"Missing," she corrected. "They are temporarily missing." With a tight smile, she stuck her hand out. "I'm Suzette Kraemer. And I really am happy to meet you. I would be happier if I had your books."

Miranda shook her hand and introduced Adrien as her bodyguard.

"Who was the last person to see the books?" he asked.

"They were in storage and shipping. Juan Carlos, the shipping manager, just called me to say he was about to arrange the delivery to the rotunda for tonight's event, and they were gone. Eight boxes can't just vanish into thin air. But according to Juan Carlos, they have." She indicated the door with one hand. "Want to join me on the hunt at the loading dock and storage warehouse? It's in the back."

On the way, Suzette did her best to make small talk about the museum and the room setup they'd planned, and then she gushed about the article that had appeared in yesterday's newspaper about the event.

"There was an article?" Miranda asked.

"A nice one, in the *UT*—the *Union Tribune*." Suzette's heels tapped on the terra-cotta floor as they walked down a long hallway. "The reporter talked about your theory about the Long Count calendar and how your book is going a long way toward dispelling a growing worry about December 2012. I'm sure it will drum up a good crowd tonight."

Adrien and Miranda shared a look as they reached a steel door that Suzette opened without a key. Inside the warehouse area, one whole wall was an open garage door and cement delivery dock, where sunlight streamed over cartons, crates, and an empty forklift.

"Juan Carlos!" she called. "It's Suzette! Snuff the butt and get in here!"

From below the delivery platform, a heavy-set Latino man came around the corner, crushing a cigarette and blowing a puff of smoke. He hoisted himself up with surprising ease, considering his size, and approached Suzette with a sheepish grin.

"You have that I'm-going-to-kill-JC look in your eyes." He chuckled, the laugh of someone who's shared a lot of inside jokes and mini-crises through the years, and Suzette's twinkle confirmed that.

"That's because this time, I really am going to kill you, JC. But first, let me introduce you to Dr. Lang. The *author*." She ladled shame over the word. "They're *her* books you lost, my friend."

He wiped his hand on dark trousers and then reached out to shake her hand. "I am sorry, Dr. Lang. We have very expensive and rare works of art come through this department, and we've never lost anything before."

"When were they shipped?" Miranda asked. "Are you certain they actually arrived?" Perhaps the prob-

lem was with Calypso Publishing and not the
Armageddon Movement.

Juan Carlos dashed that hope. "I had them, I
counted them, I inventoried them." He pointed to a
receiving area where other boxes were stacked. "Right
there. On Friday afternoon of last week. Wait here,
and I'll get the paperwork."

Adrien walked over to the boxes and poked around,
checking out the area where trucks backed in.

"Anyone can get in here," he said to Miranda.

"That's really not true," Suzette replied. "There's a
guard at the back drive, and everyone's ID is checked.
It's not that easy to get back here. We had the Dead
Sea Scrolls, for heaven's sake! Security's not lax. Anyway," she added, setting her hands on the pencil skirt
that hugged her narrow hips, "who would want 192
copies of a book? That's an odd thing to steal, don't
you think?"

No, Miranda thought ruefully, stealing her books
had become someone's favorite pastime this week.

"I found one!" Juan Carlos's victorious exclamation
rang out through the warehouse. "I must have forgot
to log this box in. Can you have your event tonight
with one box?"

Suzette dashed off toward him. "Maybe we can give
IOUs, Dr. Lang, or maybe you can sign brochures or
bookmarks for them or something."

Disappointment pulled a frustrated sigh from
Miranda. Along with a sense of dread.

"What should I do?" she asked Adrien. "He may
not show up at all if he thinks I'm going to skip the

event like I did in LA. But maybe the boxes are really lost or hidden, and he's planning to blow this place up, too. We can't jeopardize people like that."

He nodded. "I was thinking the same thing. But tonight's event hasn't been canceled, and people will be here. I think you should be, too. I'll alert the security team here and order police backup. They'll need to check every backpack and bag. I'll watch the door—there should be only one entrance and exit. Not that I want you as bait, but it could be the best way to draw him to us." He stepped closer and took her hand off her chest, where she didn't even realize it was covering a thumping heart. "Unless you want to skip it and cancel."

She shook her head. "No. I'll do my reading and sign whatever books they have. You'll catch him, then find out who he is, what he's up to."

"You're absolutely sure that's what you want to do?"

"Absolutely."

She wouldn't be beaten by Wild Eyes. Not this time.

CHAPTER
THIRTEEN

"I DUNNO 'BOUT this, Miss Lucy." Wade Cordell purposely loaded some serious drawl into his voice, mostly because he knew it amused her, and she'd always appreciated the disarming power of one of his most deadly weapons. People generally thought a Southern boy who talked slow and walked slower couldn't be much of a threat. "You sure you want *me* on this assignment?"

"I know this isn't the kind of thing you left your cushy government job to do," Lucy said, her subtle sarcasm not lost through the cell-phone connection. She knew the consulting jobs he'd done after he left the Marines were anything but cushy. Deadly, fierce, and shrouded in black but not cushy.

"I don't have an investigator in the Bay Area right now, and I know you can handle this. It'll be a nice change."

Any change from what he'd done for the government would be nice.

"Then you'll be happy to know I am parking across the street from Kroeber Hall, the anthropology department at UC Berkeley, and I'm about to interview"—he glanced at the notes he'd written—"Dr. Adam DeWitt, one of Miranda Lang's colleagues who might have some information on Fletch's target."

"Good. And if you talk to Fletch before I do, tell him that Sage checked out the bookstore clerk. There's an Ophelia on staff, but she had called in sick that night. The manager was under the impression the bookstore was closed and no one was there."

"So maybe their target didn't set the bomb off. Maybe someone impersonating Ophelia did."

"Or he had an accomplice. I've had Sage's group going through all of the online databases for the Berkeley anthropology majors and graduate students, and they've pulled all possible pictures and will e-mail them to Fletch. When I hand this person over to the FBI, I'd like to be very thorough."

"Got it." He climbed out of the Navigator and scanned the campus. "And if we have any leads from the photos Sage is uploading to Fletch, I'll check them out. I don't mind a little field investigation work."

"Thanks, Wade. When you're done with this, let's talk. I have some ideas about your future."

"That sounds ominous."

"I'm trying to decide between an ambassador on

vacation in Nice or an advance security run for a client traveling on the *Queen Mary 2*."

He choked playfully. "You're killin' me, Luce."

"I want more than consulting, Wade."

"I know." And so far, security consulting for the Bullet Catchers beat the holy hell out of what he'd been doing before. "We'll talk when I can get to New York. I have to, uh, do some work over in Europe first."

"I heard."

Did the woman know *everything*? She must have some serious connections in the Agency still.

Inside the building, Wade brushed his hand over the S&W 1911 under his jacket. Not that he expected to need it, but habits died hard. Upstairs, down a dimly lit hallway lined with labs and classrooms, he found the main office, where he faced the back of a heavy-set woman working on a computer. Her desk was a mess of papers, almost covering the plastic nameplate. She didn't turn, even when he cleared his throat.

"Dr. Rosevich is in a meeting," she said over her shoulder, her fingers clicking wildly.

"Actually, ma'am, I'm looking for Dr. DeWitt. Am I in the right place?"

"I don't work for Adam." *Clickity-click.*

"Well, then, perhaps you could tell me where to go."

She paused just long enough for him to figure she would do exactly that.

"I'm a private investigator."

That got her to turn, a scowl stamped on her wide,

fifty-something features. "Oh . . . a private investigator?" she asked, losing the fight to check him out.

He smiled and reached a hand toward her. "Sounds more glamorous than it is. My name's Wade Cordell. I'd like to see Dr. DeWitt, if that's possible."

She held his hand a second too long, a sweetheart of a flush rising. "Is he in trouble? No, no." She waved her hand, the color rising to her cheeks. "Not my business. Um . . . let me call his office. I don't know if he has office hours now, but—"

"If you'd just direct me, I'll pop in and check."

"Sure. Yes. Right out there, to the left. Second, no, third door." She caught her breath. "Wade."

"Thank you." He winked. "Donna."

"Come back if he's not there, and I'll help you."

"I just might do that."

She was still smiling when he left. He knocked on the third door to the left. When there was no answer, he tried the knob, and it opened up. He walked into the small, windowless office, scoping the room for clues about its inhabitants.

One whole wall was bookshelves, and at the farthest end of the bottom shelf, red letters jumped out at him. Dr. Miranda Lang. Was this the book Fletch's principal had written? He leaned over and pulled it out, curious. *The Cataclysn't: The End of the Myth, Not of the World.* He flipped it over, looking at the picture on the inside back cover. Pretty girl. He skimmed her biography. Brainy, too. No wonder Fletch was dragging this nonassignment out.

He opened to the middle of the book, glancing at

a few sentences, then fluttered some pages to colored photos of ancient ruins and a chart. He turned another page and blinked in surprise at the red ink all over it, scratches over words and handwritten editorial markings. Had Dr. DeWitt reviewed the book for her?

He flipped a few more pages. On almost every page in the book were vicious red swipes, question marks, notations that said "confusing" and "inaccurate" and "absurd"—underlined three times.

At the sound of rushed footsteps in the hall, he slipped the book back exactly where it had been, locked his hands behind him, and copped a blank expression.

"Can I help you?" Adam DeWitt practically ran into his office, a look of distrust on his angular features and a set of purplish circles behind rimless glasses. "Donna said you're looking for me."

"My name is Wade Cordell. I'm a private investigator." Wade flashed ID and noticed the already pale skin lighten even more.

"What's the problem?"

"No problem," Wade assured him. "I've been asked by a client to identify someone who was in the audience at a book reading and signing at the Page Nine bookstore on Friday night. I understand you were in attendance."

"Miranda? She's your client?"

Nerves. He could practically smell them.

"You were there, correct? At the reading for the book *Cataclysn't*?"

"Is Miranda okay?"

Did he really care, this colleague who'd picked apart her entire book? "She's fine, but there was a man in the audience that night who caused quite a bit of trouble, and Dr. Lang thinks—"

"What? That I had something to do with that? God, she's too much."

"—that you might be able to give a description."

DeWitt widened his stance and got his balance. Which, unless he had something to hide, shouldn't be gone in the first place. "If you mean the long-haired guy with a tattoo and an earring, I have no idea who that was."

That would be Fletch; Wade had met him once a few months ago, and the description for the Aussie was dead-on. "I'm delighted that your powers of observation are so keen, Dr. DeWitt, because that's exactly why I'm here."

"I'm very late for an appointment." He crossed his arms and stepped away from the doorjamb, a silent invitation to leave.

Wade sat down in the guest chair, stretched out his legs, and crossed his ankles. It had the desired effect on the professor, who practically snarled as he made his way around Wade's legs to get behind his own desk.

"You want to find that other guy," DeWitt insisted. "Because she was staring at him and ran out of the room with him. A little while later, I saw her leave with him."

"You saw her? Were you watching her?"

"I just happened to see her." When Wade added nothing but an interested look, DeWitt closed his eyes. "She's my friend," he said. "We work together."

Wade filed the defensiveness away. "Truth be told, sir, I'm more interested in a man who initiated the trouble for Dr. Lang than the one she left with."

"The guy who stood on a chair?" Adam gave a mean little laugh. "I told her she could expect that."

"Why was that?"

"Let's just say she invites controversy. She's young, and not really qualified to be published on such a huge subject."

Wade nodded, then glanced at the bookshelves. "Are you published, Dr. DeWitt? I suppose most professors are writers," he said. "Publish or perish, isn't that the expression?"

"Some of us are content to teach."

And watch the others get the adulation. "I realize you're busy, but we need to get you to sit down with a police sketch artist, if you observed the man in question."

"There are *cops* involved?"

"She's specifically looking for information on the people who were disruptive," Wade said. "And we intend to find them."

"I don't know. There were a lot of people there. I didn't see anybody that well. I was paying attention to Miranda. I didn't see people in the back."

Wade lifted one eyebrow. "You got a pretty good read on the hair, tattoo, and earring."

"You know," DeWitt said, trying to act casual. "I don't really have time for this. I'm sorry if Miranda's getting harassed, but it isn't my problem."

Wade leaned back, getting more comfortable as his target did just the opposite. "Are you aware of the bombing that occurred in Los Angeles last night?"

He froze. "No. I mean, yes. I had nothing to do with that."

Wade lifted one brow, real slow. "I don't believe I implied you did."

"Your very presence here implies something."

A gentle knock on the open door pulled their attention. "Is this about what happened to Miranda the other night?" An older man, easily in his seventies, hunched in the doorway, an olive-green suit matching the color of his eyes.

Wade stood. "As a matter of fact, it is," he said. "I'm investigating the incident. And you are . . ."

"Stuart Rosevich." He gave Wade a hearty shake. "Department head. Did DeWitt tell you how badly they treated her? I was there, and it was just an atrocity for that poor woman."

"That's what I understand," Wade said. "We believe there could be a connection between some individuals in the audience and the bombing that occurred in Westwood, which happened to be a bookstore where Dr. Lang was scheduled to speak."

The older man's eyes widened. "Is she all right?" His concern, unlike Adam's, was genuine.

"She is. But we're trying to find people who can

remember the troublemakers well enough to help create a sketch that might lead to an ID."

"Oh, I remember the worst of the bunch. The one who stood on his chair. I'll help you. And Adam, you got a good look at him."

"I . . . I could probably remember him," he back-pedaled.

"You talked to him for a good five minutes after Miranda left," the other man said. "Of course you could describe him. Where do you need us to go?"

"I'll arrange for an artist to come here and interview you both," Wade said. "Will that fit in with your schedule, Dr. DeWitt?"

"Of course it will," Rosevich answered for him. "Miranda should be enjoying the fruits of her hard labor and well-deserved success right now, not fending off these lunatics who want to prove her wrong. Right, Adam?"

Adam nodded. "Absolutely."

Wade stepped to the door, then pointed to the book on the shelf. "I see you have Dr. Lang's book," he commented. "Did you enjoy it?"

DeWitt half shrugged. "I haven't had a chance to really read it yet."

"I have," Rosevich said, nudging Wade into the hall. "It's brilliant. Absolutely brilliant. Of course, I'd expect no less from Miranda. She's a star in the department."

Wade sent a bland look at Adam. "Thanks for your time, Dr. DeWitt. I'm sure Dr. Lang will appreciate the help from such a supportive colleague."

When Adam just stared back at him, Wade shot him a Southern charmer smile.

"Could he hate you enough to orchestrate a campaign to see you fail?" Fletch asked, opening up his laptop on the bar in the suite's living room after he'd reported Wade's conversation to her.

Miranda looked doubtful. "He has issues, no question. He's tried to write books himself and has had trouble even getting his papers published. He's having problems and sees tenure slipping further away every year, but I don't think he's so jealous that he'd go as far as sabotage. He's petty but not . . . menacing."

"We're going to watch him."

She leaned forward, clearly interested. "What else do you guys do?"

"Well . . ." He tapped a few computer keys and entered a password she couldn't see. "We have a database that can tell you just about anything you want to know about anyone in the world. It's run by the head of our Research and Investigation Division, Sage Valentine."

"And any of you can access it?"

He clicked a few more keys and pulled up the file on Miranda. "See?" He turned the computer toward her, letting her see the stats of high school, college, graduate school, address, and phone number.

Her jaw dropped. "You had that before you met me?"

"Yes. I knew you lived on Regent Street, so you fooled me when you brought me up the shortcut." He smiled at her look. "We don't have everything. There are some limitations and some people who are canny enough to erase their info. This is first level. If we want to go deeper, Sage's team gets involved."

She studied the screen. "It's all accurate, too."

"That's the way we like it."

"What else?"

He thought for a minute. "We have a GPS-based locator system that can tell my boss where any Bullet Catcher is at any time, assuming they have a certain code punched into their cell phones."

"Show me."

He pulled his slim phone from his pocket. "I'm not working now, so I don't have it on." He punched in the code, then opened the program on the laptop, typed in his name and Bullet Catcher ID number, and a map of San Diego appeared, with a star at the street corner where the hotel was located.

"So, if I have that, I could track you after you leave me tomorrow and see where you go, couldn't I?"

"It's not that simple, luv." He reached over and took her hand. "But I'd be more interested in seeing where you are."

She slid off the bar stool. "I'm going to get dressed," she said, heading toward one of the bedrooms off the spacious suite.

When she disappeared, he just sat there staring at the empty stool.

Damn Jack Culver and his search for long-lost adoptees. After tonight Fletch would *have* to leave.

He walked across the room to the balcony, taking

in the rolling green hills and pristine beauty of San Diego. Over the harbor, a tangerine sun hung suspended, ready for touchdown.

What sunset would he see tomorrow night? The next woman on Jack's list was in Bend, Oregon, if he recalled correctly. About as far away from Miranda in San Diego as he could get and still be in the same time zone.

He tried to rationalize why this was a good thing. He couldn't ever let this mutual attraction go to the next level, because he knew she was adopted, and if he never told her, especially if they were in a relationship of any kind, then he'd be lying by omission. And if she learned the truth and realized he'd known all along, then she'd probably hate him. It would hang over his head.

But he couldn't tell her. Why destroy her childhood or strain the love she obviously had for her parents? No matter what happened tonight, tomorrow he'd fly to Oregon, and she'd drive off to her next destination.

And that left him feeling . . . unsatisfied. Maybe if they—

"Can you help me?"

Miranda had showered, made up, and turned into a vision in white.

"God save the queen," he whispered under his breath. "You look incredible."

"Thank you."

"I love that dress." It was so feminine, tied in the front across her narrow frame. The V-neck exposed plenty, a style that was both sweet and sexy, especially with her hair pulled up with only a few tendrils touching her neck.

She held a silver chain out to him. "Will you fasten this for me? It's an ancient clasp and a little tricky to do alone, which is why I never wear it. But since you're here . . ."

He took the ends of the chain, holding the tiny, circular pendulum at eye level. "It's an opal, the national gem of Australia," he said, moving the chain so that the iridescent stone and the tiny semicircle of diamond chips caught the light. He lowered it to look into her eyes. "These are unlucky. Did you know that?"

"I've heard." She turned, offering him the back of her neck. "This was my mother's. She gave it to me when I left for California, to have a piece of her with me all the time."

He lifted the necklace over her head and brought the two ends of the chain together. "So you don't believe the folklore about opals?"

Her shoulders lifted in a shrug. "I respect folklore; I just think this particular legend is based on the fact that the stone is soft, so the gems tend to break easily. Do you believe in things like luck? You strike me as awfully pragmatic for that."

"I lived with Aborigines for two years. I'd believe anything is possible." He used his nail to catch the clasp, which was old and one good yank from breaking. When he rested the chain on her skin, he couldn't resist a brief kiss and caught a whiff of something sweet.

"Mmmm. You don't just look beautiful. You smell

and taste beautiful." He dragged the word out, just because he knew she liked it.

She tilted her head, offering more skin. He ran his tongue along her nape, curled his hands around her shoulders, and pulled her closer so she could feel how instant his response was.

He threaded his fingers through those wispy hairs, admiring his ability to give her a million goose bumps. "You know I have to leave for Oregon tomorrow."

She let out a soft, gentle moan. It could have been disappointment. It could have been resignation. It could have just been that she liked the sensation of his breath on her skin.

"But tonight," he said softly, leaning back to see the way the setting sun added a bit of auburn to her dark hair. "Tonight . . ." He caressed her neck, sliding one finger into that soft hair, imagining how he'd slide into her.

God, she made him hard fast. She dropped her head forward and sighed, and he bent his face to take another nibble.

And then his heart stopped, and his eyes widened, and his throat closed.

Holy. Bloody. Hell. There it was. No bigger than a fingernail, hidden an inch from her hairline, buried in dark brown tresses, impossible for her to see.

The tattoo.

"Miranda." His voice must have sounded strained to her, too, because she glanced over her shoulder.

"Yes?"

"Did you . . ." He took a slow, even breath. "Do you know you have a . . . a mark? At your hairline?"

She touched it. "Yes, it's a birthmark."

Oh, no, it isn't. "Are you sure?"

Laughing, she turned. "Yes, I'm sure. My mother said I've had it all my life. I can't really get a good look at it, but my hairdresser said it says 'hi.' Which cracks her up."

"Let me see it again." He spread the hair at the roots and studied the strange mark. It did look like a lower-case *h* and an undotted *i*.

Miranda stepped away, indicating his worn jeans and T-shirt. "You probably need to change your clothes, too."

"Right," he said, his brain spinning a million kilometers a second, trying to figure out what to tell her. How to tell her. When to tell her.

"I don't want to be late for my own reading. Especially since that amazing Suzette went out and found another forty copies of my book in San Diego."

He couldn't tell her now. That was sabotage of a whole different nature and would ruin her night just as effectively. Later tonight, he'd tell her.

She placed a single fingertip on his lips, scrutinizing his face as carefully. "You're thinking about something, Adrien. I can tell."

"I'm thinking about later tonight."

She gave him a sexy smile and stood on her toes to kiss him lightly on the lips. "Me, too."

She was oblivious to the pain he was about to inflict.

CHAPTER
FOURTEEN

JUST WHEN MIRANDA thought she *got* the man, he changed.

Adrien had abruptly left the balcony and returned in minutes in a sharp sports jacket and dress trousers, the ends of his hair damp from a lightning-fast shower. He'd barely put his hand on her to lead her through the lobby for their walk across Balboa Park.

The sun had just set, but the air was still warm and rich with the scent of greenery and life. They took their time, holding hands as a peacock strutted past a mazelike garden, then dipped into the shadow of a covered walkway, following the balustrade-lined path back to the Museum of Man.

At a quarter to seven, the tower bell tolled, mournfully matching the sadness that had settled over her.

"So, what happened?" she finally asked.

"What do you mean?"

"Twenty minutes ago, you were licking my neck. Now you can't even make eye contact. You morphed from boyfriend to bodyguard in three point five seconds."

"I *am* a bodyguard right now. I'm working. Your safety is my number one concern. I have to—"

"Stop." She pulled away from his grasp and crossed her arms, keeping stride past an open area of free-form sculptures and bright red bottle-brush trees. "Are you holding back because you're leaving tomorrow?"

"A bit, maybe, yes."

"Oh, that was definite." She laughed. "You know, Adrien, we don't have to . . ." She wet her lips, swallowed, plunged. "We don't have to live in the same city. There is such a thing as a long-distance affair."

His lips lifted in a wry smile. "With a woman who doesn't fly?"

There was that. "I . . . suppose . . . I . . ."

"Please, Miranda." He lowered his voice and draped his arm around her shoulder, pulling her into the steely muscle of his side. "If you tell me you'll get on a plane for me, I'll know you're lying. Don't commit yourself to something you can't or won't do."

He felt warm and smelled good. Good enough to fly for? "You could come to Berkeley."

"Yes, I could. I spend quite a bit of time in a corporate jet since the Bullet Catchers have a few to ferry us around the world. Would you ever get on one?"

A corporate jet? A little tin can? "No."

"Shouldn't it go both ways?"

She blew out an exasperated breath. "Do you make

every woman commit to a year's worth of dinner dates before you have a fling with her?"

He pulled her tighter. "I don't want to have a fling with you, Miranda. And neither do you. You're better than that."

Like hell she didn't want a fling. She wanted it *bad*. "I know what your issues are," she said. "It's the mother thing, isn't it?"

He stopped. "What?"

"What you told me about her. That she had loose morals."

"Forget the morals, luv." He twirled his finger in a circular "crazy" motion at his temple. "She had loose screws."

"When was the last time you saw her?"

He veered them across the lawn, toward the museum entrance. "You want to chat about my mum, then?"

"Unless you'd rather talk about mine."

"Right now, I don't want to talk at all." He tugged at his earring, as he did whenever he was uncomfortable. "I want to do everything I can so that you enjoy a safe and memorable signing."

She tightened her grip around his waist, stepping in front of him so close that with one breath, their chests would touch. "And after that?"

He lowered his head and kissed her lips, very sweetly. The whole time, his finger circled one tiny spot on the back of her neck, and he looked more unhappy than a man who was being seduced should look.

"After that, I'm gonna make your heart pound and your breath tight and your pulse race."

Heat bubbled right between her thighs, regardless of the note of hesitation in his voice. "Is that a promise or a threat?"

"I'm afraid it's both. Turn around, Miranda." He put his hands on her shoulders and pivoted her. "You've gathered quite a crowd, luv."

Dozens of people filled the stairs and the entrance to the museum, and more streamed in. Anticipation tiptoed up Miranda's back . . . or was that because Adrien had his finger on her nape again?

He dropped one more kiss right on that spot and whispered, "Good luck, then."

Son of a bitch, she still had the muscle with her.

The stud was right next to her when Miranda Lang floated into the museum like a swan in white. The dude was a hired blade, with rock-star hair and Hollywood stubble. He wore gradient aviator shades that any of the museum patrons would think were the ultimate in hip, but Eddie Dobson knew better. They were designed to hide the eyes.

Eddie had been a little worried about the heightened security when he'd arrived twenty minutes earlier but not surprised, after what they'd pulled off in LA last night. No matter. He'd never carried a gun in his life, although his aim was pretty deadly, and he'd proven it on every level. But he'd bet his next version of Halo that the bullet stopper who was tracking the hot doctor had a Walther or a Glock hidden under his expensive jacket. The bodyguard was obviously on a first-name basis with security, so they probably knew he and his weapon would be here tonight.

That might make things a little trickier, might take the level of play up a notch, but since he was only there to let the author know there was a higher power in charge, he could still accomplish his goal. He reached into his pocket and fingered the wireless sensor, fighting a smile.

He had control with a button. That's what he loved about this. It was like a video game, only he was *in* it. He looked around the cavernous rotunda, at the massive columns of fake Maya carvings and the maze of half-walls that spilled off the main area to other exhibits.

It was a typical role-playing game environment, complete with unknown models and textures. And he was the First Person Shooter with a button in his hand. Maybe he could have some fun with Hollywood Boy while he was at it.

A spunky blonde in a skinny skirt started the festivities with an introduction, while Eddie stayed in the back of the crowd of San Diego's effete intellectuals. Skinny, young, and undetectable, he'd be noticed by no one. That was his power; he was invisible. And like the winner of any good game, he was invincible, too.

The bodyguard moved through the crowd while the speaker introduction was made, then made his way closer to the podium. Eddie had to give the guy props. He was unobtrusive, wary, and smart. Which added considerably to the game play.

It would be cool to see how good he was, just for laughs.

Eddie shifted in his sneakers and cleared his throat, purposely zeroing in on the author, who stood to the side of the podium while Spunky Blonde read her bio. The bodyguard did a visual scan, and Eddie could feel his eyes boring the proverbial hole. Eddie shifted again and, with pretend deadly intent, lifted his hand. Then, timed just for effect as he did with that slick move when he played level seven Gears of War, he reached inside his jeans jacket.

He saw the bodyguard tense instantly, his elbow bending like he was going to whip out his weapon, waiting and ready.

They locked eyes. Barely managing not to smile, Eddie lifted a handkerchief from his shirt pocket, shook it like a magician to prove it was empty, and then blew his nose, hiding his chuckle in the cotton.

He probably shouldn't have gotten on the guy's radar, but it was irresistible. That dude was big and armed and had the looks that probably got him laid more in one month than Eddie'd gotten in his whole life.

But today Eddie had the power. Right in his pocket.

The introduction ended to polite applause as Dr. Lang stepped to the podium. She was pretty in a Julia Roberts meets Andie MacDowell kind of way, the kind of woman who wouldn't notice Eddie if he stripped naked in front of her and waved a million dollars and the keys to a yacht. But she *was* a professor; if he'd gone to college, she might have liked him because he was a geek, and geeks were smart.

When the applause died down, he took a few steps closer to the stone tower in the back of the room. His game strategy started and ended right at the top of that thing called a stella—or stelae—something Latin.

He had to be very close when he pressed the button, but it would work. Then he needed to get the hell out within twenty-three seconds, but he'd planned his escape route this afternoon. He'd been so invisible he'd walked right in front of her and even talked to her, and she didn't see him.

He had a little time to listen to her spiel. She started off soft, her gaze darting from an imaginary focal point in the back of the room then back to the bodyguard. The dude had positioned himself close enough to the podium that he could throw himself on top of her if he had to, and though he was attentive to the crowd, he looked at Dr. Lang like he would definitely enjoy throwing himself on top of her.

"There will be no cataclysm, there will be no doomsday, and there will be no cosmogenesis that marks the end of one time and the beginning of another," she droned. He didn't even listen. God, he heard enough of that crapola from the Moonies.

With each sentence, she loosened up a little more, and after a few minutes, she hit her stride. Her voice rose with confidence, and she no longer glanced toward her bodyguard. The snobby crowd seemed mesmerized. What a bunch of idiots.

Still, she had them, and she knew it.

Sorry, Doctor. We're taking things to the next level here.

"On ten-four-zero-zero-zero, or January 18, 909, the very last Long Count stela, so much like the very monument we see here, was erected at Piedras Negras." She made a gesture to the twenty-something-foot monster column next to him. The one he'd been on top of just that afternoon, right after she'd left with Hollywood Boy to find out the books were history. Somehow they solved that problem, but they wouldn't be able to solve this one.

He waited until every eye was back on her, until she began to read the passage about how they could all sleep like babies when December 2012 bore down upon them all. They could sleep—forever. He was following the king. Well, the money trail the king left behind.

Time to remind her of who was in charge here. His heart rate sped up, and his fingers itched the way they did when he opened the cellophane on a new game. He abso-fucking-lutely couldn't wait to start playing. To beat a level, to make a kill, to outsmart whatever Dot-popping, Coke-drinking, pasty-faced genius invented it all.

A few beads of sweat dampened his collar and temples as he took careful, slow, backward steps to the half-wall that surrounded the rotunda. He glanced up at the top of the biggest of the three stone columns, squinting at his target. Every ounce of attention honed in on the one spot, the place where it would start. His hand shook a little, and he wiped his upper lip and his mouth.

Here goes, kids. So slowly that no one could see his arm moving, he dipped his fingers into the pocket of his loose cords, sliding down the inside until he felt the handmade controller. His thumb grazed the button, his pulse hammering. He lifted his eyes to the mark again. *Four. Three. Two.*

"You'd better be in there looking for your balls, mate, 'cause you're going to need a pair when I get done with you."

Shit monkeys!

The voice in his ear was harsh, low, and accompanied by the barrel of a gun pressed in his lower back. Eddie's bowels turned to water.

"Now, I know you keep your hankie in your top pocket," the Australian accent continued. "And you got through security with no problem, so I'm guessing you don't have any hardware in that pocket, do you?"

"I don't know what you're talking about." He turned an inch, but the bodyguard jammed the gun and stayed right behind him, not giving him a chance to see his face.

"Take your hand out of your pocket, or I will put a bullet through your kidney."

Eddie closed his eyes and made a decision. If he pressed the button right now, he wouldn't have failed, and failure was unacceptable. The fact that the bodyguard knew took a little of the mystery out. She'd know, too, but no one else would. And then they would accomplish the goal of emptying this room. Fast.

"Show me both hands."

Eddie pulled his left hand out but smashed his thumb on the tiny button in his right pocket. Then he lifted both hands to show he was unarmed. He had twenty-two seconds to get out of there. "I just wanted to hear the speaker, but if you'd like me to leave, I will." Right now.

He fought the urge to look up but breathed when the weapon at his back moved an inch away. "We'll go together," he said. "Now."

Eddie took a step to the side and looked at the bodyguard, who had him by about four inches and forty pounds of muscle. But size didn't matter anymore. Speed did.

"Sorry to bother you, man," he said, holding the gaze of a man who clearly took no shit from anybody. "I'll be going now."

The bodyguard lowered the gun but didn't put it away. Eddie took a few more steps backward, circled around the edge of a half-wall, and headed straight for the door. He'd just cleared the entrance when he heard a loud, collective gasp, a few female cries of "Oh, my God!" and one piercing female scream.

He broke into a run, wishing like hell he could have seen the brilliant invention at work but knowing that the bodyguard had a good enough look at him to be trouble.

But he'd done his job for the cause.

When he reached the parking lot, he pulled the device from his pocket to admire it again. This baby worked like a charm. He slipped it into his jacket pocket. He had one more stop to make that night— another treacherous level of game play.

As he drove past the museum, he saw Hollywood Boy at the top of the stairs, scanning the crowd as it dissipated. Resisting the urge to honk and wave, he secretly gave him the finger instead.

Game over, bodyguard. You lose.

CHAPTER
FIFTEEN

IF IT HADN'T been so absurd, Miranda would have laughed.

They had imagination, she'd give them that. And they knew the secrets of the Maya.

The bright blue ball of light had ricocheted from the top of the stelae around the curved ceiling of the rotunda, emitting a strange smell and eliciting gasps of disbelief. Enough people in the room knew of the ghostly "Indian light" that many Maya believed held the ancestral souls and the "energy light" that supposedly meant one of the gods was present. *Kyopa*. It was the stuff of fantasy and folklore, something many had heard of but few ever witnessed.

They still hadn't. But it had been a clever, ingenious imitation of the lightning ball, a brilliant way to attract all the attention in the room. Even Miranda had stared at it, captivated by the laserlike effect, as everyone in the room had been. Although that might not have been enough to ruin the reading, the odor it left in its wake smelled enough like gas to send plenty of the audience straight to the door.

Once again, some unknown, unnamed force had managed to crush her message and squash book sales.

"I have no idea what that was," Suzette said, making her way to the podium through a group of people who were headed toward the door. "But fire code says we have to get everyone out of here and investigate the cause of that stink."

The bitter smell lingered, although the light had disappeared. "It was an optical illusion," Miranda said. "We must have had a magician in our midst. Who was up there today?"

"There were workers everywhere today. I'm not exactly sure what they were doing or who they were or who even approved their work, and I don't have time to find out now."

'Scuse me, Doctor. The voice of one of them— one who knew her—floated back in her head. He'd been right next to her, with a ladder. She hadn't even questioned how that man had known her title; she'd assumed he worked for the museum and knew she was the night's speaker. Or she could have been inches from someone trying to ruin her tour. But it hadn't been Wild Eyes; she would have noticed him.

Suzette gave Miranda an apologetic squeeze on the arm. "I'm sorry, but you're going to have to leave like everyone else. We're closing the building, and the fire department is on its way." She waved her hand in front of her nose. "Whew, that's quite a stench."

Miranda started gathering her notes, then scanned the room for Adrien. She found him between the murals in the front, walking toward her with a dark expression.

"You gotta give them credit," she said calmly when he reached her, despite the black anger in her stomach. "They're creative."

"And I've got one now, so let's go." He took her elbow and headed her toward the door.

"You got one? Wild Eyes?"

"Not even close. This guy was younger, darker. I've never seen him before, but I know who did this. And we need to hurry, because we want to get him before he discovers my cell phone in his jacket pocket."

Her jaw dropped. "You didn't."

"I did."

"That's totally brilliant."

"Or monumentally stupid." He inclined his head to the door. "Let's run back to the hotel and check the locator software. Then we go."

"Where?"

"Wherever that little weasel goes." He urged her through the crowd. "Timing is everything now."

As they headed south on the freeway, Fletch gave Miranda instructions about the software, and she typed on the computer on her lap.

He punched the address into the GPS system, then studied the map that appeared on the small screen built into the dash of the Range Rover. "This isn't the tony section of San Diego."

Miranda shrugged. "So what exactly did this guy look like? And what did he do?"

"He's young, thin, and geeky, but this bloke had a much calmer demeanor than Wild Eyes—more calculated and focused. And he was hiding something; I knew it the moment I saw him."

"How did he do it, do you think?"

"Smoke and mirrors, operated by whatever he was fondling in his pants pocket." Fletch took the exit to K Street. He'd need to keep his weapon very handy here. Behind the weather-worn housing and inside the pimped-up cars, bad news was everywhere. Street lights were blown out. Windows were boarded up. A few unsavory characters loitered at the corner, making no effort to hide their interest in the big black beast he drove through their turf.

"No security specialist in his right mind would bring a woman he was protecting here," he said, cursing himself. "I want to get in and out of here as quickly as possible. Just give me the closest address you can get."

She clicked a key, having quickly got the hang of operating the satellite image. "K Street and . . . Jefferson, I think. There." She pointed to a street sign. "K Street. I think we have to go about six more blocks east."

Two gangsta types sitting on a wall watched them make the turn. "Stay very low, Miranda," he said. "In fact, you should be lying down on the floor of the backseat."

"You need me to work the computer."

"His location hasn't moved for forty-five minutes."

"Do you think that means he found the phone and ditched it?"

"Or took his jacket off and left it somewhere."

She sighed. "We are so close. He's here, somewhere."

At the next corner, Fletch slowed down. "Staying here tonight, I'd guess." The two-story motel looked like the definition of seedy, with two letters of its plastic sign missing and no security lights. It ran perpendicular to the street, and the rooms farthest away were deep in the darkest of shadows. At the front, the lobby—not much more than a room with a counter—appeared deserted.

Fletch parked the Range Rover where they could see the whole side of the motel.

"We're not going to knock on doors," he said.

"Want to try the lobby? Maybe there's a phone to reach management."

He threw her a look. "That's assuming there *is* management."

She wrapped her arms around her waist and squinted through the windshield. "What would he be doing in a place like this? What would anyone be doing?"

"Crack. Meth. Prostitution. The list is long."

She turned to him, her eyes bright. "How do we find him?"

"We just did." Two people had emerged from one of the rooms upstairs, and one was the right build and hair color to be the geek from the museum, without his jeans jacket. The other was a flippin' monster.

"Is that him?"

"The little one," he said. "I think so."

They came down the steps together, deep in conversation, then walked to a red sedan parked outside one of the first-floor rooms. They talked some more. The bigger guy lumbered to the door of the room, unlocked it, and went inside. The littler one climbed into the driver's seat and started the engine.

As the big man came out carrying a large square box, the driver flipped open the trunk from inside. The other man dropped the box in, then climbed into the passenger side, and away they went.

"Are you going to follow them?" Miranda asked.

"Look at that." He pointed to the motel-room door, which was still open. In the doorway was a young woman, wearing nothing but a short white T-shirt and underpants, her cigarette burning in the dark. She watched them leave and closed the door.

"Let's follow them," she said.

Fletch blew out a breath. "Or talk to her."

"Come on," she insisted, banging her door in frustration. "These guys are at the root of whatever or whoever is after me. She could be anybody. And he doesn't have the jacket on, so we might not get a signal on them. If we talk to her, we could lose them."

She made good sense. But still, he could hear Jack's voice. *I have it on very good authority that someone—I don't know who, so don't ask—knows we're looking for Eileen Stafford's daughter, and she could be in real trouble because of it.*

"Adrien, please, I want to know why they have targeted me. I can't sleep until I do."

And another voice. That bunyip that growled warnings in his ear.

He closed his eyes and put the car in drive. "Right. Let's roll."

They stayed far enough behind the target not to be observed, but Fletch kept the taillights in his line of vision.

"The locator is moving, too," Miranda said. "He must still have your phone. It's probably in the car."

"Perfect, because he's getting on the freeway, and we could lose him very easily."

Even at this late hour, the wide California freeway was crowded as they followed the Taurus south. Fletch memorized the license plate and would get the Bullet Catchers to run it tomorrow.

He threw a glance at his passenger. "You could quit the tour, Miranda. You could . . . do something else this summer." *Like go meet your real mum.* "This is a fool's errand."

"I can't believe you would say that," she shot back. "This is my career. I really believe what I wrote in that book. I really believe that there are misguided people who are already going to ridiculous lengths because they think the world is going to end in 2012. I can save—oh! He's getting off."

He swerved quickly into the right lane.

"Faster," she demanded. "He's flying down that exit ramp."

He squinted into the night and swore. "We lost him. Which way?"

"He went east," she said, sitting forward, gripping the laptop.

"All right, let's just follow the locator, then." They did, and it stopped completely after five more blocks. "Give it a second," he told her. "See if he moves again." The signal stopped. The phone, at least, was still.

Ten minutes went by, and he could sense that Miranda was ready to bolt from the car and run after the damn phone. She shifted and tapped and sighed heavily as they waited.

"All right, all right," he said. "Let's find it."

A few minutes later, they spotted the Taurus parked on a side street between two massive warehouses.

"Dangerous ground, Miranda," he said as they turned down the street. "Very dangerous ground. I am not going into a warehouse with or without you. Not happening."

"Just drive by the car. See if he's hiding in it."

He wasn't. No one was around, anywhere. Fletch drove around the block again, U-turned, and, one more time, drove up to the Taurus, positioning the vehicles so that the drivers' windows faced each other.

From his high seat, he could see right into the little car. "The jacket's in the backseat."

"Are you going to get it?" she asked. "Because you could open the glove box and maybe get some ID."

"It could be a trap."

"He obviously doesn't know we're following him, or he'd have ditched the phone."

Fletch pushed down his window and listened.

Nothing but the distant sound of traffic on the freeway and the murky smell of the harbor less than a mile away.

"When they left the house, the car was unlocked." He opened his door and put one foot on the ground. "I'm hoping the geek is a creature of bad habit."

He was, and Fletch had the jacket in his hands in two seconds.

"The glove box," she insisted, leaning over the console to whisper to him. "Just try."

The instant she said it, a light flashed, a gunshot cracked, and the windshield popped with the impact of a bullet. Fletch dove toward Miranda, shoving her down to the floor as he yanked the door behind him and threw the car into Drive as a second shot *thwumped* right into the leather seat.

"Stay down!" he bellowed, stomping his foot on the accelerator and screaming down the side street. A gunshot at the back window told him he was going in the right direction—away—and he kept the pedal on the floor as he made a wide right so fast only the power of his pull on the wheel kept them from toppling over.

Miranda was silent as he flew through the street without another hit, running a red light and whizzing through two stop signs. He headed straight back to the freeway, barreling up the ramp without even a glance in the rearview mirror, watching the traffic through the spiderwebs that spread out from the two bulletholes.

The only reason she wasn't dead was that she'd

been leaning over into the driver's side, and the bullet missed her. The *only* reason.

They were two more exits down the freeway until he was certain no one was following them. "You can get up now, Miranda." He reached to pull her back up, closing his hand over her narrow wrist, feeling her pulse pounding through her skin like a jackhammer. "C'mon, luv. Just be careful. There might be some glass. We're all right, though."

"All right is relative." She slid into the seat, taking a tentative peek over her shoulder before pulling on the seatbelt. "They shot at us!"

Yes, and he had her there, right in the middle of danger. Impulsive and stupid merged into one bad move.

"Who in God's name *are* they?" She turned to look out the back, as though they might appear.

"Dangerous. Deadly. Doesn't matter who, we're not going onto their turf anymore."

She lifted the jeans jacket from the floor. "So we got the phone back, but we're no closer to identifying them than we were before." She sounded disgusted as she stuck her hand in the pocket. "Ow!" She jerked her hand out and pressed it to her lips. "Something cut me."

He took her hand and tried to see it in the light.

"Damn, that hurts." She gingerly set the jacket on her lap, and Fletch turned on the dome light to help her see. "It's a piece of glass," she said, inching out a bright sliver that glinted in the light.

"Windshield?" he asked.

But she just sat there, staring at a pie-shaped piece of glass that glinted and shot a reflection of the dome light into his eyes.

"No." She lifted the shard, moving it so the light danced over two large lemon-yellow stones set in silver, as blood oozed between her thumb and index finger. "It's a piece of Taliña's *toli*."

CHAPTER
SIXTEEN

"IF THE SIGHT of blood makes you panic, luv, you might want to keep your eyes closed when we unwrap your hand." Fletch slid the hotel room deadbolt and glanced down at the blood-splattered white dress, covered from her view by the tourniquet she'd fashioned from the jeans jacket.

"I'm fine," she assured him.

She'd held it together for the past twenty-five minutes, but that could change, Fletch thought wryly. As soon as he told her the truth.

"Why don't we go in the bathroom and take a look-see." He shrugged out of his jacket and stashed it with his gun on an end table. "I'm fairly handy with a first aid kit, and I bet we can get one from the hotel."

"Good thinking," she said over her shoulder as she headed to the closest bedroom and, presumably, the bath. "Because from the way this feels, we'll definitely need something."

She'd need something, all right. Maybe a shot of whiskey when she found out she was adopted on the black market, tattooed by her birth mother, and had to fly across the country to meet the woman who happened to be dying in a prison where she was finishing her life sentence for first degree murder, unless, of course Miranda happened to agree to donate healthy bone marrow. If she matched.

And don't forget the bit about him knowing about it since the night they met, and how he spent the better part of a few days trying to get her naked so he could prove it all to her.

"You better come in here." She called from the bathroom. "This is worse than I thought."

In an instant he was in the bathroom, his arms around her as soon as he saw blood dripping into the white porcelain sink.

"Let me take a look," he said, flipping on the water to wash his hands. "Do you think you can stand to rinse it?"

She braced herself against the marble vanity, then gingerly placed her hand under the water, letting out a soft *ugh* of pain. The gash ran from the base of her index finger at least four centimeters to her thumb, taking a decent slice out of the skin but not the muscle beneath it.

"Do you have mobility in that thumb?" he asked, lathering his hands, then rinsing. "If you've damaged the muscle or nerves, we should get to a doctor."

She wiggled her index finger, and barely moved her thumb. "It's okay," she said. "I just need to get it cleaned and bandaged."

He took her hand in his, studying the cut. "You're going to have a scar." He caught her reflection in the mirror. "A good ER plastic surgeon can make sure that it's small and fades with time. It's a cosmetic thing, but you have particularly lovely hands and I'd hate to see them ruined."

She shook her head. "I don't need to go the ER. I heal easily."

God, he hoped so. Because what he had to tell her was going to leave the deepest scar she'd ever known. And she'd blame him, of course. He was the messenger, and she'd hate him for the message he carried.

She closed her eyes and blew out a long, slow breath. "Just clean it and wrap it, okay?"

He guided her hand back under the water, then grabbed clean towels and washcloths from the shelf.

"Oh, God, that hurts."

His stomach constricted at the pain in her voice. "I'm sorry, luv." With as much tenderness as he could muster, he rinsed again, working to keep the water from going directly into the gash and stinging.

"I'll go down and get the first aid kit, rather than wait here for it," he said. "Maybe they'll have a butter-fly bandage. That'll help with the scar. Otherwise you look at this hand for the rest of your life, and you're going to remember—"

"You."

He looked up and met her eyes, warm with affection. A knife of remorse twisted in his gut.

"I'll remember how you took care of me and helped me and didn't leave me," she said softly. "I'll remember how good you were to me, how you went headlong into trouble to find whoever is trying to hurt me."

The knife in his gut twisted harder. "You dodged the bullet all by yourself, luv. Give yourself some credit."

If only there was some way out of the inevitable. A delay. A change in plans. A reason not to tell her.

But there was none.

"Let's wrap this in a clean towel, and I'll go get the first aid kit. Unless you want to change your mind and hit the hospital."

And give him another few hours before he had to break the news.

"No, I think a butterfly bandage will do the trick."

"Up you go, then." He tapped the wide marble counter next to the sink. "I'll do my best so you don't have a horrid slash on pretty hands and say 'that bastard should have taken me to the ER.' "

She laughed softly, scooting her backside onto the marble. "No, I won't."

No. More like 'that bastard ruined my perfectly nice life with information I was quite happy not having.' He started wrapping a washcloth tightly around her palm and knuckles, making a clean, tight tourniquet that stopped the flow of blood.

"I'll say that bastard shouldn't have taken so long

to get me in bed." She reached to tuck a strand of hair behind his ear.

Now there was a worthy delay. Guaranteeing that she'd hate him in the morning. "A wounded woman with one hand? I'm not that much of a sook."

He finished by tucking one corner of the washcloth into another so that she wore a white terry boxing glove. Her expression was a little hungry, a little brazen. A woman ready to ease the horror of near death with sexual pleasure. The invitation in her eyes made his groin stir.

"There you go, sheila. You want to lie down a bit?"

She just lifted one eyebrow, silently saying that she wanted to lie down, all right—under him. The thought kicked him up to semihardness.

He cleared his throat and stepped back. "Want me to pour you a drink? Something to dull the pain?"

She shook her head, her eyes cloudy with a hurt that had nothing to do with the gash on her hand. It slayed him.

"You think I can take a shower with this wrapping on?"

"Wait for me. You might need help."

"Now you want to help me shower?" A smile curved her lips. "You are one confused man, Adrien Fletcher."

He laughed softly at the accurate and surprising assessment. "Not confused, really." Dreading the inevitable, aching to kiss that mouth, wondering like hell how he could tell her the truth and not be the messenger she'd want to shoot. He shrugged, still smiling, tugging at his earring. "Yeah. Maybe confused."

She reached up and closed her hand over his. "You know that you do this"—she pulled on the fingers that clasped the gold hoop—"whenever you are uncomfortable and not completely honest."

"Do I?"

She nodded.

He flipped his hand to hold hers. "I'm not uncomfortable, luv. Unless you count the fact that every time I'm six inches from your body, no matter what the hell is going on around us, all my red blood cells take the train south."

She smiled at that, a little twinkle of victory in her eyes. "Then you're not being completely honest."

Too right.

"So there's not someone else, and you admit you're physically attracted to me. And just a few hours ago, you promised you'd make my heart pound and my breath catch and my pulse race."

He grinned. "And didn't all of that happen during our little adventure?"

She gave a frustrated laugh. "Never mind. I'm not going to beg, Adrien. Go get the bandages."

Beg? She didn't need to beg. All she needed to do was walk into a room or look at him with those blueberry eyes or brush his cheek with a touch, and he wanted her. Couldn't she tell that his entire being ached for how much he just wanted to lean forward, cover her lips, and hold her so tightly they could feel each other's blood flow? Any other time in his life, he'd tear that bloodied dress off her and lick her clean. Then he'd throw her onto the bed and root himself so deep into her neither one of them would remember their names.

Then, when the sun came up and she wanted to go another round, he would tell her the good news. *Let's talk about you mum, luv.* Wouldn't that be some fine postcoital conversation?

"Why are you staring at me?" she asked softly.

He tugged his earring. "Because I'm confused and uncomfortable?"

"I didn't say that. I said uncomfortable or dishonest." She narrowed her eyes to underscore the last word. "Now, go." Her voice cracked a little as she pushed off the counter and stood. "Hurry. My hand hurts."

He left, closing the hotel room door before he spilled out the whole bloody truth.

Or worse, before he didn't and hurt her more by doing exactly what she wanted.

For almost five minutes after he left, Miranda didn't move. Finally she looked down at the splatters on her white silk dress, and then up, to see wide, haunted eyes in a pale face, surrounded by a chaotic mess of hair tumbling halfway down her shoulders.

With her left hand, she reached into the bodice of the dress and pulled the single string that held the wrap in place. It opened, revealing her completely bare skin. She'd dressed with *undressing* in mind.

So much for that fantasy.

The one where he gasped with shock and delight

when he realized she'd been naked underneath that dress. For him.

"Good onya, luv," he'd say with that whiskey splash of danger in his eyes. "All ready, are ya?"

But once again, it wasn't going to happen. Heat pooled low in her stomach, and her breasts ached, heavy with desire. She opened the dress and let it fluff to the ground.

She touched her lips and her throat and lightly fingered the bud of her nipple. What would it feel like for Adrien to touch her there again? For him to lick and suckle her, pull her breast to an agonizing peak, then tongue, kiss, and suck hard and furious, until she spread her legs and let him inside her?

Her knees wobbled, and her body clenched. God, she wanted him so much it truly hurt. She wanted his mouth on her. She wanted his hands on her. She wanted that giant, imposing man *inside* her.

But what did he want?

He wants your soul.

Miranda froze as she remembered Taliña's prophetic words, the warning buried in every syllable of her lilting Mexican-accented English.

He wants something you have. He's not with you by accident or chance. He will ruin your life. Give him your flesh, not your soul.

But he didn't seem to want her flesh, so why was he sticking around? Was he just protective, a professional bodyguard down to the bone? Or had Taliña seen something dark and dangerous in Adrien . . . in her *toli?*

Miranda practically dove for the jacket she'd

dropped on the floor. A jacket owned by someone who knew Taliña, who had been at Canopy, who'd followed her here, who'd ruined yet another event for her.

The splinter of mirror told her that Canopy was the connection to the Armageddon Movement. She was certain of that. Just as certain that she'd go back there tomorrow, taking that piece of mirror and demanding an explanation. As soon as Adrien left.

A ferocious disappointment gripped her. She didn't *want* Adrien to leave.

Is that what Taliña meant when she said he would steal her soul? That she would fall so hard for him she couldn't stand to see their unexpected encounter end? What had the shaman seen in her bejeweled magic mirror?

Miranda carefully reached into the pocket, sliding out the offending glass with two fingers. She sat on the cool tile floor, folded her legs, and stared at the gaudy topazes along the edge of the thick, jagged shard that had wounded her.

What had Taliña seen when she examined Miranda in this mirror?

She lifted the pie-shaped mirror, looked at the fractured image of her eye. The pupil was so wide that only a rim of her normal deep blue iris showed. She tilted the mirror, watching her nostrils flare slightly with each breath, her lips open, wet, quivering. Angling the mirror down, she studied the flushed color of her neck and chest and the hard, round bead of her nipple. And lower, down to the wet curls and ripe flesh between her legs.

She didn't know what Taliña saw that night in
Santa Barbara, but tonight, naked and crosslegged on
the floor of a bathroom, Miranda saw a woman utterly
and completely aroused.

And utterly and completely alone.

She set the mirror down and touched her breast
again, skimming down the skin to her stomach and
lower, to the moist folds between her legs.

Alone and aroused.

She dipped her finger into the flesh, then made a
small circle around her clitoris, the sudden intensity
making her twitch. Only then did she realize how fast
and labored her breathing had become, how loud the
pulse of blood in her ears had grown.

Like on the night he'd found her in the crypt,
excitement shimmered through her, blinding her temporarily. She'd been possessed, so needy for him it was
beyond an ache.

Was it the glass? Did it have that kind of power?

Or was this just the result of a lightning strike in
every erogenous zone in her body from being around a
man she wanted so much?

She stood on shaky legs, pushing damp strands of
hair behind her ears, her brain shortcircuiting with
flashes of need, with images of Adrien's mouth, his
hands, his hair . . . his dark, menacing tattoos.

With a soft groan, she put both hands on her face,
not surprised to feel the heat of her skin and a sheen
of perspiration. Facing the mirror she ran her hands
down her throat, over her chest, onto her breasts.
The rough terry of the makeshift bandage scraped her

tender nipple and whipped more desire between her legs. She dropped her head back, closed her eyes, and rubbed her body, breathing, sighing, longing. Losing the fight to a fantasy.

"Miranda."

She opened her eyes to see . . . reality. Or, at least, a reflection of her fantasy in the bathroom mirror.

Adrien stood in the doorway, his eyes as dark as hers, his chest rising and falling with the same strained breaths that she took. He was every bit as aroused as she was.

For a long, hot moment, they said nothing. Then he reached out his hand, and she turned and let him guide her into the darkened bedroom. He sat her on the edge of the bed and stood directly in front of her.

Do you want my soul? Why are you here, protecting me? Torturing me?

He unbuttoned his shirt, shaking off the sleeves to reveal the full width of his shoulders, the carved planes of his chest, the dip and cut of his abdomen.

She forgot speaking and just *looked.*

He unbuckled his belt, unsnapped his pants, and, in one easy move, kicked off his shoes and removed his trousers and boxers. His body was a masterpiece, his manhood fully erect and swollen, the jagged antlers of a shadow black-stag climbing up his lower abdomen, his legs solid and strong and dusted with golden-brown hair.

He closed the space between them, lowering himself to the bed and guiding her body up to the middle as he did.

And still, he hadn't said a word.

Was this a fantasy or a man who wanted her soul?

It didn't matter. Nothing mattered but the first, indescribable moment that his naked body covered hers. He inhaled deeply, and she did, too, to share the scent of them together, of heat and sweat and skin. He lowered his head, opened his mouth, and kissed her so gently a sob caught in her throat.

Every touch was *tender*. His hands, his lips, even the slow dance of his hips over hers. All tender.

He didn't attack with his tongue or grind his arousal into hers. He didn't plaster his hand on her breast and knead it while he licked the other. He didn't do any of the things that she'd imagined.

Instead, his kiss was somewhere between adoration and amazement, so whisper-soft that at times she wasn't sure their lips were touching. He held his whole body in check, suspended close enough to warm her but not crushing her with impatient desperation.

Was this how someone stole your soul? With infinite tenderness?

"Miranda." His sexy accent drew the syllables out, making the sound a sigh, a song of her name. "Miranda."

She wrapped a leg around his and opened her mouth for more of him, and he obliged, deepening the kiss and entering her mouth with a slow tickle of his tongue. His fingertips grazed her nipple, and then he cupped her, lowering his head to feather kisses and blow soft, sweet, warm breaths on her breast.

A helpless whimper shook her chest as fever rolled

up her spine and back down into her womb. Unable to stop, she arched up, her hips jutting into his, her stomach taking the full pressure of his erection.

He stroked her skin, down her ribs, around her hips. He flattened his hand on her backside, rubbing her flesh, heating her with his palm. She rocked again, in a primal, uncontrollable need to move against him. She pushed his hair off his face and kissed him, her eyes open, their gazes locked.

If he wanted her soul, at that very instant he had it. He had her. She spread her legs, slid herself up and down his shaft, splayed her hands over the steel of his muscles, still kissing, still gazing.

Electricity zinged through her, between them, around them, snapping at her flesh, firing her from her eyes to her toes. She lifted her hips again and captured the tip of his penis with her thighs. His mouth opened, his breath caught, his eyes sparked like golden flints.

She took him into her with one continuous move, filling herself with heat and fire and Adrien. He finally closed his eyes, letting out the defeated, relieved groan of a man who had lost a very tough battle.

That instant, everything changed.

He rose above her, tenderness transformed into raw sexual fire, his hands at either side of her head for balance. The softness in his eyes disappeared, replaced by an animal gleam. His jaw set, his hair falling into his face, he started to pump.

She raised her hips, meeting his thrusts as he rammed himself against her pelvis.

A wail of victory caught in her throat, along with a gasp at the power he'd just unleashed. He grabbed her shoulders and pulled her to him, burying his face in her neck and hair, as lost as she was.

Feverish, frantic, he pounded his flesh against hers. She dug her fingers into his shoulders, then her teeth, tasting salt and sucking in the scent of sex, licking the tattoo that painted his muscle. Pleasure swirled through her, pulling her tighter, throbbing, squeezing, driving against him. Her moans became helpless cries for release.

Her climax started as deep inside her as he was, burning and burning as she rolled against him and wallowed in it. She couldn't bear it but couldn't stop. She parted her lips, moaned his name, and finally let go for the long, sweet, agonizing fall over the cliff.

"Miranda," he murmured, kissing her throat, her chest, sucking her skin, all the while plunging deep, pulling out, plunging deeper. "Miranda, luv, please don't hate me."

Blood thundered in her head as she came.

"I don't hate you," she gasped, riding the last of the wave. "I don't. You . . . I . . ." Her voice cracked, and tears rolled down her face. "Come inside me. Please. I *need* you to."

She forced him deeper and he threw his head back, growled, and exploded violently.

Wasted, he fell onto her with a long groan, the sound of resignation, of surrender and . . . despair.

As she tightened her arms around him, Taliña's words floated in her head. *He's not with you by chance or accident.*

CHAPTER
SEVENTEEN

REBECCA AUBRY'S BRICK ranch sat just off a busy highway in West Ashley—probably once a very desirable suburb of Charleston but now solid working-class and not even a blip on the radar screens of the city's up-and-comers.

Jack liked it. Lots of trees, unassuming side streets lined with small houses that had the kind of screen doors he remembered slamming as a kid. This was a neighborhood without any of the pretentiousness of other parts of Charleston, none of the old money, none of the new. Not much money at all, to be honest. Just dinged-up cars in driveways and lawns that showed care but no fuss.

He also liked sitting in the unmarked car, drinking heavily sugared coffee, sunglasses on, window down, a target's house in his field of vision. He felt like a cop again—even though he was only staking out an old lady who'd once worked as a nurse in a farmhouse near Holly Hill. He'd decided to wait when no one had answered his knock, since he doubted a seventy-year-old woman would be gone that long.

It hadn't been hard to discover where Rebecca lived. Sweet, young Toni Hastings had pulled up the info in minutes, and over fried clams and beer in a noisy waterfront restaurant, she'd agreed to let him borrow the picture of Rebecca holding the baby.

Jack's coffee was cold by the time a late-model Buick pulled into the driveway. The petite frosted blonde who loped around the back of the car after climbing out of the driver's seat was clearly not Rebecca Aubry. Then she opened the passenger door and offered a hand to an older woman, who had to be the one he wanted.

Rebecca looked weary and bowed. Birthing babies, falsifying documents, lying to unwed mothers, and then ratting on the woman who'd employed her for a decade mustn't have been easy. Long before Eileen Stafford's trial, Rebecca had built herself quite a little police file, although she was in the files as Becky Santoulian. That's why Jack hadn't put two and two together when Eileen mentioned Rebecca.

Now it was time to take Rebecca on a trip down memory lane.

Sliding the *Post and Courier* photo into his jacket pocket, he climbed out of his car. As soon as he slammed his door, the younger woman whipped around, straightened her shoulders, and stared at him. Rebecca didn't appear to have heard him.

"Ms. Aubry?" he called.

The young woman pushed a pair of sunglasses up to hold back some of her hair, a protective arm tightening around her charge.

"What do you want?" she asked.

"I'd like to speak with Rebecca." Always better to let the gatekeeper think you're on a first-name basis.

But this gatekeeper just shook her head. "I'm so very sorry, sir," she said, her thick Carolina accent accompanying that tight, fake smile that usually preceded something like "Bless your heart, dear." "Miz Aubry won't be able to entertain your sales pitch today. Perhaps another time."

He continued toward them. "I'm not selling anything, ma'am, but I have a few questions for Ms. Aubry. It's very important—and personal."

As he got closer, he saw that she wasn't quite as pretty as her lithe silhouette and blond hair promised; her skin was rough, and her mud-colored eyes were small and unadorned by makeup.

"My name's Jack Culver," he said. "I'm a private investi—"

"Miz Aubry doesn't speak with investigators." There was no trace of the fake smile now, and she was using some force to keep Rebecca facing the other direction. "If you're seeking information about an adoption, y'all need to go to other channels. She turned over everything she knew to the police many years ago, and she's not able to help with specific cases."

In the middle of the recited speech, the older woman turned, and Jack noticed she wore a pair of dark plastic sunglasses from an optometrist's office. "Who is it, Betsy?"

"Just a salesman, Miz Rebecca." She shot him a warning look. "Not now," she whispered harshly. "She's just been to the doctor."

"Who are you?" Rebecca asked, with the loud bellow of the deaf. "You're handsome. Isn't he handsome, Betsy?"

Betsy looked pained.

"My name is Jack Culver, Ms. Aubry. I'm investigating an adoption."

Her slight shoulders sank even more, and she reached up with a shaky hand to pull down the plastic sunglasses, but her caretaker jumped in before she answered.

"You need to rest, Miz Rebecca." She looked at Jack and spoke softly. "Her memory is gone. She's deaf, old, and, today, partially blind. You won't get any answers you can rely on from her. I don't know why you people insist on bothering her. I told the same thing to a man who was here just yesterday. She doesn't remember that far back."

Rebecca took a step forward but stumbled, and Jack swooped forward to catch her other elbow and prevent a fall.

The sudden move knocked the plastic shades off, making Rebecca blink, blinded, startled, and scared.

"Ms. Aubry," Jack said loudly as he picked up the fallen glasses. "Can I schedule a time to talk to you about a Sapphire Trail baby?"

"Oh, I don't know about that, dear. Betsy's right. I don't rightly recall that much anymore."

"Please," the younger woman said, peering over the stooped shoulders between them. "Have some pity for an old, sick woman."

"I do," he told her. "In fact, I'm here on behalf of Eileen Stafford." He said the name loudly and directed it to Rebecca, whose chocolate-brown eyes widened instantly.

"Did you find one of them?" she asked.

"Did I find a Sapphire Trail baby?"

"Miz Rebecca, please don't do this to yourself," Betsy said insistently as she tried to urge the woman forward. "You can't help every one of these people who come knocking at the door or lurking in the driveway waiting to attack you for information."

But Rebecca blinked at Jack, fighting for clear vision. "Eileen Stafford is still in jail, isn't she?"

"Yes. Do you remember her, Ma'am? Do you remember the baby? The parents who adopted her?" Would she admit she was at the trial? Would she reveal the name of the baby she held?

She shook her head. "Poor girl never got a break in life."

"No, never did," Jack agreed. "Eileen Stafford is dying of leukemia, and her daughter might be the only person who can save her life."

"Her daughter? Is that what you said?" Rebecca asked, lifting a hand to indicate her bad ear. "Daughter?"

"Yes," he practically shouted. "The records are sketchy, but I have names of girl babies who were sold during the month when Eileen's daughter was born. I'm trying to locate her."

"Most of the records were destroyed."

"I have a picture," Jack said, pulling it from his pocket. "Perhaps this photo from the trial will jog your memory."

She froze and looked at his hand as if he'd drawn a weapon. "A picture? Of . . ."

"Of you." He showed it to her.

She blinked, wiped her eyes, then shook her head. "I can't see."

"This isn't just another case of a separated parent and child," he said. "Lives are at stake. Not just Eileen's. Her daughter could be in danger, as well."

She reached for the picture but pulled her quivering hand away before she touched it.

"I don't believe she's guilty, Ms. Aubry."

A hesitant smiled pulled at the woman's mouth. "I believe she is a woman who would do anything for her . . . child."

"Would she take responsibility for a crime she didn't commit?"

Rebecca suddenly looked very old and very tired. She held her hand up to Betsy as if to ward off an argument. "Let him come in for five minutes."

"Miz Rebecca, you're tired. You're sick."

Her face contorted with self-disgust. "Yes, I am, child. I'm sick and tired of *lying*. Come." She beckoned Jack with one hand. "I need to show you something."

The house was dimly lit and smelled of lavender and cat. The cause of the latter was a sneaky tabby that mewed at its owner, then curled up on a blue sofa in the living room to watch Jack.

The two women disappeared into a back part of the house. After a few minutes, Betsy came back in, her expression grim.

"I don't know why she wants to do this," she said, "but she does. The minute she gets even slightly agitated, you have to leave. Is that clear?"

He nodded as Rebecca came shuffling back into the room, a brown envelope in her hand. His heart kicked up a notch, and he imagined an answer it held.

"I'd like to make you a deal, Mr. . . . what was your name again, sir?"

"Culver. Jack Culver."

With a disgusted sigh, Betsy left the room.

"What kind of deal, ma'am?"

She held out the envelope. "That picture for this paper."

"What is that paper?"

She opened the envelope very slowly, with a palsied shake, then slid out a single piece of paper. "This is the petition to adopt, signed by a Charleston County notary on August 21, 1977, granting final adoption of Baby Stafford."

Jack took it, scanning the Courier font made by a manual typewriter, the parchment feeling very much like an original, the seal of the State of South Carolina embossed and still a little shiny, even after thirty years. "Whitaker," he said, focusing on the last name of the adopting parents as he read. "From Virginia."

"You'll know her when you find her," Rebecca said, "because she has a tattoo."

Now his heart did kick up. He'd *found* her. Finally.

Whitaker of Virginia. That wasn't even one of the names on the list he'd given Fletch. "Yes. Eileen told me about the tattoo. Do you know where it is?"

"Hello, Butterscotch." Rebecca sat on the sofa and tunneled her fingers into the cat's fur. "Of course I do. I put it there."

He drew back, surprised. "You did?"

"Some of the mothers want to, so that they might be able to identify their children years later. Some put their initials, some put their names."

Jack frowned at her. "So these kids . . . they have names and letters on their bodies?"

"Usually in a place where they can't see it." She touched her nape. "Right here, under the hair."

"If I find her, will she have a tattoo there?"

Rebecca nodded.

"Do you remember what it was?"

"Not precisely." She closed her eyes. "That girl, that Eileen, she wanted numbers. Now, that was unusual. Most wanted a picture of something, a cross or a heart Maybe initials. I never did numbers before or since."

"Numbers? Do you—"

She shook her head. "No, I don't remember."

"Ms. Aubry." Jack took to one knee in front of the woman and held out the picture from the newspaper library. No one would miss it. "I will make that trade."

Rebecca snapped up the picture and held it to her breast, closing her eyes. "I'm tired," she said suddenly. "I want you to leave."

As if on cue, Betsy entered the room.

Jack stood, folding the adoption paper in half,

and slid it back in the envelope. "On behalf of Eileen Stafford, thank you."

She nodded, still clutching the picture. "Thank you, Mr. Culver," she said with a dreamy smile.

The minute he walked out the door, Jack checked his watch. It was barely seven A.M. in California. Was that too early to call Fletch and tell him he didn't have to go to Oregon? Would he go to Virginia and find the Whitakers?

Maybe Fletch could tap into Lucy's database for information. Then he'd make a trip to Camp Camille to see Eileen with the good news. It would—

Across the street, a young man waited next to his car. The cop in Jack went on high alert.

Male. Caucasian. Black hair, military cut. Mid-twenties, five-eleven, dark hooded sweatshirt, jeans, boots, sunglasses.

And, Christ, armed—the pistol was pointed directly at him.

He considered reaching for his own weapon but figured he'd be shot before he drew.

Son of a bitch. Nothing said this was the kind of neighborhood where you'd get rolled at ten in the morning.

"Can I help you?" Jack said calmly as he approached the car, holding his hands far enough from his sides to show he wasn't going to shoot.

"Give it to me."

Jack had worked the streets for too many years to be upset by a hold-up. He carried very little cash and no ID of consequence in his wallet; anything he really needed was stashed in his car.

"All right. I'm going to get my money now." A sudden move could cost him his life. He reached for his money clip and pulled it out. As he handed it over, the kid grabbed the envelope in his left hand.

"I'll take that, too."

"Hey!" Fury shot through him. "There's nothing in there you want. It's paper."

The kid lifted the gun to Jack's face and stepped away from the car. "Shut the fuck up, and get in the car."

Jack opened the car and slid behind the driver's seat, his eyes on that envelope. He knew the name of the family and the state. Did he need more than that? The papers would make it easier, but it wasn't worth getting shot over.

"Now close the door and drive away," the kid instructed. "This gun will be aimed at you until you're gone."

Jack turned the key in the ignition, drove down the street, and turned the corner. When he circled back around, the guy was gone. And so was the car in the driveway.

There was no answer at the door when he knocked again.

He pulled his phone out to call Fletch and tell him he had the wrong girl. None of the names on the list matched Whitaker of Virginia. Unless Rebecca Aubry was lying, that's who adopted Eileen Stafford's baby.

But his instinct, that motherless bastard, said she was telling the truth.

CHAPTER
EIGHTEEN

MIRANDA STARED AT the bunyip on the back of the man she'd made love to all night. Fletch was asleep on his stomach, his arm firmly around her waist, his face turned away so that all she could see was a mass of dark caramel hair, the muscular slopes of his arm and back, and the artwork that rolled over his shoulder blade.

The bunyip was a menacing thing, with wide-set yellow eyes, pointy black ears, and ferocious teeth. There was nothing gentle about this creature, nothing protective or proud like a falcon or an eagle. None of the authority and power of the classic Maya jaguar, none of the fertility and life force of mythical creatures that sprouted horns and exaggerated genitalia.

The bunyip was purely mean.

Why would a man who was so protective, so willing to help another person, and so deeply passionate that

he could make her weep every time he entered her
sport such a wicked, malevolent image on his body?

Miranda, don't hate me.

She lifted her hand toward him, the one with the
tight bandage he'd made for her in the middle of the
night. Her finger was less than an inch from the bunyip and the relaxed muscle under it. She could feel
the heat of Fletch's body, almost touch his back as it
moved with each breath.

"Careful, luv."

She jerked her finger back as he slowly turned his
head to peer at her through sleep-narrowed eyes.

"He might bite ya."

He grinned, deepening the dimples she'd explored
with her tongue the night before, a strand of golden-
brown hair falling over his eye and landing on the
angle of his cheekbone. He kissed the finger still extended in his direction. "G'day, Miranda."

"G'day, mate."

He laughed at her Aussie accent and folded her
against him. "So, what's your professional opinion of
my bunyip?"

"That he's in an elite group of cultural symbols that
exist solely to scare people. Like gargoyles. Why did
you pick that particular image?"

"I got it at a time when I needed to scare people,
because"—his grin faded, and he held her gaze with
one so intent and honest it looked right into her heart
—"so many had scared me."

She caressed his cheek and the soft growth on his
strong jawbone. "What happened to you?" she asked.

His erection was like steel against her stomach, their legs instantly intertwined. But he didn't seem consumed with need, just resigned to talk.

"Here's my life story, luv—all thirty-eight years of it. I had a shitty childhood, got the snot knocked out of me on a regular basis, ran away from home when I was sixteen and still pretty small, lived with natives in the bush, where I basically grew up physically and more, went back to Tassie to square with my dad, but he was too drunk to deal with me, so I joined the police, worked my way up the ranks, got my ass saved by a bloke who became my best mate, landed a job in the States with the Bullet Catchers, and just last night"—he to smiled that killer grin again—"I had the best sex of my life."

She just stared at him.

"Not that this is just about sex or anything," he added.

"Oh, no. I can tell." She moved against his aroused body, not yet ready to slide from self-revelations to sex. "You told me when and how you got that monster on your back but not why."

"Well, I guess the monster on my back is . . . the monster on my back."

She frowned. "I don't get it."

"It's a reminder of my weaknesses."

"You have them?"

That made him laugh and kiss her. "As if you didn't see evidence of my world-class impulsiveness when I threw you on this bed."

"No," she disagreed, sitting up to make her point.

"You've shown nothing but restraint. If anyone has been impulsive these last few days, it's me, diving into danger."

He eased her back down, into his warmth. "We're good for each other that way." He ran the pad of his thumb over her cheek. "And it *was* the best of my life. Honest." He leaned closer to kiss her, but she drew back.

"I want to believe you."

He gave her an insulted look. "You *want* to believe me? Why don't you?"

To be fair, he'd done a masterful job of erasing her doubts the night before. He'd kissed and nibbled and loved her into multiple orgasms, the kind that no man could give a woman unless his heart and soul were into the act.

"I didn't tell you everything that Taliña said in the crypt the other night."

He rolled his eyes. "Whatever it was, it was bullshit."

"She said . . ." She hesitated, not wanting this to come off like a woman needing reassurance. "She didn't trust you. She said you wanted my soul."

His expression changed so subtly and quickly that if she hadn't been staring at him, she wouldn't have seen it. "That's probably a bit more of a commitment than I'm ready to make," he said, going for lightness but not achieving it.

"She said," Miranda continued. "that you aren't here by chance or accident. And I kept thinking about that when we made love last night."

His body tensed, and for the first time in about twelve hours, his erection didn't seem quite so intent on being attended to. Slowly, deliberately, he made some space between them.

"Nothing happens by chance or accident," he said. "The Aborigines taught me that."

He inhaled the breath of a man about to jump off a cliff, then let out a soft groan that was somewhere between misery and dread.

A steel band circled her chest. "What's the matter?"

"Miranda, I have to tell you something. I can't delay it any longer."

She tensed.

"This is going to be extremely difficult for you."

"Oh, God, please don't tell me you're married."

"No, I'm not married. I swear. Not married, not involved. Not committed, not anything."

She closed her eyes. "You scared me for a second."

"But you are going to ha—"

"Just tell me whatever it is. I'm not going to hate you for leaving or announcing that you don't want a long-distance relationship with a woman who doesn't fly. Just tell me."

His phone buzzed on the nightstand behind him, and he frowned as he looked at the ID. "I'll call him back. This is more important."

It sure is. "Why do you think I would hate you?"

"Because I knew who you were long before you knew who I was."

She flipped through every possible reason in her head and came up with only one that would result in *hating* him. "You're one of them? You're with the Armageddon Movement?"

"No. It's actually much worse than that."

"Worse?" she croaked.

He rolled out of bed and grabbed the duffel bag he'd been traveling with. After rooting around the side pocket, he yanked out a piece of paper.

She sat up and pulled the sheet over her, watching as he perched on the edge of the bed and smoothed the paper in front of her.

The phone rang again, and he glanced at it for one second, then back at the paper.

"What is that?" she asked, skimming a list of women's names. Oh, this couldn't be good. Nothing about this could be good.

"These, Miranda . . ."

Miranda Lang. Daughter of Dee and Carl Lang, Marietta, Georgia. What kind of list was this?

"Are the names of babies who were adopted."

She stared at the paper, then at him. "What are you talking about?"

"The birth mother of a baby who was born in July 1977 and sold through black-market adoption is searching for her daughter. That's why I'm here. I'm looking for her."

She backed up slowly, drawing herself further from him, deeper into the bed. "You think . . . that's me?"

"I know it's you, because you were tattooed at birth." He reached up and slid his hand around her neck, tapping her hairline gently. Her mark.

Hi? She could hear her hairdresser laughing. *It says hi on your head, Miranda.*

"When I met you, I was looking for that mark so I could be sure I had the right woman."

Blood pounded in her head and she almost couldn't hear him.

Adopted. You're on this list. Black-market adoption. Birth mother looking for you.

"Then I found it, and I had to tell you."

"You weren't going to tell me?"

He closed his eyes. "Obviously, your parents didn't want you to know. I felt I had no right . . . until I found it."

No right? She couldn't even process that. A million thoughts raced through her head, none of them coherent.

Mom. Dad. Home. Life. Love. Security. Genes. Self.

Oh, Lord. Who *was* she?

She was *adopted*.

"This is a mistake," she said, shoving the paper away. "A big, fat mistake." Wasn't it? It had to be.

"No, Miranda, it's an accurate list." He started to reach for her, then seemed to think better of it. "I'm sorry to be the one to tell you this."

Her head vibrated. No, that was his phone. Again.

She pressed her hands to her temples to organize her wild thoughts. "She's my *mother*, Adrien. I don't care if there's even a remote possibility that she didn't carry me for nine months. She's my mother. He's my father. They're my parents, far better and more wonderful than most parents."

The trueness of that washed over her, warm and comforting.

"You are so right about that, Miranda. I'm sure your parents love you unconditionally. And believe me, that is worth everything in the world."

Taking the paper, she studied the names and dates, her hands shaking. "What is Sapphire Trail?"

He explained about a farmhouse in rural South Carolina, where babies of young, unwed mothers were given new birth certificates and sold to parents who weren't able to get babies by any legal means.

Not just adopted. *Illegally* adopted. Black-market baby.

"They were forty," she said when he finished. It was all she could think of. A defense of their indefensible actions. "My parents were too old to adopt legally."

He nodded. "Thank God they found you, right?"

"Right." She meant that, down to her soul. Didn't she? *Oh, God.*

"Miranda, I'm sorry you have to face your loving mum with this information."

Face her with this information? "I have no intention of telling my mother." Or maybe she did? She hadn't decided yet. But this man, this damn near stranger who'd infiltrated her life and her bed and her heart, he had *no* right to tell her what she was going to do or not.

Another reality hit: he'd set this whole thing up

from the beginning. He really was here to steal her soul. At least, her identity.

"She sent you, didn't she? My . . . the woman who . . . is looking for her child. She put you up to this whole thing, didn't she?" Nausea pulled at her.

The phone rang again, and he swore under his breath, seizing it. "Not now," he growled into the phone. He paused for a minute, his face dark. "No. I can't talk."

"She sent you," Miranda repeated when he threw the phone onto the bed.

"No. As a matter of fact"—he nodded toward the phone—"that bloke who's been calling all morning did. Jack Culver."

"Who is he?"

"He's working for . . . he's trying to help your . . . Eileen Stafford."

Miranda put her hands on her ears to shut him out. "I don't want to know her name. I don't want to know anything." Not yet. Not until she could understand this.

"She needs to meet you."

"Oh." The word was a sigh of abject misery. How had this happened? "I'm not going to meet . . . her. This woman. My—no, she isn't my mother, and I have no desire to bring her into my life. I don't want her to know who I am, understand? Because this is a huge mistake. Huge. Tell her or whoever the hell sent you that you didn't find me. I can trust you to do that, can't I? After this . . ." She gestured toward the bed and her naked body. "I can trust you to be on my side and not hers or your friend's, right? I can trust you, can't I, Adrien?"

Oh, please, please, please say yes.

He just stared at her. "You can't just ignore this woman or act like you were never found."

"Who says I can't?"

He let out a breath. "Because you don't know everything yet."

She didn't want to know everything. She didn't want to know *this*.

"Your birth mother is dying of leukemia and needs a bone-marrow donation from a child. That's why she wants to find you."

Her jaw dropped. Oh, this just kept getting better and better. "You're lying."

"Of course I'm not." He reached for her, but she ripped her hand away.

"*That's* why she wants to find her child? Because she's dying? Why wouldn't she want to find me before she needed me? What a horrible woman!"

"It gets worse."

How could it possibly?

"She's in jail for murder."

She absolutely couldn't speak. She dropped her head back, closed her eyes, and told herself this was a bad dream. She hadn't awakened yet. She hadn't laid eyes on that bunyip, that . . . that monster who preyed on children.

"Miranda, I—"

She slowly stood and gathered the sheet around her. "I'm going to leave now. I'm going to pack my bag and walk downstairs and get a cab. I don't want you to come after me. I don't want you to call me. I don't want you ever to seek me out again." She finally looked at him, her throat so full that she could barely speak. "And you are not going to stop me."

She stepped away from the bed, just as his phone rang again.

She turned and nodded to the phone. "I would appreciate it if you would tell that man I am not the woman Eileen Stafford is looking for. I am not her child." She sought out his gaze and looked hard into his eyes. "If last night meant anything at all, if you have a heart in that chest, if you have any pity or warmth or affection or just plain common sense, then tell him that for me."

She walked out of the room, and the phone kept ringing even after she'd closed the door.

In the other bedroom, she pulled on jeans, sneakers, and a T-shirt. She threw whatever she'd left in the bathroom into her bag, zippered it, and rolled it across the salon. Behind the closed door, she could hear his voice.

Would he respect her wishes? She stopped and listened, only able to make out a few words.

"This is really a stupendously bad time, Jack," he growled. Then nothing for a minute.

Come on, Adrien. Do this for me.

"No, I've bloody got her right here," he said. "And I've told her already." Another pause. "Bloody hell, you've got to be kidding me."

Well, could she blame him for having loyalties to

his friend and not her? Still, it hurt. She rolled the bag behind her, then stopped when he spoke again.

"Not possible. I have her. I've seen it. I've just got to think of some way to get her to go—"

Silence on his end. A long silence.

He wants your soul.

Well, he couldn't have it.

She left, clunking the bag through the door and down the carpeted hallway. She pressed the elevator call button and stepped inside when it arrived.

"Miranda! Wait!"

She stabbed the Close Door button with her bandaged hand, over and over and over. *Come on. Close, door.*

"Miranda!"

Punching so hard she broke a nail, she pictured him running naked through the hall, cell phone in hand, plea on his lips. The doors *thunked* and swept closed.

There.

She'd never have to see the monster again.

CHAPTER
NINETEEN

BLOODY, BLOODY HELL.

Fletch stood in his grundies staring at the closed elevator door. She'd be in a cab and gone before he had time to go back and pull his pants on. A string of curses boiled up in him.

God damn Jack for not calling sooner. Well, he had, but he'd ignored the phone.

She wasn't Eileen Stafford's daughter. Some woman had proof of that. Some woman who tattooed babies for a living, who might have tattooed "hi" on Miranda's nape, but that didn't make her the one he wanted.

He almost roared with fury. The whole fucking thing could have been avoided if he'd waited ten more minutes to tell her. He kicked at the air. If he had just answered the bloody phone and talked to Jack.

It vibrated again, and he almost threw it down. But it could be—

"Yeah?"

"Hello, Fletch."

"Hey, Luce." He started the walk down the hallway, to where he'd left the dead bolt holding the suite door open.

"I need you on an assignment. Now. And before you tell me you're all wrapped up in Jack Culver's problems, let me tell you that you brought this one on yourself, so you're handling it."

"What is it?"

"We've been doing the background checks on the Blakes, as you requested."

"Yeah." He walked back into the bathroom, as if Miranda might have magically reappeared.

"Interesting development. A lead in Victor Blake's background sent me to a friend and sometimes client, Anthony Bellicone, the CEO of Northgate, Inc."

"Northgate? Don't they publish magazines?"

"More than a dozen, the biggest names in the business. He knows Victor Blake all too well. Evidently, Blake made his millions by selling magazine subscriptions—not just Northgate magazines but every other one as well. He has a massive, nationwide network of subscription crews and made a not-so-small fortune from this shady, but not illegal, business of using crews of runaway and lost teenagers going door-to-door to sell magazine subscriptions."

He squeezed his eyes shut. He couldn't go on a case now. He couldn't. "I know about them," he said. "It's damn near slavery, in some cases. But Lucy, I—"

"It's profitable as hell, and the bane of my client,

because most of the subscriptions are never fulfilled, the money is lost and laundered, and the magazine publishers are left with nothing but a PR mess of unhappy customers. Anthony Bellicone wants us to get something on Blake."

"I know exactly where he is," Fletch said quickly, "if you want to send someone in to question him. But I—"

"You," she interjected. "You are going to get something on him."

He took a step, and his foot hit something sharp. The mirror shard. He bent over and lifted it, angling it to catch the light. "What do you have in mind?"

"Track down one of the magazine crews, and get something to connect it to Blake. We believe there are several working in Southern California right now. They stay in low-cost motels."

Kids in cheap motels? He fingered the glass that had come out of the jacket pocket of someone who'd visited a cheap motel last night. That was a connection to Blake, at least to his wife. And somewhere, somehow, there was a connection to Miranda.

"I might have a place to start this morning," he said. "If I can connect one of these crews to Blake right away, you mind if I finish what I'm doing?"

"This is a high priority for an important client, Adrien." *In other words, forget the business you're fooling around with now.* "Once you've successfully completed this, I'll see what I can do about helping you find this woman Jack wants."

"We don't need to make deals, Luce. Anyway, he's found her," Fletch said. "But I've lost another one, and I'll need some time and maybe some help."

"Fulfill this client's request, and you can have all the resources you need."

"I know where to start." He glanced at his laptop and prayed Miranda had her phone on. Lucy was already helping him. She just didn't realize it yet.

When he turned off the freeway at the exit they'd used the night before, Fletch decided that the two radial fractures and bulletholes in the windshield of his rented SUV fit the neighborhood perfectly. He'd known the place was seedy last night, but in the daylight, it was worse.

Magazine crews. They'd gone after some sub crews, as they were called in Australia, when he was on the police force, and he'd seen some of the handiwork of the more aggressive managers. Not pretty.

Usually, some thugs ran a group of low-IQ, abused, or addicted teenagers, giving them false hopes and a sense of family, along with disgustingly low pay and poor conditions. The kids traveled around the country together, usually in dilapidated vans driven by questionable individuals. They were dropped off in neighborhoods to knock on doors and sell magazine subscriptions. Most of their sales were made out of pity, and most of their profits—always cash—were turned over to the manager. If they didn't perform, they were beaten, tortured, raped. They stayed because they were desperate and scared to leave.

He'd very much like to pin a mess like that on Victor Blake. And then help Miranda.

He threw the car door open and headed for the dingy lobby, shrugging into the hooded sweatshirt he wore to cover his weapon.

Just before he got to the lobby, he saw the curtain move in the window of the room they'd watched the night before. Screw the management. He slid his shades into place and went right to the motel room.

He rapped twice, but no one answered. He probably could kick it in with no problem, and just as he debated the merits of that, the door opened.

She was practically a child.

Although her height and body under her baggy shirt were those of a grown woman, this girl wore the wide-eyed terror of a kid about to get the crap kicked out of her. She hadn't seemed so terrified the night before, when she stood smoking in this doorway.

A bitter smell wafted from behind her. Stale cigarette smoke, pot, beer, and . . . meth. Maybe she was too stoned last night to be scared.

"I swear to God," she said, her voice so soft he wasn't sure he heard right. "I can't go today. I just can't. I can't." She tried to look tough but failed. "And don't hurt me."

"I'm not going to hurt you."

Her look was wary as she pushed a strand of straight, stringy hair behind her ear, and he saw three violent red wounds on the side of her palm. "Then what do you want?"

"I'm looking for someone."

"Frankie?"

"I don't know his name, but he was here last night. Not very tall, light brown hair, wire-rimmed glasses. Kind of a nerd."

"Eddie Dobson." She shook her head. "He's one of the tech guys. He mostly just comes for the money, and Frankie gives it to him or takes him . . . wherever they take the cash. I honestly don't know that end of the business at all."

"The business of . . ." He let his voice trail, hoping she'd fill in the blank.

But she just gave him a look he knew all too well. Stricken. He'd seen it in the mirror when he was seven. "He ain't here."

She started to close the door, but his foot was too fast. "You can tell me. Or I can tell the cops. Your choice."

She shrugged, but he thought she probably didn't feel as cavalier as she acted. "Nothing against the law," she said. "No drugs, no shit like that."

Right. "Then what generates the money?"

Her pale blue, red-rimmed eyes tapered. "None of your fucking business. So get your foot out of the door and leave."

He lowered his head and his voice. "Does he use cigarettes or a joint to burn your hand like that?"

She froze, and color drained from what would be very pretty cheekbones if she didn't have the gaunt look of a user. "Like I said, none of your fucking business."

He wedged his foot in further. "Is Frankie the boss?"

She snorted. "No."

"Who does he work for?"

"The company."

"What's the name of the company?"

"No clue." She looked past him, scared. "Look, Frankie loves to come back unannounced and shit, and he will *really* not like it if I'm talking to you, so could you please leave now?"

"Frankie's the large fellow who left with Eddie last night?" He might be the connection to Blake, not this young girl.

"He's the size of a house, yes." She wrapped her arms around herself. "And happy to remind us that he's in charge."

He stepped back, allowing her to close the door if she wanted. "You can go home anytime, you know. You can get help."

She snorted softly. "Maybe I don't want to go home."

"I got that," he said. Christ, he'd chosen to live in the bush rather than with his father. "Will Eddie or Frankie be back soon?"

"I dunno. Sometimes Frankie comes here during the day, but mostly he's following the crew. Especially now, since they need a van for the demos."

"Demos?"

A little more color faded from her face. "I already told you too much. You could be a cop or a reporter, for all I know."

"I'm not either one. But let me ask you something. Do you need money to get home, or to get to a phone?"

She straightened and wiped her mouth with the back of her hand. "This is a test, isn't it? Frankie put you up to this to see if I'd take cash and leave? He'd do something like that."

"No, it's not." He reached for his back pocket. "I met a bloke once who worked for a crew, in Tasmania." At her frown, he added, "That's part of Australia."

She nodded, watching him warily.

"He just wanted to get home." He pulled a few twenties from his wallet. Too much, and she'd be scared. Not enough, and she might stay. She might stay anyway, but it made him feel better to try. He handed the money to her.

She stared at it.

"It's not a test," he said. "Just keep it. If you want to go home, you can get a bus or a train."

She snatched it and slammed the door closed. He'd have to wait for their manager, who might have a connection to Blake. He started to the car when he heard the door open.

"Hey, Crocodile Dundee."

He turned to see she held out a cardboard box. "This is for you."

As he walked back, she added, "Like, in case I have to explain where I got that money. I'll just say you bought this, okay?"

The box was plain, about the size of large shoe box. "What is it?"

She smiled. "You want the shtick? Okay." She cleared her throat and lifted her chin like a child about to recite the Lord's Prayer. "A couple thousand years ago, a civilization lived that was very advanced, called the Mayans. They were unbelievably smart, like really, they knew all this stuff about astrology and had an advanced language, and they were all scientists."

He stared at her, his jaw loosened.

"Anyway, they had this calendar, and no other people, ever, in the history of world or before ever had such an accurate calendar. They could see the future. This is true," she added, crossing her heart like a little girl. "They counted exactly how many days the earth would be around before it . . . ended." Her eyes widened. "Do you know that's going to happen in, like, less than four years?

"Really."

"Seriously. December 21, 2012. Do you know how close that is?" Fervor and sincerity changed her face from a stricken, lost teenager to an evangelist. "Some people will survive. Only the people who are prepared. That"—she pointed to the box—"is a start. It has things in it you will need. Information, tips for being safe, all sorts of proof about the Mayans' calendar, and a Web site you can go to and buy more things like generators and computers that won't fail. Phones that will connect you to the other living people on earth. Guns, because you might need them. Remember Y2K?"

He nodded.

"This is going to be *so* much worse. People have to have this. There's more, but this will get you started."

"This is what you're selling door-to-door?"

"We're not selling anything," she insisted, her face flushed now with commitment. "We're saving lives. Trust me, this has been proven over and over, and anybody who says it's not true is just stupid."

Anybody . . . like Miranda Lang.

He held the box up. "How much does it cost?"

"Well, that's not a complete package, because they cost, like, ninety bucks. But that's a demo with some more information, and it's only twenty bucks. It'll send you to this amazing Web site, and not everyone can get on it. You need a password; that's in there, too. And you can buy all kinds of stuff there, stuff you'll need, I promise." She stepped back, cracked her knuckles, and suddenly seemed like a shy girl again. "I, um, actually sell a lot of them."

"I'll bet you do. And what are you going to do in December 2012, when the world ends?"

"I'm going to be saved."

"Is that right?"

"Everyone who sells a certain amount is going to this really special place, it's like, um, the birthplace of civilization. And there's going to be a king and a whole new world. And we'll be part of it. You can be, too."

"Where is this place?"

She squinched up her features. "I think Canada. I've heard Frankie talk about it, and I think he said Canada."

"Could he have said Canopy?"

She brightened. "Yeah. Canopy. That was what I heard."

Too right. He got it all: what Lucy needed and what Miranda needed. Proof in his hands, a Web site that no doubt sucked credit-card numbers like a vacuum cleaner, and a connection to Victor Blake—his home.

"Thank you," he said, indicating the box.

"That'll really help you," she said with an expression of pure sincerity.

"You have no idea."

He hustled to the car, threw the box onto the passenger seat, and checked the laptop he'd left open. He had time. He still had time.

CHAPTER
TWENTY

FROM THE CAB window, Miranda saw a plane landing, so close she could read the word DELTA on the side.

Her heart jumped like the turbulence she imagined the passengers endured, jerky and sudden and fast enough to send her stomach on a free fall. Could she do it? Could she get on that machine and fly?

She hadn't answered that question yet; she was too busy trying to come to terms with all the others.

Adrien Fletcher had used her in the worst imaginable way. He hadn't been lying all those times he said it wasn't about sex. It *wasn't*. And when she told him she wouldn't meet this woman, this Eileen Stafford, he'd upped the stakes to a life-or-death situation.

From the beginning, he'd tried to get her to stop the tour. When she wouldn't, he'd stayed with her. Watched her. Scrutinized her body. Saved her from a gunshot . . . sort of. For all she knew, that whole thing could have been staged by some secret organization just to make her trust him or believe him.

But could she believe him? Only one person knew the truth. Well, two. Mom and Dad had to know.

There had to be another reason.

The Armageddon Movement.

What if he really was part of them, and this preposterous story was just a way to make her quit? Right now, with her head spinning and her heart reeling, anything seemed possible.

Miranda, Miranda, please don't hate me.

She closed her eyes, and when she opened them, her gaze landed on the sign for National Car Rental. Oh, wouldn't that be the easy way out? She could drive anywhere.

She could get on Highway 10 and head due east to Atlanta. Or she could head out for Phoenix and continue on her tour. What difference would a few more days make? It wasn't as if she was dying to have this conversation with her mother.

Better yet, she could drive down to Mexico, see ruins, and get lost in the ancient culture that comforted her. Or San Francisco. Or Alaska or Peru or *anywhere* but Terminal 2 at the San Diego International Airport.

But none of those trips could erase the impact of Adrien Fletcher's words. Or the rotten way she'd left him. Or the fact that now she was contemplating running—no, *flying*—home to Mommy.

How long would she let fear dictate her every move?

"Delta, right?" the driver asked.

Delta flew into Atlanta a million times a day. She could leave here and in a few hours be in the comfort and safety of her family. Home to Dee and Carl Lang of Marietta, Georgia.

Oh, Lord above, were they even her parents?

Adrien Fletcher had planted a seed that might never germinate but would always be there under the surface, torturing her.

"Ma'am? Delta Airlines?"

She dragged herself back to the moment, to this decision. "Yes, I'm flying Delta." No words could sound more foreign coming from her mouth.

Except maybe *Are you really my mother?*

She toyed with the corner of the bandage Adrien had so lovingly wrapped around her last night. In between hours of sex and kisses and cooing Australian, he'd bandaged her as neatly as a surgeon.

Was that the act of a man out to ruin her?

Then the cab pulled to the curb, and she felt like a spectator, watching someone else wait in line at a counter, talk to an agent, purchase a ticket, show identification, check a bag, use the ladies' room, and sit in a bustling place where a million trillion zillion *normal* people went every day.

For an hour in the same navy-blue leather seat, she sat motionless. Mothers with babies, businessmen with laptops, teenagers with iPods, families and grandmothers and flight attendants streamed by, rushing to their planes or their luggage, on phones or drinking or eating. Laughing, talking, and normal.

Her heart was remarkably calm, her palms surprisingly dry, her stomach amazingly settled.

Until the announcement that Flight 516 to Atlanta was ready for boarding.

"Now boarding zones one through four," a friendly, efficient voice said. "If you are seated in zones one through four, please proceed to Gate A-9 for boarding."

A group of travelers stood, checked paperwork, admonished children. Miranda flipped the worry-worn corner of her boarding pass. Zone seven.

Heat and dread prickled at her neck, down her arms. She sucked in a slow, even breath.

A million people did this every day. No one died. No one fell out of the sky. No one—

"If you are in zone five, please proceed to the gate."

How many of those millions got on the plane having just found out they might be adopted? Or that the man they'd lusted after and slept with the night before could be a traitor sent to wreck everything? Or that—

"Now boarding zone six. If you are on Flight 516 to Atlanta, Georgia, and seated in zones one through six, you may proceed to the gate."

Breathe, Miranda. You can do this.

Well, at least Adrien had forced her to face her worst fear. She could thank him for that. And those five mind-melting orgasms last night. And all that laughter, and tenderness and byu-ee-ful—

"I'll fly with you."

She gasped, opening her eyes to see him on one knee in front of her.

"I will, luv. I'll fly with you and hold your hand and make you feel safe and get rid of every bloody fear you've ever had." He squeezed her hands gently and fluttered a boarding pass.

All she could do was stare into his steady, sincere golden-brown eyes and drink in the sight of wind-blown hair and a heaving chest that had to have been caused by one hell of a run through the airport.

"Miranda, I've found the Armageddon people, and I know why they're doing what they're doing, and I want you to have the satisfaction of taking them down with me."

He found them? "How did you find me?"

He tapped her phone, tucked into the corner pocket of her handbag. "That locator system. I dropped a chip into your phone the other day."

"You *what?*"

"Please," he said, placing his finger on her lips. "Give me two minutes to tell you this, and then you decide what to do."

She was vaguely aware of people staring, a few "ahhhs" and some smiles. Obviously, they misunder-stood the man on his knee pleading his case before the woman boarding the plane.

He pulled her closer, as though he could physically bend her to his will. "It's Blake," he whispered ur-gently. "You've gotten in the way of a money-making scheme."

She searched his face, waiting for more.

"He—and I'd bet a million quid his shaman wife—are running a cultlike thing to sell 2012 survival kits. They're probably siphoning credit-card numbers off the Internet, and we're checking on that now. Miranda, *that's* who wants want to stop you and your book. It's too easily understood and accepted by the very people they are trying to fool. You're educating the gullible people they're using to bilk millions. You're in the way of their scam."

She just stared at him. "After what you told me this morning, you expect me to believe this?"

"Yes."

The tinny voice on the loudspeaker broke the silence between them. "If you are holding boarding passes for Delta Flight 516 for Atlanta, Georgia, you may now board with any zone number."

He gripped her tighter. "Miranda, I talked to Jack Culver. He was trying so desperately to call me because he found additional information." As her eyes narrowed in distrust, he squeezed her legs, willing her to hear him out. "Eileen Stafford's child is someone else. He was shown a birth document that proves it's not you."

"I'm not adopted?"

"You're not Eileen Stafford's child—he found that person. But . . . you are one of the Sapphire Trail babies."

She dropped back into the chair, staring. "I just don't know what to believe anymore."

"Believe this: I really do care about you. I want to help you. I want to nail any and everyone in the Armageddon Movement and help you succeed. I want to be with you like we were last night a thousand more times. I want to take you on your first flight, and teach you the wonders of travel and a long-distance or short-distance or no-distance relationship." His eyes were bright with determination, his hands were clenched, and his words were tearing her apart.

Her whole body wanted to reach out to him, to believe him, to hold him. She ached for it but held back, her head spinning.

"Please," he whispered, closing his hands over her wrists. "Don't go home yet. When you do, if you do, I want to go with you. I've caused the misery, and I want to help you through it. Please, stay with me. I'm going up to Canopy. I'll have backup support, and we're going to get to the bottom of the Armageddon Movement and put them out of business. Let's do this together. Please. When it's settled, and you're ready, I'll take you to Atlanta or wherever you want to go. Oh, bloody hell." His voice cracked. *Cracked.* "I don't want to lose you."

Her heart felt full, and utterly certain. She didn't want to lose him, either.

"All right, Adrien." She stood and he did the same, holding her close. "Let's get the bastards."

"Ohh. The juice is loose."

Lucy ignored the sexy voice, refusing to let that familiar low laugh pull her out of alignment of the warrior three pose, her back leg steady and straight, her entire torso perfectly perpendicular to the ground. She held the yoga position an extra thirty seconds before she bent into a downward dog, then folded onto the mat, rolled over, and finally faced the only man who could get away with calling her Juicy Miss Lucy.

Dan Gallagher ambled into her workout studio in the basement of her estate, and lounged on a weight-lifting bench. He grinned that lopsided, careless smile that made women swoon just before he seduced them, and criminals wet their pants just before he shot them. He tossed back a lock of sun-kissed hair, his green eyes twinkling.

"Good morning, Luce. Hope I'm not too late for exercise class."

She laughed. How could she not? Everything about Dan was light, bright, fun. Sharp and brilliant and alive, he was levity and life. The polar opposite of the man she'd been thinking about for the last half-hour: Jack Culver. And in many ways, the opposite of her.

Which is what made him her perfect right-hand man and the closest thing Lucy had to a best friend.

She crossed her legs and extended her arms to each side. "Exercise class is over."

He winked. "I'll just watch you stretch, then."

Only Dan could flirt with her like that.

She stood, dabbing her face with a towel. "Fletch is waiting for our call."

"Good. I just got off the phone with some friends at the feds, and I have plenty to tell you both." He gestured toward the door and let her pass first, holding her gaze until she was in front of him.

Upstairs, they headed into the Bullet Catchers War Room adjacent to Lucy's library, the one room in the Hudson River Valley manor where English country style was sacrificed for technology and the tools of their trade. Sage Valentine, the head of Bullet Catcher Research and Investigations, greeted them with one raised finger as she faced a monitor and pushed an earpiece to her ear to listen to someone on the other side.

Since Lucy had scheduled a phone meeting, the flat-panel conferencing screen was black, but the bank of computers and the half-dozen plasma display panels were blinking and alive. As she took her seat at the head of the table, Lucy scanned the Bullet Catcher locator screen, giving her an instant, worldwide snapshot of the whereabouts of every person on her staff.

Alex Romero was in Colombia, undercover with Jazz Adams. Chase Ryker was in Colorado Springs on a government assignment. Four more were detailed in Europe, two others in Asia.

Sage ended her call and spun around to face the table. "Hey, Dan."

"Hello, Sage." He nodded toward the locator screen. "How's Johnny liking that stint with the ambassador in Salzburg?"

Her brown-green eyes sparkled at the mention of her live-in boyfriend. "He says the food's good, but he's ready to come back."

Lucy shared a look with the niece she'd once lost but now spent every day with. "He wants to make us all Wiener schnitzel."

Before he took a seat, Dan playfully nudged Sage. "He wants to make this one pregnant."

"So he threatens." Sage tugged at her long blond

ponytail and stood, winking at Lucy. "We're negotiating a nursery on-site here at Chez Sharpe, right, Luce?"

"Whatever it takes to keep you from taking maternity leave," Lucy said, still scanning the locator board. "Oh, there's Fletch," she said, spotting his code on the screen. "On his way to Santa Barbara. Who's with him?"

"Unidentified third party," Sage responded. "I've been tracking that signal since yesterday. I thought it was his principal, but they were separated for some time but back together now."

How long would it take for Dan to put the clues together and come up with Jack Culver? Knowing Dan, not long.

He studied the screen as well. "I could have sworn you said he wanted to take some time off and head home, Luce."

"He did," Lucy replied. "He got distracted."

"Blonde, brunette, or a rugby tournament?"

"He's doing a favor for a friend."

Dan's green eyes flashed with curiosity. Not unusual, since she routinely kept him in the loop on all the assignments, in an informal backup capacity.

"I've got him on the line," Sage announced.

The communication unit on the table lit red, and Lucy pressed the button to turn on the speakers. "Hello, Fletch."

"G'day Luce. Sage."

"Dan is here as well," Lucy told him. That ought to keep Fletch from mentioning why he was in Southern California. "How far are you from Canopy, Fletch?"

"Can you read my locator?"

She looked at the screen. "We can, but the entire compound doesn't show up on the map."

"I've found some dark green on satellite," Sage interjected. "But it's so densely wooded that it's really impossible to see the place. I'm setting up an infrared filter, but that'll take a few minutes."

"I should be there soon," Fletch said.

"Great. Dan has more to report."

"A lot more," Dan said. "I was just talking to some friends in the FBI. The Mexican authorities have been looking for a woman by the name of Juanita Carniero for two years. She was part of a powerful Mexican crime syndicate that started in the eighties, selling illegal identity documents all over the world. The bulk of the business was done on the streets, recruiting young people in very much the same way magazine distribution syndicates run subscription crews. Over time, they moved into much more sophisticated forms of fraud, including telemarketing and Internet scams."

"Don't tell me," Fletch said. "Juanita Carniero is Doña Taliña Vasquez-Marcesa Blake."

"Precisely," Dan continued. "Juanita was just in charge of the street operations. Evidently, she wasn't a favored member of the syndicate because of her tendency to dabble in witchcraft, shamanism, and various other activities that didn't make money."

"But her street recruitment skills could be very appealing to Blake's business. They'd make a formidable team. When did she leave Mexico?"

"She was arrested about five years ago on a very

light sentence and released on bail in hopes that she'd turn over the real leaders of her syndicate to the Mexican authorities. Then she disappeared. Some family members claim she married and moved to the U.S., some say she's dead."

"So why don't they use Blake to get Carniero?"

"Because Victor Blake hasn't actually done anything illegal. And to complicate matters, he's not married. Not to anyone, by any name. He's a widower."

Fletch was silent for a moment, and Lucy suspected he'd hit Mute to fill Miranda in.

"The connection to the survival kits you uncovered is key, Fletch," Dan said. "We suspect that if Blake and Carniero have hooked up and brought their joint skills to the table, they may be selling these as a ruse to obtain credit card numbers fraudulently."

"Why don't the feds go to Canopy and get them?" Fletch asked. "They're not exactly living in hiding."

"She disappears. And they have nothing on Blake— who isn't even married, so he has no reason to produce her."

"She won't disappear from Miranda. My plan is to drop in and surprise them. Look around, question them."

"Absolutely," Lucy agreed. "Get on the compound, find anything incriminating you can, and we'll put together a case for the FBI to nail Carniero and, at the same time, help our client, Mr. Bellicone. I've alerted Wade, who's on his way by helicopter with Bullet Catcher backup if you need it. But if she suspects anything, Carniero will likely disappear."

"She's a master at it," Dan agreed. "According to a lot of people, she really is some kind of Mexican witch, and Blake is a hobbyist sharp-shooter, so watch your . . . principal."

"Got it," Fletch told them. "I'll be reporting in to Sage; keep the lines open."

After discussing some logistics, they signed off, and Lucy pushed away from the table, but Dan reached over and grabbed her hand. "Damn convenient that Fletch just happened to be there, isn't it?"

"It's working to our advantage," she said vaguely.

"Especially since he's supposed to be on personal leave this month," he added.

"His activities in California are most definitely personal," she said. "His work protecting Dr. Lang on a book tour is on his own time. She is not a Bullet Catcher client."

Lucy turned to the locator screen to end the conversation. But Dan had a hand on her shoulder before she even realized he was behind her.

He leaned very close. "Just a wild-ass guess, Juice. Does this have anything to do with Jack Culver?"

Chapter
TWENTY-ONE

SOMEWHERE BETWEEN LOS Angeles and Santa Barbara, after he'd debriefed her about his phone call and they'd spent an hour speculating about Taliña and Blake and another on Jack Culver's search for Eileen Stafford's daughter, Miranda lost her doubts about leaving the airport with Adrien.

She also gave up the fight not to hold his hand. He'd threaded their fingers together in the space between them, maintaining contact for the hours it took to wend their way north along the coast. May Gray, the overcast skies that settled above coastal California, draped the Pacific Ocean in silvery dreariness. The cliff-clinging ride along the Pacific Coast Highway, with the wind-whipped waters of the Pacific on their left and the rolling California mountains on their right, added to the sensation that she was hanging on the edge of the world.

Which gave her even more reason to hold that rock-solid hand.

She understood so much now—about his search to help a friend, about a woman who had given up a child for an illegal adoption and how he needed to find her, about her name on that list. And as the hours and miles passed, she started to understand a little bit about her hyperprotective mother, who no doubt lived in dread of the day Miranda would learn the real circumstances of her birth.

"I always took their love for granted," she admitted, leaning against the headrest as her mind flipped through snapshots of her childhood.

"And no piece of paper can take that away from you, Miranda. Count your blessings, luv, and all that."

She heard the little twinge of emotion buried in that gentle accent. "I can't imagine what you went through, Adrien."

He shrugged. "Made me what I am, you know?"

"And what you are is"—the list of adjectives was so long, she simply seized the first thing that came to mind—"fearless," she whispered, squeezing his hand.

That earned her a flash of his dimple and a sexy glance from under his eyelashes.

"So what's going to happen when we get to Canopy?"

"Remember, we'll have surprise on our side, since Taliña is not expecting you."

"And what do you want me to do? Distract her while you hunt for evidence that connects them to the magazine subscription crews?"

"We'll have to be flexible and take our cues from them," he said. "I'd like to stay together. It might be a simple matter of cornering her, letting her know we know her real identity, and getting her to make a deal. It might be trickier than that. We have to be ready for any contingency."

"Don't you wonder why they're faking being married?"

Fletch frowned. "I was just thinking about that, and I don't believe I heard him refer to her as 'my wife' or vice versa. Not once. Did you?"

She thought for a moment, replaying their conversations. "I think she did. I recall her saying, 'My husband is delayed in Los Angeles.' Remember?"

"I do—but Blake was there, not in LA." He checked the rearview mirror and passed a slower truck. "I suppose she's just a liar who comes from a family of liars and cheats. I didn't trust her from the beginning—all that *toli* bullshit. I threw it in the glove box, by the way, when I left the hotel."

She opened the latch and took out the mirror shard, turning it over on the bandaged hand it had cut. It felt heavy, much heavier than a regular mirror.

She held it up to her face, seeing her reflection. What had Taliña seen? A fool? An impediment to her goal?

"Here's the turn to Maya Land," he said.

"It's a shame that a place so awe-inspiring and brilliantly constructed was funded by fraud," she said wistfully. "The place should be used for more than parties, it's like a museum. Students of the Maya could come here and learn so much. Or anyone who'd like a chance to see ancient history unlike anywhere else on earth. Archeologists and anthropologists." She shook her head, considering the vast possibilities. "It would be so much better to teach Maya studies here than in a classroom."

She was still thinking of the idea when they reached the gate, and he inclined his head for her to come closer. "Let her hear your voice."

But nobody answered their buzz. Adrien pressed the button again, holding it down, then glancing around at the wall that surrounded the property. "I could climb that."

"Let's do it."

He grinned at her. "I think I've been a very bad influence on you. I love the spirit, but let me get in and see if I can open the gate from the inside."

He left the engine running and climbed out. The wall didn't appear that imposing, considering it was built to house a fugitive. In a matter of a few minutes, he hoisted his muscular frame to the top, shook back his hair like a victorious warrior, and crouched and leaped to the other side.

She slid over the console to the driver's seat while Adrien disarmed the gate. In less than five minutes, it rolled open. He climbed into the passenger seat with a cocky grin.

"Very impressive, Mr. Fletcher. Like everything else about you."

She drove around the curved road, then up the steep hill to the precipice where the first view of Canopy was visible.

Miranda studied the vista with a wholly different eye this time, seeing it as a museum and educational center, getting a little zip of excitement as the first threads of a tapestry started to weave in her mind.

"Would you ever leave the university?" he asked, watching her expression.

"It would be tempting," she said. "I love teaching about the Maya. I hate the cutthroat atmosphere of academia."

The end of the drive narrowed to a paved path where the branches met overhead, forming a tunnel. On a cloudy day like today, it seemed almost nightlike, oddly eerie. Suddenly, dramatically, it opened up to the mind-blowing vista of the pyramid-shaped palace with its soaring tower and the two smaller temples that flanked the home to the north and south. The last time they'd arrived, at least a dozen cars had been parked at the base of the massive front stairs. Today there were none. Canopy felt as deserted as the real city of Palenque, centuries after its famed inhabitants had died.

"Where is everyone?" she asked, her tone as hushed as the grounds around them.

No graceful, gorgeous woman descended the long, steep stairs. No well-dressed staff bustling about, no sounds of life. Miranda parked, dropped her phone and the piece of the mirror into her shoulder bag, and climbed out.

Once again, she marveled at how much the stucco and stone building replicated Palenque at its height of glory, ingeniously proportioned to fit into the hills as though Mother Nature herself had built the palaces.

But this monument to the past was built by a Mexican criminal whose partner indulged her passions.

Where was she?

Adrien stood with his hands on his hips next to her, his sunglasses hiding eyes that she knew missed nothing. "Something isn't right."

"It does feel abandoned." She sniffed as a bitter odor reached her nose. "Do you smell—"

"Smoke," he finished. He pivoted, scanning the horizon.

"If we go up to the main floor of the palace, we can see into the jungle. Maybe there's a brush fire in the hills on the outskirts."

"It's closer than that," he said. "But okay, let's try."

He drew his weapon and pointed it downward, his hand on her back while they trotted up the steep stone stairs. Under the vaulted portico, the curved wooden doorways that led into the labyrinth of rooms were all locked. He tried every one as they followed the veranda around the side of the structure, to the back that overlooked the pavilion and the two temple-like structures. The height allowed a direct view over the canopy of trees.

"There," he said, removing his sunglasses and pointing southwest. "Not exactly a brush fire."

Almost a mile away, a single plume of smoke curled into the sky. It rose, then stopped, then another puff followed. Three in succession, then none. Then three more.

A breeze wafted over her, carrying the scent of smoke, but that wasn't what caused the tiny hairs on the back of her neck to stand. "Somebody wants something from the gods," she said, taking his hand. "They're bloodletting."

He turned to her, his eyes piercing in disbelief. "What?"

"That isn't a fire. It's the ritual smoke of bloodletting, a form of sacrifice to make a plea to the gods. For the Maya, it was a way of life."

"What's burning?"

"Paper drenched in blood, taken from whatever part of the body is involved in the request. It was usually done by the king, who would cut his ear if he wanted to hear something or his tongue if he wanted someone to say something." It got worse, uglier, and far lower on the body, but she skipped that. "They dripped blood onto strips of parchment made to burn very slowly and let the smoke rise in a ritualistic rhythm. The theory was that the smoke would reach the gods in the overworld, who consumed it and granted the favor."

"How much blood?"

"How big a favor? If the crop was a disaster or a civil war was brewing, a human could be sacrificed through bloodletting." She studied the next three tendrils that curled into the sky. "That looks pretty small out there."

"Taliña?" he asked.

She chewed on her lip, nodding. "That'd be my guess."

They started down the steps together. As they crossed the pavilion, she sensed that Adrien was alert and ready. He scrutinized the horizon, the jungle, the entire area, then turned and looked over his shoulder at the tower.

"Bloody hell," he whispered, pushing her hard. "Run!"

She did, toward the darkness of the jungle foliage, tearing across the stone.

The first shot made her stumble, but he had her by the arm and didn't let her fall.

"Hurry!" he cried, thrusting her in front of him, blocking her as another shot cracked the concrete about two feet away.

Miranda felt a scream tear at her throat, her leg muscles burning as she ran as fast as she could, her sneakers barely touching the ground. Adrien turned, his weapon raised, and shoved her to the cover of the trees.

"Shoot!" she told him.

"I can't hit him with this." He urged her deeper into the thickness of the jungle. He stopped when they had solid cover behind trees, both of them crouching low and peering toward the buildings.

"Blake's profile says he's a sharp-shooting hunter. That wasn't a professional sniper, or we'd both be dead. But it was someone handy with a Remington."

"Taliña's out in the jungle bloodletting, and he's up there firing at houseguests?"

"Looks that way," he said, already pulling out his cell phone and dialing. Before he completed the call, he reached over and touched her cheekbone with his thumb. "You okay?"

"Yeah." She shifted on her haunches and tucked some hair behind her ears, catching her breath. "I really want to get these guys."

His mouth curved in a dark smile. "Me, too."

He stabbed the Send button and put the phone to his ear, turning to watch the tower through the trees.

"I'm at Canopy," he said. "We have a shooter. Tower of the main building. I'm with my principal in the woods, about two hundred yards from the house. How close is Cordell in the helo? I could use his sniper talents about now."

He listened, his gaze shifting from the palace back to her while he finished the conversation.

"If we just wait here, Taliña will disappear," Miranda said.

"They might both go on the run. And the heat on them might stop their credit-card fraud business, but it won't necessarily stop them from harassing you, or worse." He wiped his mouth with the back of his hand and studied the tower again, then the jungle that surrounded the pavilion. "If I follow the line of the trees and stay covered, I can get to the other side of the house without him seeing me."

"You mean without him seeing *us*."

His shook his head hard. "I can't take that chance, Miranda. You need to hide."

"Here?"

"How about that little stone house where I found you with Taliña the other night?"

"Pakal's Crypt."

"Right," he said. "There was only one opening, and if I close you in—"

"Please don't do that."

"I need to be sure no one can get in there and hurt you while I'm gone."

There had to be a better way than closing her in a cement building. "I can stay here. I won't make a noise. I won't move."

"No, he knows our general location. Come on. We have to hurry."

He was right. She should stay under cover. They hustled through the forest toward the northwest quadrant of the property, a good distance from where they'd seen the smoke, reaching the ten-foot-tall rectangular structure in a few minutes. Holding her a little behind him, his gun pointed ahead, Adrien circled the jade-colored building to examine it carefully.

"Like I thought, one way in and out." He approached the slender opening between two stone walls, up a few stairs. "Come on."

Inside, the walls were tall, beveled outward, and green with moss that Miranda hadn't seen in the dark the other night. They had elaborate Maya carvings, as did the slab of concrete in the center of the floor, which was a perfect reproduction of Pakal's sarcophagus lid, a famous work of art that showed the great king falling through the jaws of the underworld.

"Not the most cheery of hiding places," he said, "but you should be safe here."

"Don't close off the opening, Adrien. I'll stay flat

against the wall, right there, where no one can see me. No one will know I'm here."

"I'd feel better if no one could get to you."

"But then, if I had to escape, I couldn't."

She could tell by his expression that she'd won the battle. "Don't turn your cell phone off, okay? I need it on to keep track of you."

"I promise."

"And if anything happens, if you hear a noise or anything at all, press Star on the phone. It won't make any sound but it will alert me, and Bullet Catcher headquarters, that you've got trouble. Whatever I'm doing, I'll be here. Don't move, don't leave, don't run. Be smart, not brave"

"Right." She used his accent, and he smiled, then kissed her quick and hot and hard.

After he left, she pressed herself against the cool stone wall of the crypt, totally hidden from sight. She unclipped her phone again, checked it, and re-clipped it.

One, then two long, silent minutes went by. Then five. Every second there was no gunfire, she felt better. She imagined him returning to the edge of the jungle, snaking his way along to get to the house . . . and then what?

Still no gunfire.

One more time, she pulled the phone out to check it, turning it over to make sure the chip was still in place. Just as she did, the ground rumbled with a low, unearthly growl of stone against stone.

She froze, and watched in horror as the slab below

her feet wrenched. It thudded, cracked, and rose from the ground so fast it knocked her off her feet, jolting her sideways, her hands smacking on stone just milliseconds before her face did.

Her phone tumbled into the hole that had suddenly formed in the ground.

Slowly, noiselessly, like an apparition, a man rose from the hole below. A scream caught in Miranda's throat as he climbed steps from underground in a deliberate, measured rhythm. His face was painted with the bright blue of sacrifice, slashes of color on his cheeks and throat. He was naked but for a loincloth, and a massive jade pendant hung over his sunken chest. And there were red blood streaks everywhere. Dripping from his earlobes and his shoulders and, when he raised them to her, oozing from his palms.

"I asked the gods to solve my problems," he said in a low whisper. "And they sent you to me."

She was staring at a living, breathing, menacing Maya king.

"Miranda." He sneered at her, wiping his chin with a bloody hand, smearing red on the blue stains of his face. "You have been chosen to make the ultimate sacrifice in the name of the gods."

Paralyzed with terror, she looked up from the floor into pale blue—and horribly familiar—wild eyes.

CHAPTER TWENTY-TWO

THE BUNYIP TURNED fierce in Fletch's head, spewing a nasty bit of scurrilous scolding.

Shouldn't have left her. Should have waited for the helo. Wade could take that guy out from the chopper with his eyes closed. But no. Fletch had to be an impulsive larrikin trying to save the world, get the girl, and win the respect of his boss, too.

He spat, trying to rid himself of the voice and the unpleasant aftertaste of dirt and jungle.

Screw the 'yip. He had to do this.

He stayed under cover, circling the outer structures, staying out of the tower's view by remaining very close to the north wall of the main building. He'd like to step out and get a better look at the layout of the top of the tower, but he didn't take the chance. Even if he saw the shooter, his Glock couldn't make a hit that far.

Confident that he hadn't been seen, he rushed up to the veranda and, flattened against the building, started rechecking every door. All locked. He didn't want to fire and give away his location.

He realized he was right below the balcony of the rooms he and Miranda had shared. All the fancy carving and Maya faces and jaguar heads made a decent ladder on the stucco, and in a minute, he yanked himself up. He hung from the balcony enclosure, then he flipped his lower half in the air and, with a solid grunt, vaulted the wall and landed on his feet.

The drapes behind the glass doors were drawn, but he touched the door and silently thanked the staff member who forgot to lock it. Then he drew the weapon he'd holstered for the climb and inched the curtain to the side. The bedroom was dark, empty. He went straight to the door and slipped into the vestibule that joined this room and the next, pausing to visualize the layout of the second floor.

The central stairs to the tower ran right up through the middle of the building, but access was limited to the main living area. From memory, he found that room one floor down, tucked deep into the heart of the building. It was cool and dark, thanks to closed shutters, and so dim he could barely make out the rough-hewn furniture and bright woolen wall hangings.

It was empty.

At the far end of the room, another heavy jade mask hung on the door he knew led up to the tower. Except for a four-story drop to the solid concrete pavilion, he didn't think there was any other way out. But he wasn't certain.

It wasn't locked. Mildly surprised, he stepped into the darkness, his gun straight ahead and his finger on the trigger, taking a second to adjust to the blackness. When he did, he could make out the carvings on the wall and a constricted stairwell that curved tight and steep, reminding him of a newel staircase in a medieval castle. He followed it up, his footsteps silent on the stone, on deadly alert as he took the spiral up without knowing if the barrel of a rifle would be around every turn.

But it wasn't.

At the top, the stairs ended at a small wooden door that had no knob, no lock from this side. If he shot, the answer could be a rifle blast in his chest. If he did anything except attack, he'd probably end up dead.

Bracing himself on the floor, he aimed the gun and threw his weight against the door. It flung open.

Victor Blake spun around, took one look at the gun aimed at his heart, and threw his rifle down. "Don't shoot me."

That was easy.

Fletch stepped into the lookout. Just ten square feet, with only a half-wall enclosure on the three open sides, it providing a panoramic view of the jungle. "Why the hell shouldn't I? You shot at me."

"I'm hunting."

Fletch almost choked. "For houseguests?

"What do you want, Fletcher?"

"Your wife. Where is she?"

"My wife died of a brain tumor about twenty years ago."

Oh, so he wanted to play games. Fletch didn't. "I meant Taliña. Or do you call her Juanita?"

When his jaw set and he didn't react, Fletch lifted the gun and pointed it right between his eyes. "I've got nothing to lose, mate. You're the one running an Internet scam. You're the one this close to being accused of a bombing in a major metropolitan city. No one would care if I pulled this trigger. Where is Taliña?"

"Where she always is. Hiding in her jungle."

"Letting blood and blowing smoke?"

He wet his lips. "Maybe. Probably. She's a complex woman."

"She's also wanted in Mexico. But you know that."

"She's not my wife." He lifted one defiant eyebrow.

"But you wanted me to think she was. You wanted everyone to think she was. Why's that?"

Blake sneered. "I don't care what you think. You're nothing to me."

"I'm the very impatient person holding the gun in your face. Where is she?"

"She's probably . . . with her husband."

Fletch took a charging step forward, and Blake held up both hands to stop him. "My son," he added. "She's with my son."

"Who is . . . ?"

"The person you should be holding a gun to," he said, disgust darkening his voice. "Victor's the mastermind. He's the fanatic—the one with the drive and ideas and ambition. Taliña and I just work for him."

He glanced over the canopy of the faux rain forest, where the smoke trail had stopped. How long had he been gone from Miranda? And where was Cordell in that helicopter?

"You met him a few days ago," Blake said, as if that would prove he wasn't lying. "I'm surprised you don't see the likeness."

Fletch glared at him, scrutinizing his face for a recollection of someone who looked anything like this pompous, gray-haired, fat-jowled older man. None came. "Was he here, at your party?"

"Most people don't forget young Victor," he continued. "He's so enthusiastic, so convicted. His interest in history started right after his mother died. He felt disconnected, I think, and lost, as any ten-year-old would, and he glommed on to this ancient studies stuff. I encouraged it at first, but then . . ." His voice trailed off, and he leaned back, away from the gun that Fletch hadn't moved. "It was no surprise to me when he married an older woman. Freudian, I suppose. The replacement for his mother and someone as passionate as he was about all that Mayan business."

Realization hit. "Wild Eyes."

"He built this, you know." Blake notched his head in a move meant to encompass the entire compound. "His mother, my wife, left him everything, and it was iron-clad. I got nothing for all the years I nursed her, but the kid got every dime. I guess that made up for the crazy brain he inherited from her. The day he turned eighteen, he started buying land and building monuments."

More pieces fell into place. Wild Eyes was married to Taliña. That was the connection to the Armageddon Movement. And Wild Eyes—Victor Blake, Jr.—was no doubt the leader he and Miranda had been seeking.

"So you're working with her by combining your sub crews with her experience selling fake identities on the street. And your son's the idea man, is that right? What a quaint little operation."

"He won't last long." Blake actually looked sad. "His tumor will take him, and he knows it. He likes to think he's . . . immortal, but he's going to die very soon."

"That's a shame." Fletch didn't bother to hide his sarcasm. "Where is he?"

Another shrug. "Cutting himself somewhere."

"What?" Fletch demanded. "What does that mean?"

"He's always slicing his arms, his legs—he even makes his freaking cock bleed. He calls it a sacrifice, but really, it's the only way he can cope." Pain darkened his features as he looked out to the grounds. "And now he knows that she and I . . . but Christ, it was only a matter of time until he faced the inevitable. He brought her here. He put us together."

"Don't tell me," Fletch said. "He knows you're screwing his wife."

Blake closed his eyes. "He had to know she was better with me. We think alike, and we're closer in age. It was part of our deal."

"Whose deal?"

"I cover for her." He turned slowly, looking at the jungle. "And she . . . rewards me. She has a colored past, which is, I guess, part of her charm."

"A colored past? She's part of one of the biggest crime families in Mexico. She married your son because he was a ticket out of a Mexican jail."

"All true," he agreed. "And that's why I was firing the gun. Honestly, I wasn't trying to kill anybody. After he . . . found us, he made everybody leave. She ran into the jungle, and he threatened the staff and went berserk. I came up here and saw him go after her. You showed up about half an hour later. I just wanted to warn her that he was out there, looking for her. It's our signal for her to come here, to the tower. But she has to escape him—"

The heat of the hunt turned to ice-cold fear in Fletch's veins. "He's out there?"

"Yeah, and he knows every inch of the place. No one could hide from him out there for very long."

Fletch backed up, his every instinct to kill this guy and run for Miranda. Instead, he lowered the gun and braced it on Blake's chest, using his other hand to ball his collar and push him back, tipping him over the wall. "You've got one chance to live, pal. If you want to buy yourself a lighter sentence and a chance to spend your golden years somewhere other than jail, tell me exactly where I can find them." He pushed him so far Blake's back arched, and his eyes bulged. "Now."

Only a lifetime of control kept Fletch from touching that trigger. That and the distant thump of a helicopter. "Tell me where he is, or you're dead before that thing lands."

The chopper rumbled closer, the rhythmic thump of the blades flattening the tops of the trees and whipping its own wind.

"He's with me," Fletch said when Blake turned his head just enough to see the helo. "And he doesn't care if I shoot you point-blank or he takes you from the chopper. Believe me. If anyone can do it, he can."

Blake closed his eyes and whispered something too low for Fletch to hear over the sound of the helicopter.

"Where?" Fletch demanded, stabbing the gun hard and shoving him so far only his knees held him in place.

"Pakal's Crypt."

Jesus God, that's exactly where he left her. Fifty feet away the chopper hovered, and over the deafening thump of the blades, he heard a man holler.

Wade Cordell braced himself at the open hatch, a rifle pointed directly at them. If rumor was right, Cordell could hit Blake square in the head, even from the bird. But their client just wanted him stopped, not dead.

Fletch waved him off. "Land and come up here!"

The helo landed on the open space of the pavilion, and Wade Cordell rolled out, two guns drawn, Rambo-like, gobbling up the pavilion in a few long strides, his expression fierce even from four stories up. A gunshot knocked a door off. Footsteps thudded on the stone stairway and Wade swiftly appeared.

"He's all yours," Fletch said without greeting his colleague. "Get him into the helo, and meet me in the jungle."

Wild Eyes.

It took Miranda a few minutes to comprehend what she was seeing. The paint, the blood, and the costume threw her, but she'd recognize those eyes anywhere. Watery blue, when they weren't glinting with a hint of insanity. She remembered them from her signing in Berkeley and from the streets of Westwood and from the TV after the bombing.

"What are you doing here?" she managed to ask, still on her knees before the open vault he'd climbed out of.

"I could ask the same of you, Miranda. What are you doing on my property?"

"Your property? Where's Taliña? She owns Canopy."

Disgust registered on his face, intensified by the cobalt paint streaks. He put both hands on his hips, drawing her attention to his torso, which was so thin you could count the sharp outlines of his bones, but wiry strong. The only things that looked soft on him were the wisps of pale blond hair that fell over his forehead—so oddly out of place with the costume.

"I own Canopy," he said, drawing out the words as though he were talking to a child.

She lowered her head as if considering her next move but surreptitiously searched the hole in the ground for the phone. She'd seen it fly into the air and knew it was in the grave this animal had just climbed out of.

No sign of it. Was the signal still working? She met his gaze, trying to think, trying to stay calm enough to figure out a strategy. *Be smart, not brave.* "What do you want from me?"

"I want to stop you." His voice was steady and sure, sending an eerie feeling right down to her bones. "You know that."

Slowly, she righted herself and stood. "Who are you, and why are you following me?"

"Who am I?" He curled his lip in disgust. "I thought you were a student of the Maya, Dr. Lang. I thought you were an expert." He said the last word as if it were as filthy as the dirt between his bare toes.

She studied his pendant and the glyph carved into it. "Pakal?" she asked, suddenly feeling as if she were at a costume party.

He smacked her so hard and fast her head snapped back, and she stumbled again. "I should sacrifice you for that alone."

She touched her lip and tasted blood, her brain spinning in desperation as she tried to psych him out. "You're the leader, aren't you? Of . . . the Armageddon Movement."

"I am K'inich Ahkal Mo' Nahb."

Oh, Lord. Crazy didn't even begin to cover it. "The great-grandson of Pakal."

He tilted his head in cocky acknowledgment. "The rebuilder of a weak and splintered civilization. The revitalizer of Palenque. The recreator of a crumbling world."

"And you . . . follow me around to my book signings so people won't listen to me. You blew up a building in Los Angeles. You staged some fake mystical energy appearance in San Diego. Why?"

He gave her an incredulous look. "Because you are spreading lies and heresy. Because you are sowing seeds of doubt. Because you are wrong about everything, and you and people like you are ruining my plans."

"Your plans? To save the world?"

"My plans to start again. Right here, in the New Palenque. With a new breed of followers. I've already found many students. They follow me, they speak my word, they will be saved."

He was a cult leader, a psychopath with extreme delusions of grandeur. And she'd made the mistake of getting in his way. But why was he here?

"Do you know Taliña?"

His face fell into disgust. "Not anymore."

"But you did? You do?"

He nodded.

"Is that why all my books were here? Is she part of your movement? Does she work with you?"

"She was my queen. She was the magnet that drew in our followers. She was a healer, an interpreter." His eyes filled as he looked at his hands, then back at her.

"Was?"

"She is gone." He said it so softly she wasn't sure she caught the words. But the finality of them, and the blood on his hands, made her go numb with fear.

He moved in closer, trapping her. His chest rose and fell quickly as he got closer. Too close.

She dropped her gaze and saw the loincloth tented with an erection. Drawing back, she almost gagged.

His blue eyes darkened, and the vein in his forehead jumped. "Taliña is gone," he repeated. "Like all women, she could not be trusted. They prey on love and need. They give you life, they let you suckle at their breast, then they lie and spread their legs for anyone."

Miranda backed against the wall, bracing her palms on the stone. Right behind him was a deep chasm. She'd kick him in and run like hell.

"Did she lie to you?"

As soon as he got emotional, *wham,* right in the nuts. Then, when he was off balance, she'd push him backward.

But he slammed his hands on either side of the stone behind her head, his breath hot on her face, beads of sweat over his lip. Just as she lifted her leg, he jammed himself in between, trapping her and ruining her kick. "You will not say no to K'inich Ahkal Mo' Nahb."

The ridge of his penis pressed against her. "No." She tried to push him back, but he was surprisingly strong for how thin he was. A wrestling match could end up with her in that hole instead of him.

Her purse thudded against her hip. *Be smart, not brave.* "Okay," she whispered.

His mouth turned down. "You're a whore, too."

"Just don't hurt me." She took a deep breath, her

plan forming in her head. "Why don't we . . . lie down?"

He took a step back, distaste in his expression. "Get on your knees like the animal you are."

She closed her eyes. "Please, don't hurt me."

He tightened one bloody hand around her shoulder, poking his thumb painfully deep into her flesh. "On your knees."

She visualized where the purse would go if she knelt. Right by her hand.

He pushed her to the ground hard with a grunt.

Her hands slammed on the concrete again, and her purse clunked to the ground next to her face. The zipper was still open. She could see the *toli*.

"Take your pants down," he ordered, kicking her thigh and tearing at the loin cloth. "Now!"

She lifted her hand as if she were going to do it but instead grabbed the mirror and turned, brandishing the weapon hard and fast, slashing everything in her way.

He screamed as she swiped his thighs and stomach and the erect penis he'd exposed. He fell, slamming one knee into her chest and crushing the air out of her lungs.

Swearing and bleeding, he rolled her, and she fought to hang on to the glass and get him again. Arms everywhere, blood and paint smeared out of focus as they wrestled next to the hole. She tried to kick, to bite, but he was more powerful.

With a roar of fury, she jabbed him in the neck, making him jerk backward in shock. But he had her right next to the edge of the grave, and with one brute shove, half her body hung perilously over the edge. She stabbed again, missing the artery but leaving a gash below his collarbone.

He twisted her arm back so hard she braced for the break. Then he kicked her. Her head cracked against the cement, and the shard went flying out of her hands.

Blood dripped onto her face, into her mouth, and she spat. Blood thumped in her head and she cried out when he aimed his foot at her stomach.

No, that wasn't blood thumping. It was a *helicopter*. Before she could open her mouth, he kicked, loosening her grip, and all she heard was the sound of her scream as she fell, weightless for one second, then hitting the ground with a solid *thwack* on her back.

At first, she felt nothing. No pain, no shock, no sensation at all. Then she opened her eyes and looked up. The light was about ten feet above her and he peered over the hole, directly over her head.

A drop of something wet hit her cheek. His blood.

"The gods have answered all my favors," he said, his strained voice eerily echoing in the tiny tomb. "I only have one sacrifice left to make."

She opened her mouth to cry out, but when she saw the stone slab sliding overhead, her voice evaporated. He was trapping her, and Adrien would never find her under that slab. He would never know it covered a grave . . . *her* grave.

In the waning light she could see the steps, and she threw herself forward as the grinding of stone against stone filled her ears.

"No!" she sobbed, just as he pushed the flat stone an inch from completely closing. All she could see was his painted face—his sneer, his eyes, flat and deadly.

"I wouldn't go poking around in the dark. You might disturb something. Although it really shouldn't go off until after you're dead."

What shouldn't go off?

The stone slid into place with a thud. Miranda took a breath, expecting the pressure of panic. But there was no panic. No squeezing of her lungs as she fought for air.

Because there was no air. And no sound.

Except for a steady whisper of shoosh. Shoosh. Shoosh.

The soft, even breaths of someone—or something—trapped in the tomb with her.

CHAPTER
TWENTY-THREE

FLETCH SMELLED BLOOD—ONE of the many skills he'd learned in the bush. He catapulted up the few steps of the crypt and shouldered into the slender opening, only to freeze and stare.

Blood, mixed with something peacock blue, puddled in the crevices of the stone floor.

He spun around, surveying the place, before dropping to his knees to touch the blood, determine it was very fresh, and smell the other substance. Paint. Oil-based. Also fresh, and mixed with what he'd guess was human sweat.

If this wasn't Junior's blood, then it was Miranda's.

Fury and fear welled up in him as he followed the trail of blood, out of the crypt and into the jungle, headed due south. He lost the trail a few times, but every few minutes, he'd find more blood.

If Wild Eyes had captured her, he didn't want to

risk alerting them that he was following, so he fought the desire to holler Miranda's name as he followed the trail. Without losing momentum, he called Sage Valentine to get a location.

"The locator hasn't moved, Fletch. It's exactly where it's been since you last called me."

But she was gone—or she'd left her phone behind. Could it have been on the floor of that crypt and he missed it? Someone made this trail of blood. If it didn't lead to her, then it had to lead to the last person who saw her.

"Call me if her location changes." He flipped the phone off and burrowed deeper into the jungle, running as fast as he could when he realized the trail was taking him directly to the place where they'd seen the smoke.

Sure enough, there was another thin trail curling into the sky. He studied the rectangular stucco building, this one painted green and decorated with more jade masks, a different carving over the door.

Slowly, stealthily, he approached the structure. He circled once, then came back to the front entrance, certain it was the only way in or out, except for the chimney on the flat-topped roof.

Underfoot, more blood and blue paint pooled in the dirt.

He placed his hand on the solid stone door and pushed. It didn't budge. He tried to slide it from one side to the other, but it was immovable. And bullets would bounce right off.

How the bloody hell could he get in there? He ran

to the back again, where a few carvings jutted out enough for him to scale the building, which couldn't have been ten feet high. He doubted he could be heard from the inside, since the structure was solid rock.

He got to the flat roof and peered into the chimney, not six centimeters wide and long. Directly below him, a man sat crosslegged in front of a bowl, a small fire burning in it. He extended his arm, and a knife blade glinted in the firelight.

Blood oozed from his wrist and forearm. He sliced a sliver of skin that hadn't yet been cut, and fresh blood dribbled into the bowl.

Victor Blake, Junior.

Head lolling, Victor lifted a piece of paper, dropped it into the bowl, and let out a low, long sound that was half song, half growl. Fletch backed up as a puff of smoke shot through the chimney.

If the freak killed himself in there, how would Fletch get in? How would he find Miranda? If she wasn't dead already.

He smashed the possibility and considered calling for backup. They could storm the stone door. Blow it up. He had to do something. He had to draw the bastard out before he killed himself.

Victor wailed again. This time, Fletch could make out the words. "Show me the answer. Give me a sign."

He wanted a sign? Fletch wedged his gun into the chimney, aimed for the bowl, and fired, shattering it and throwing his victim backward.

Fletch shot again, and in less than three seconds, he heard the scraping sound of the stone door being opened from inside. The minute he stepped out, Fletch jumped off the roof, rolling Victor to the ground and giving him a knee to his stomach that earned him a grunt in pain and eyes wide with shock.

It was him, all right, painted up like some kind of freak.

"You bloody mongrel," Fletch spat. "Where is she?"

"Dead."

Fletch squeezed the scrawny throat so hard blood oozed from a wound. She couldn't be dead. She *couldn't* be.

"Where is she?" He jammed the gun into his neck. "Tell me, or this'll be your last breath."

"Then let it be." There was total surrender in his words.

Fletch shook him hard. "Tell me where she is!"

"Watch for the light in the sky."

"Don't give me that Maya crap. Where is she?"

"Light . . . in the . . . sky." He closed his eyes, and died.

And a piece of Fletch went right along with him.

Fear closed in on Miranda, squashing her lungs. Instead of giving into it, she put her hands on the cold, wet earth, rose to her knees, and gingerly crawled toward the sound of breathing.

She had to be calm. To think. There had to be a way out.

Her hand hit something, and a whimper caught in her throat as it moved under her fingertips. A smooth human leg. She patted higher, touched wet cloth, heard the softest moan.

"Taliña?"

Another low groan and a gurgle. "M'randa. You . . . came . . . to . . . me."

"What did he do to you?" she asked. "Where are you hurt?"

"Cut. Stabbed. He killed me."

"Not yet," Miranda whispered. "Where did he stab you?"

"My heart. My side. Go. Get out."

"How? We're trapped in here."

She moaned, but Miranda couldn't understand her. She blinked and tried desperately to see in the dark, but it was impossible. She could only smell earth and blood and feel the pressure of an airless, cool tomb.

For one long, defeated moment, she gave in, wrapped her arms around her legs, and squeezed, fighting tears and wishing with everything in her that she could hold Adrien just one more time before she died.

"Unn . . . ell." Taliña's sound was urgent and incomprehensible.

But Miranda's need to connect to someone—even a criminal who'd probably masterminded all of this— was too strong to ignore it. "What are you saying, Taliña?"

She grunted, not even a word.

Miranda couldn't just let her die. On her knees, she crawled closer, placed a hand on her chest, and cringed at the warm, thick blood that covered it. She pressed. Taliña moaned again, the sound stronger this time.

"Does that help?"

"Help."

She added more pressure. "We need to stop the bleeding somehow." With her other hand, she felt the material of the dress, imagined how to wrap the wound, but it would be useless. "We have to get out of here. Do you have any idea how to open that sarcophagus lid?"

Taliña groaned. "He won't . . . he won't let us."

"Who is he, Taliña? Who is that man?"

"My . . . husband."

"What?" Miranda let off the pressure in surprise.

"Victor . . . son."

He was Victor Blake's son? "Why did he try to kill you?"

Taliña took a deep breath, then grunted with the pain. "He believes in twenty . . . twelve. I don't."

"Then why are you doing this? Selling these kits? Bringing kids into a cult?"

"I am a shaman."

"Oh, please." She'd keep up the charade to the death? She pressed on Taliña's bleeding chest, kneeling to get a better angle. When she did, a sharp pain stabbed her knee, and suddenly a laser light shot across the tomb, the bright round light bouncing off a stone wall.

Miranda gasped, staring at it, recognizing it from the museum. "Taliña," she whispered. "The light."

In the ambient glow of the light, she could see Taliña turn her head and flutter her eyes open. And almost smile. "*Kyopa*."

Sharp pain ripped through her knee again, making Miranda lurch to the side. Instantly, darkness descended. "What the . . ." She patted the ground where her knee had been and touched the sharp, cold stones of the *toli* shard.

"It's a hologram," she said, picking it up and pressing the jewels with shaking fingers. "That's what he used in the musuem. An optical illusion made with laser light." She squeezed the topaz stone and the blue light shone, like a ball floating through the air at the end of a laser beam. She angled it to Taliña's wound and bit her lip at the jagged, bloody mess at her chest. She would die. And soon.

Still shaking, she aimed the light on the walls, getting just enough brightness to make out the carved glyphs and painted images. It was a perfect replica of Pakal's tomb.

"M'randa . . . find . . . tunnel."

Hope punched her stomach. A tunnel? There was no tunnel in Pakal's tomb, was there? She squeezed her eyes shut, recalling the funerary crypt she'd visited five years ago, reviewing her thesis on the hieroglyphs inside the tomb.

She spun around, directing the light to the Nine Lords representing the nine nights, carved into the wall exactly where they appeared in the real monument.

"I am . . . shaman," Taliña said. "I see things."

"I'm sure you do." Miranda pacified her while she crawled across the dirt. At the stone wall, her fingers glided over the glyphs. "I wish you could see the tunnel."

She lit the ancient words with the laser light, they slid her hands over the last glyph. "Is it here? Is this the opening to a tunnel?" She threw herself against the wall.

"Tunnel."

It didn't move at all. "Where does it lead?"

"Temple."

"Do you know how to open it?" She shoved and scraped at the stone, reading the glyphs for clues that weren't there.

"Shield."

"A warrior's shield?" Miranda forced her hands to slow, to feel the nubs and grooves. Frustrated, she used the light when the skill of her hands wasn't enough to read. Her heart raced and blood pulsed in her head. She realized her own breathing was getting tight and labored.

Panic pressed down, and she shuddered to shake it off before it took hold. *Not now. Not now.*

Her fingers grazed a cieba tree. A quetzal. A . . . shield! "I found it!" She pressed hard directly in the middle, and the wall inched back. "I did it, Taliña! I'm opening it."

Miranda pushed with every ounce of strength she had, grinding her teeth with the effort, and finally, the wall moved enough to reavel a well-constructed tunnel about six feet high and almost as wide. There was probably a whole series of these underground.

Joy and hope surged. "I'll get help," she promised. "I'll be back, Taliña."

A soft hum, then a beep from somewhere near Taliña was the only response.

She froze. *You might disturb something. Although it really shouldn't go off until after you're dead.*

"He's set a bomb," she whispered, mostly to herself. "Just like the one in LA."

Taliña groaned. "Go."

"I can't leave you here! It's going to explode."

"You . . . can't. Go."

It beeped again. Twice. What did that mean? Two minutes? Two seconds? "I'll drag you," she said, scrambling back through the hole. She couldn't just leave her there to die.

"Here." She found Taliña's arm, as well as she could while still holding the mirror that gave her light. She couldn't risk dropping it. "I'll pull you. We'll get out of here."

Taliña didn't move. "No. Go."

"I can't, Taliña. I can't just leave you." No matter what she'd done, for she didn't deserve to explode in a hole in the ground. Miranda yanked at her arm, but Taliña resisted.

"Let me die."

Three beeps.

"Let me die, and you . . . go to your mother."

Miranda stilled, an inexplicable chill going through her. "What?"

"She needs you."

"Please, Taliña, don't do this. You don't know anything about my mother. You're not a real shaman. You don't see things. Stop and let me take you with me."

Four beeps.

"I am. I see. I know. Go to your . . . mother. She is going to die." She squeezed Miranda's hand, weak but insistent. "Your . . . mother . . ." She wheezed, moaned. "She will die if you don't help her."

Five long, extended, horrific beeps.

She dropped Taliña's arm and lunged for the opening, slipped through, and ran as fast as she could, her thoughts racing.

What if Taliña did have true sight? What if that woman in jail really was her mother, and that's what she meant? Or was someone going to hurt Dee Lang to get Miranda Lang to stop? Or were those the ramblings of a delirious, dying woman?

If she could just get out of this place alive, she'd get on an airplane and fly to her mother. Determined, unafraid, and at top speed, she ran smack into a concrete wall, so hard she saw a flash of white just before the world went silent and dark.

Fletch dropped Victor Blake, Jr.'s lifeless body and stood. The crypt. That's where the locator said she was.

He ran, flipping fronds and branches out of his way, hearing the helo overhead. He pulled out his phone, called Wade, directed him toward the crypt, and barreled on through the foliage.

Look for the light in the sky.

The chopper blades whirred overhead, whipping air through the canopy. In a clearing, he signaled to Wade, pointed in the direction of the crypt, and continued running.

What had Blake done to her? Where did he hide her? Was she dead?

Look for the—

The explosion was so loud, bright, sudden, and hot that it threw Fletch backward. Brilliant orange flames and smoky black clouds filled the sky in front of him, right where the crypt was. Where the crypt had been.

Sickened and heartbroken, Fletch ran toward the small brush fire caused by explosion, already petering out from the wetness of the jungle. Giant chunks of rock and stone, jade and mother-of-pearl carvings, orange stucco and green paint littered the area around the exploded crypt. All that remained was a cracked and shattered slab of the floor.

He sidestepped debris and some hot spots to get closer, realizing that beneath the slab was a deep hole, a mess of dirt and concrete, and—his stomach turned as he saw the charred head of Taliña Blake. She'd been buried under there. Buried alive. Had Miranda been in that hole, too?

He ran down broken stone steps, digging through the rocks and dirt for a sign of Miranda. Anything. Anything.

And then he saw the little silver phone. He picked it up, turned it over, touched the tiny chip that located her. Throwing it in fury, he dove into the dirt and debris, digging and only finding more dirt and debris.

He dropped to his knees, fought the urge to howl, and dropped his head to look straight up through the blasted ruins to the helicopter he heard overhead.

Instead, he saw a mystical blue sphere hovering in the sky.

Miranda clawed and forced her hand through the water-logged earth. The ground that had buried her after the explosion was soft and wet and full of . . . worm holes. She was trapped in an opening not much wider than her body, but light shone through tiny holes in the earth right above her head. She was almost close enough to the surface to dig her way out.

Using the glass shard, she furiously swiped at clumps of wet earth, revealing more and more light with every desperate stroke. Finally she broke the surface, but she was trapped too tightly to pull herself out. She stuffed her bandaged hand straight up and prayed someone would see the signal she sent by pressing the button on the holographic *toli*.

Please see the signal. She could hear the helicopter blades, she could hear men shouting, but she had no idea how far from the crypt she'd made it before the explosion, how far she'd run until that stone wall had knocked her out . . . or how long she'd been out.

She'd awakened when the ground rumbled and shook and fell around her, and she'd started to dig her way up to the diffused light.

Her arm ached. Her finger ached. But most of all, her heart ached.

She knew Adrien was out there searching for her, calling for her. Would she ever get a chance to tell him how fearless she'd been down here? How she'd overcome the panic and the terror and did everything he would have done to save herself?

Her arm burned; her finger felt as if it were on fire from the effort it took to activate the topaz stone. If he would only see the light. Earth rolled down her makeshift hole, sending clumps of dirt into her face. She spat it out, wiped her mouth, and waved her hand again.

If he saw the light, could he find the source? Was there a beam, as there'd been in the dark, or just a ball of light? *Come on, Adrien. Come on!*

More dirt fell. The narrow opening she'd made was getting darker. The air seemed to thin out with every breath. Her thumb could barely hold the jewel down. Her eyes started to close . . .

No. No. She bit her lip. Tasted blood. "Help me. Adrien . . . help . . . me."

"Miranda!"

Bits of earth rained over her face.

"Miranda! Hang on!"

A beautiful, distant, accented voice woke her up. A hand closed over her hand, another over her wrist, and strong, solid, loving arms reached down and pulled her up from the ground, closed around her, and held her tight.

"I've got you, luv. I've got you."

She gulped air, light, safety, security. All she could do was hold the man who'd saved her, savor his kisses on her muddy face, cling to the relief that coursed through both of them.

"Miranda, I know you're going to hate this, but

you're getting onto the helicopter, and you're going to the hospital."

She gulped some air and looked into his golden-brown eyes. "I'm not afraid of anything now."

He squeezed her, smiling through moist eyes. "Good onya, luv."

"And as soon as they let me out, we fly to Atlanta to make sure my mother is okay."

He let out a half laugh, half sob, lifting to help her toward the clearing where Wade waited in the helicopter. "Whatever you want."

"And then maybe you'll help me find my birth mother."

He pulled her closer, kissing her on the head. "Anything you want. Anything."

Satisfied, unafraid, and blissfully safe in the arms of a man who'd come to change her life and succeeded, Miranda flew to the hospital, unafraid.

CHAPTER
TWENTY-FOUR

WHEN LUCY SHARPE entered the cabin of the Bullet Catchers Gulfstream IV, Miranda almost forgot that she was on a private jet ready for takeoff. Lucy was that mesmerizing. When she spoke, her voice was like silk and velvet, low-toned and a little throaty. She glided across the cabin to greet Miranda, nearly six feet tall, a cape of blue-black silk hair draped over her shoulders, the single white streak down the left side both stunning and startling. Her face was exotic and unique, with ebony eyes tilted up in a nod to an Asian ancestor and a wide, full mouth darkened in wine-red lipstick.

She dressed in dove-gray silk from top to toe, the style emphasizing everything clean, smooth, and un-broken about her. But her most compelling trait was her natural command, an undercurrent of authority and control. That must be how she ran an organization of gun-wielding alpha men.

Lucy sat on the long leather sofa that lined one side of the spacious plane cabin, an amused look on her face as she watched Adrien kneel before a built-in cabinet under the plasma TV screen, searching a long row of DVDs.

"If you make this poor woman watch the highlights of the 2006 Regional Rugby Championship," Lucy said, "you will guarantee she never flies again."

Adrien turned to Miranda. "That would be the game in which yours truly drop-kicked a three-pointer in the midst of a maul, which is virtually unheard of and hasn't been repeated in postseason play since." He flashed a distracting set of dimples. "All of the Bullet Catchers keep their favorite movies in here. The '06 championship happens to be mine."

Lucy and Miranda shared a look, then Lucy returned to the report she'd been giving them about what had taken place at Canopy after the helicopter lifted off for the hospital yesterday.

"Anthony Bellicone is extremely pleased that we've put a stop to Victor Blake's subscription crews. He's decided to give a major contract to us, for a complete security analysis of his worldwide operations." She beamed. "I've wanted that job for some time. Thank you."

"Has Dan called yet?" Adrien asked, settling into the recliner next to Miranda. "He was going to meet with his FBI contacts in the LA office."

"He had one meeting yesterday, and we're going in again shortly. They are ninety-nine-percent certain that Doña Taliña was Juanita Carniero, and her husband, Victor Blake, Jr., has been the mastermind using her and his father to lure teenagers into what he anticipated would be a cult."

Miranda shook her head. "I'm just sorry the two are dead."

"But the older Blake is cooperating," Lucy assured her. "About a dozen missing teenagers have already been located, all of them involved with the sale of 2012 survival kits. Blake and Carniero were making a lot of money, the bulk of it coming from Internet fraud. They tricked thousands of people into sharing sensitive data from credit-card numbers to social security, using that to generate millions in revenue."

Fletch reached over and took her hand. "Most important, Miranda, the Armageddon Movement Web site is now closed and under intense investigation."

Miranda blew out a breath, shaking her head. "I still can't believe they thought my book was a serious threat to a multi-million-dollar scam."

"Your book is easily understood by the layman," Lucy said, "and could capture commercial attention. If it caught on and your publicity campaign was successful, they'd have far less credibility with gullible people. Sure, some customers made pity purchases from the teenagers who knocked at their door, but the real money was through their online presence, promising satellite phones and generators and all manner of survival gear while they were pilfering card numbers and selling them on a black market. It's a huge illegal enterprise, one the FBI battles daily."

"There are more crews out there, right? More

managers who can hurt people." Taliña's warning still played in Miranda's head. *Go to your mother. She is going to die.* "One of them could be in Atlanta."

"I have my best men in Atlanta watching your parents," Lucy assured her. "You'll see that for yourself when you arrive."

"Thank you."

Lucy glanced out the window when a stretch limousine pulled up. "Here's Dan. I'm staying at least three days in Southern California, so the plane and the pilots are yours while you need them. Perhaps after you leave Atlanta, Miranda, you'll want to use it to get to your next book signing."

A man entered the cabin then, exchanging greetings with Fletch and Lucy.

Dan Gallagher's warmth rolled off him in waves as he flashed an engaging smile and reached out to shake Miranda's hand. "Fletch tells me you're a virgin flyer."

Miranda smiled back. "I'm afraid so."

"He'll keep you distracted," Dan said, a twinkle in his eyes as he gestured toward the DVD rack. "But don't expect to understand a single thing about a game where a bunch of grown men roll around in mud and bad shorts. It's incomprehensible."

"I already warned her," Lucy said, moving to make room for Dan, who dropped next to her.

"Nice work, Juice," he said. "You've saved this woman from an enormous amount of pain and suffering."

"And I'd like to save her from more," Lucy replied,

looking at Miranda. "Fletch tells me you want to launch a search for your birth mother."

A needle of panic that had very little to do with the fact that the engine of the plane had just revved prickled up Miranda's spine, and she absently touched the spot on her nape that Fletch had shown her with a mirror. It did look like "hi" but his friend Jack said it was likely a number, so they surmised it might be "14."

"I want to talk to my parents first, since they have no idea that I've learned I'm one of the Sapphire Trail babies. They have the right to know before I attempt to find my . . . birth mother."

Lucy nodded. "When you're ready, we can help you—I'd like to, as a way of thanking you for the work you did with Adrien this past week."

"That would be fantastic, Lucy. Your resources are amazing. Thank you."

"As you know, I also have"—Lucy glanced in Dan's direction, then back to Miranda—"a former employee who has done quite a bit of work with the Sapphire Trail families already. He thought you were the daughter of a client he's working for now, but, of course, he's discovered paperwork that disproves that. Still, Jack might be able to help you in the search. I'm not promising anything, but it might help shorten the process."

"I really appreciate this," Miranda said. "And I'll be happy to pay for your services."

Adrien choked. "No you won't. We cost the earth."

Lucy smiled. "But sometimes we work for free, and this would be one of those times."

She stood, and Miranda did the same. When Lucy

reached out to shake her hand, Miranda took it, but couldn't resist a quick hug of appreciation. When they parted, Lucy's expression was warm and oddly sad.

"Just remember, Miranda, this will be difficult for your mother. She might feel as if she's losing you."

An unexpected lump formed in Miranda's throat, and she blinked. "I know that. And it goes both ways."

Lucy said goodbye to Adrien and left the plane, followed by Dan. From her seat, Miranda watched them walk to a limo, pausing at the door to face each other. Dan's smile was absent, and Lucy squared her shoulders and lifted her jaw as she spoke to him.

He responded, pointing a finger at her, which she calmly eased to the side, continuing what she was saying.

Adrien took the recliner next to her. "In case you haven't noticed, she favors him."

"That doesn't look like favoring," Miranda mused. "Are they a couple?"

Adrien laughed. "Not hardly. But he is the unofficial top Bullet Catcher. She confides in him and trusts him."

"So why the fireworks?"

"Because her offer of Jack Culver's assistance was unexpected and stunning."

She pulled the seatbelt around her. "How's that?"

He fastened his own belt and reached over to make sure hers was tight. "About a year ago, Jack and Dan were on an assignment together. Two more contradictory blokes, you'd never imagine. Dan is a witty guy, always making people laugh, always seeing the bright side, sort of a one-man happy pill. Jack is"—he let out a dry laugh—"not."

"What happened?"

"They had trouble with someone attacking their principal, shots were fired, and Jack misfired. He hit Dan and nearly killed him. It was a mistake, but we're not supposed to make them."

Miranda watched as the limo pulled away. *Oh, Lord.* The limo wasn't moving; the plane was. "Is that what they were arguing about? Because she's suggesting I get Jack's help to find my birth mother?" The words *birth mother* still felt foreign, but with the aircraft taxiing toward a runway, she welcomed the distraction.

"They're arguing because Jack Culver is persona non grata among the Bullet Catchers. He's my mate and he saved my life once, so I ignore that unwritten rule. But Lucy just broke it, and in front of Dan."

"So she allows no mistakes, ever?"

"This was more than a simple misfire," Adrien said. "Jack was hiding something the entire time he worked for Lucy. He got injured when he was with the NYPD, but he managed to have the extent of the injuries erased from his record. When he started working for Lucy, he never revealed the truth. Not to her, not to me when we became friends, not to anyone."

"What was the injury?"

"The worst possible for the job we do. Some lunatic druggie slammed Jack's trigger finger in a door on a bust gone bad. He's not legally allowed to shoot a gun in the role of any kind of law enforcement."

"And Lucy didn't know this? She strikes me as someone who prides herself on knowing everything."

"She strikes you right, then. Lucy knew he'd been injured and even knew it involved his hand, but he passed her rigorous testing. Anyway, she stripped him of responsibilities and banned him from the company."

Miranda dared a peek out the window just in time to see the Spanish tile roof of the municipal airport terminal whizzing by as they picked up momentum. She clenched her stomach and hands and forced her head back to the conversation. "So offering his help is offensive to Dan?"

"There's a rivalry there, and obviously some history." Adrien reached across the armrest that separated them and took her hand. "Jack lost more than his trigger finger in the accident, and more than his job when Lucy sacked him. He lost faith in himself. That's why I want to help him on this project."

He was totally aware of her anxiety, she had no doubt. But he hadn't said a word, just kept this conversation going. A warm rush of affection filled her and made her determined to show him she could do this. She could just talk and not dissolve into a puddle of panic.

She dragged her brain back to the conversation. "Would she ever let him back into the company?" she asked despite the mad pounding of her pulse. "If he did redeem himself somehow?"

He shrugged and weaved his fingers in hers. "Hard to say. She's been known to give a second chance if it

was deserved. He's worked hard to rehabilitate his trigger finger. Although more than his finger has needed a
few stints at rehab."

The jet engines revved a little, pulling her attention
and a soft intake of breath. She dug deep for control
and for the ability to respond. Rehab? Is that what
he'd said?

"Did I tell you how I met him?" he asked. "It's an
interesting story."

Miranda finally released a nervous laugh. "Interesting enough to make me forget that this plane is taxiing
toward the runway?" Damn, they were moving fast.

"I hope so." He stroked her damp palm. "I know
this is terrifying to you and that no matter what I tell
you, you aren't just going to relax during this flight,
but you've been through far worse in the past few
days." He squeezed her hand as the wheels began a
slow, rhythmic clunking over evenly spaced cracks in
the concrete.

She curled her fingers around his. "Tell me how you
met Jack."

"Well, Jack was on assignment in Tasmania for
the Bullet Catchers, escorting a diplomat, and my
group of SOGs—the Special Ops group—was there
in response to a bomb and riot threat. Jack was . . ."
His voice drifted in and out, his words buzzing in her
head, his meaning lost.

Mechanical sounds grew louder, each clunk more
intense than the one before. Pressure pushed her back
as they barreled toward the unavoidable defiance of
gravity.

She risked a glance outside, and without missing a beat, Adrien touched a button on his chair. A shade built into the window lowered and blocked the view.

"So, anyway, his principal—that's the person you're protecting, called a principal—starts to run, which is an all-out stupid move, so I . . ."

They had to be going seventy-five now. More. The engines whined, and the steady cracks in the concrete increased to a constant click of the wheels, like a clock, getting faster and faster and faster. Her chest tightened, making her breathless, and her eyes burned with tears.

"We're taking off now, aren't we?" she asked, interrupting his story.

"Yes." He put his arm over her shoulder and pulled her closer. "And I'm failing miserably in the distraction department."

She shook her head, half smiling, half crying. "Not your fault."

In one move, he flipped off his seatbelt and hoisted himself onto her recliner. It was plush and wide enough for him to slide his knees on either side of her thighs and pin her in place as if he were a human seatbelt.

She gave a surprised laugh. "Is this you being impulsive?"

"I prefer spontaneous." His kissed her hard, covering her mouth and then invading it, pulling her up to meet him, and not letting her think about anything but his hot, demanding tongue.

Then the bottom plummeted out of her world as the plane left the ground, making her stomach drop so hard and fast that she let out a little cry into his mouth.

He rolled against her lap, his erection rising as rapidly as the aircraft. He closed his hands over her breasts, sending a shock wave down to where their hips connected. She dropped her head back against the leather seat, and he bent to kiss her throat and unbutton her silk blouse.

"Are you distracted yet, luv?" There was a little tease in his voice, but just enough concern to twist her heart.

"Mmmm." The back of the plane felt like it was falling, and at the same time the front shot up, tearing another tiny gasp from her at the very instant he unclipped her bra, lowered his head, and suckled her nipple to a painful point. Pleasure battled terror, both sensations ripping through her body so furiously she had to bury her fingers into his hair and press him harder against her.

A loud knock shook the floor under her, and she let out a cry, pulling his hair. "What was that?"

"Landing gear up." He took her hand and placed it on his erection, which was full and hard and straining his pants. "Mine, too."

She couldn't help it—she let out a laugh.

He winked, pointing a finger at her. "Looky there, I made you smile during takeoff."

She squeezed him and nodded ferociously. "Can you distract me some more?"

He obliged with a long, juicy kiss, pushing her blouse out of his way to squeeze and fondle her nipple. She arched into the sensation, but then the plane thunked and dropped, and oh, the whole freaking thing tilted *sideways*.

She visualized the wings tipping toward the ground, the inescapable spin, the fall to earth.

"We're banking into a turn," he said as he reached below her seatbelt and cleverly unsnapped her jeans. "Might make you dizzy." Hot, strong fingers slid against her stomach and rolled over the nub of her womanhood. "Or this will."

"Oh." She sucked in a breath, definitely dizzy. He entered her with one finger just as the plane righted itself, but everything seemed to slow down, suspended in the air.

His finger curled over her flesh, making her wet.

Everything was eerily, suddenly quiet. "Did we lose an engine?"

A soft bell dinged.

"No, but we can lose our seatbelts." He flipped hers open and laid her down on the sofa, easing himself on top of her. "We are alone in this cabin for the duration of the flight, and I promise you will be safe, distracted, and blissfully relaxed. Because right now, Miranda Lang, I'm about to make you forget you're flying. You'll forget you're scared. You'll forget you're in the air. You'll forget everything but me inside you."

She opened her legs enough for him to settle against her. "Good onya, mate."

He rolled his eyes at her accent, chuckling as he shimmied her jeans down and knelt above her to open his pants. "Next you'll be talking dirty strine."

He freed his erection, and she closed a hand over it with a sexy smile.

He lowered himself so that their skin touched below the waist, but her blouse was still hanging from her arms, and his T-shirt was on. With them half dressed, the act seemed so maddeningly sexy and desperate and sensuous that all Miranda could do was writhe against his heat and enjoy the sensation.

He kissed her mouth, her neck, her ears, then lifted himself, and she took him in her hands to guide him inside just as the plane banked again. She sighed, and he entered her, sliding straight into her body, filling her, taking her over.

"There now," he breathed in her ear. "Don't be scared."

She rocked once, and he plunged in again. Squeezing his steely biceps, she dug her fingers into the cotton T-shirt and wrapped her legs around his hips. Deep inside her, he mirrored the act with a slow, silky French kiss, his hands all over her body, his hips driving a crazy, heated rhythm.

They hit a bump. Then again. The plane pitched up and down, and Miranda yanked away from their kiss.

"No worries," he assured her, riding her steady and slow and holding tight until the turbulence stopped. "We're fine. Let me love you." He slid all the way in, holding her gaze with such intensity she almost couldn't bear it. Arousal coiled through her, blinding her, melting her, torturing her as she got closer and closer to a climax.

"Come with me, Miranda," he urged, the tendons in his neck tightening, his eyes narrowing with each furious thrust. "Now."

Her body clenched, and the plane bounced on another wave of turbulence. He rose and thrust again, the force of another jolt shocking her, thrilling her. She closed her eyes, held him tight, and let her whole body simply move the way nature intended.

The plane dipped, hanging in the air, suspended somewhere between earth and heaven. The climax started deep inside her, a biting, irresistible need for release and satisfaction.

The lights dimmed. Adrien grew harder, wilder, mightier. Sweat prickled, and blood boiled, and pleasure stole all control and all fear until she just . . . flew.

He ground into her, murmuring her name, digging for his own release, exploding inside her with a roar as loud as the engines that carried them.

When all the noises and the breathing and the heart pumping stopped, Miranda closed her eyes and miraculously, unbelievably, *relaxed*. At twenty thousand feet above the ground, filled body and soul by a man she . . .

A man she . . .

She fingered a lock of his hair, stroked his cheek, fiddled with his earring.

A man she could love.

"You're not scared anymore, are you, luv?"

She put a finger on his lips and smiled. "Not of flying."

When Miranda and Adrien walked into the cozy entryway of the two-story brick Colonial where she'd lived most of her life, she saw that worry had etched a line deep between Dee Lang's hazel eyes. Or maybe that was due to the man who had answered the door, a six-foot-two, muscle-bound Bullet Catcher named Nico.

An hour later, they were still gathered around the oval table in the white kitchen that felt as comforting to Miranda as the sweet tea her mother had made for them all. Her parents had accepted Adrien's presence and his role in keeping Miranda safe, as she explained exactly what had happened on her book tour and why she felt they needed protection.

But with each passing second, Miranda fought the need to say what was pressing on her heart and head.

Several times, Adrien's cell phone rang, and he excused himself to take the call. Then she heard him talking softly with Nico in the living room. She knew he was giving her time to broach the subject of her adoption with her parents.

When he left the third time, she plucked a paper napkin from the holder on the table and began to fold it neatly into squares. She opened her mouth to initiate the conversation, but her mother interrupted her.

"Exactly how did you meet this man again?"

Miranda's mother stood polishing glasses as she took them out of the dishwasher. She was a slightly over-weight blond woman with round eyes and a rounder face who didn't share a single physical trait with her. Across from her at the table, her father, well under six feet, with dark brown eyes and faded blond hair so un-like Miranda's, stirred his tea.

She was about to wreck this normal, everyday, routine moment with an accusation of monumental proportions. But she had no choice. Even though she only knew she was a name on a list . . . she still knew. She *knew*.

And now that she did, the urge to find out more had become burning.

"She said she met him at a book signing, Dee," her father said, in that tone that told her he was ready, always, to fly to her defense or be the voice of reason.

"That's true," Miranda said slowly. She'd practiced a thousand possible responses to their expected ques-tions about Adrien, from the truth that they were lovers to some parent-friendly version of that.

But she couldn't lie or color the truth or put off what had to be said for one more minute. She took a breath, rolled the napkin into a ball in her fist, and stared at her father.

"He's an investigator who is searching for children given up in black-market adoptions."

A spoon clanged into the sink, the echo reverber-ating through the kitchen. Dee spun around, her mouth hanging open, her speechlessness confirming everything.

So it was true. She was adopted, and they'd hidden it from her for her whole life. Her father reached across the table and closed his hand over Miranda's. Slowly, her heart thumping harder with each passing second, Miranda looked from one to the other.

"Miranda," her father said softly, "it shouldn't change anything."

Always, reason and sanity.

"I know, Daddy." She managed to squeeze his hand and turn back to her mother. "But why didn't you tell me?"

Tears already streamed from her mother's eyes, and her body tensed with the heave of the first sob. "I couldn't. I didn't know how. I'm sorry, honey . . . I should have . . ." She just dissolved, and Miranda leaped up on reflex to hold her.

"Please forgive me," her mother said, her arms limp at her sides as if she didn't feel right hugging her daughter. "I just never knew what to say. And I was so scared you'd . . . you'd leave."

Always fear. Always terror. Always dreading the worst. "Mom, where would I have gone?"

"To . . . your family."

"You *are* my family."

Her father had risen and awkwardly circled his arms around both of them. "We're only guilty of wanting you more than you can ever imagine, Miranda, and the truth was a mighty big thing for a child to understand."

"But I haven't been a child for a long time. And you know I love you both enough to understand anything."

They shared an odd, quick eye contact that made Miranda's heart flip.

"We know that," her mother said. "But I've always been so scared that—"

"Stop." Miranda held her hand up. "Stop being scared. I have, and I've never been so free or happy in my life. That man out there"—she notched her head toward the hall—"has taught me how to face fears, and I think it's time for you to learn as well, Mom." She looked from one to the other. "I know you've been afraid of losing me, but that's crazy. We love each other, and you'll be my parents and my family forever."

Through tears, her mother nodded. "Do you forgive me?"

"For loving me and choosing to hide the truth from me? There's nothing to forgive. It's past, and no one will ever replace you." Miranda squeezed them both. "No matter what."

"Of course not," Dad said.

"But . . ." Miranda lifted her chin and looked directly at her mother as she made her announcement. "I want to find her."

Her mother's mouth quivered. "You do?"

"I'd like to meet her, if she's alive. I'd like to know her. Know her name and my genetic history. Like Daddy said, it won't change anything. You are my parents, and I am your child. I just have to meet her." Miranda searched their faces. "It won't be easy. I understand the paper trail is sketchy. Do you know anything about her? Anything that might help me?"

Her mother's gaze settled on her husband, in obvious warning.

Seconds ticked by, and her father's face grew miserable.

Miranda stiffened. "You know who she is, don't you?"

They said nothing.

"Daddy?"

He looked defiantly at his wife. Tension zinged between them.

"Yes, honey," he said softly to Miranda. "We do know who she is."

Miranda jerked backward. "You do? You know her name?"

Her mother gave a tiny whimper.

"*Tell* me," Miranda insisted, frustration burning. "After all these years of keeping the truth from me, you have to tell me if you know her name."

"No!" Dee reached out to her husband to stop him. "She doesn't want to know the truth."

Fury boiled up. "Yes. I. Do." Miranda gripped her mother's arms. "I'm not afraid of anything. I can take it. I can handle it." Hadn't she proved that in the past week? "Just tell me."

"Randy," her father said, slipping into the old childhood nickname, "you might not be proud to find out who she is."

An eerie apprehension curled around her heart. "Is she . . . in South Carolina, by any chance?"

The look flashed again, but her father nodded.

Could Adrien have been right the first time? Or

could Jack Culver's document, claiming that someone named Whitaker had adopted Eileen Stafford's baby, be wrong? "Is her name Eileen Stafford?"

A slow exhale of defeat from her mother confirmed it.

Miranda covered her mouth with her hand, holding back another soft cry. Taliña had been right. Her mother was dying. And she might be able to save her life.

"It's okay," she said to her parents. "I know who and what she is."

From the doorway, Adrien cleared his throat, and Miranda turned from her parents. "Adrien, that adoption document that Jack saw is wrong. Eileen Stafford *is* my birth mother."

He held up his cell phone. "I just spoke to Jack. He's with her. She's slipped into a coma, and they don't know if she's going to come out."

Miranda felt a sudden, inexplicable ache. She wanted to meet her, if only for a moment. It would somehow complete her.

"But Miranda, she talked to him before she became unconscious. He told her about you and the paper Rebecca Aubry gave him, and she told him Rebecca's document is accurate. And your parents are also right about who your birth mother is."

She frowned at him, totally confused. "I don't understand."

"It appears, Miranda, that you were part of a multiple birth."

"A multiple . . ." It was like being punched in the gut. "I have a sibling?"

Her mother dipped as if she were going to faint dead away, but Miranda spun to her, unable to contain her fury. "Do I?" she shouted. "Do I have a sibling?"

How could they *keep* that from her?

"You have two," Adrien said. "You were a triplet, and you have two sisters."

Two sisters.

"Has he found them? Does he know who they are?"

He shook his head. "But we will, Miranda. If we have to move the earth, we'll find them for you, and for Eileen Stafford."

Feeling lightheaded, she stepped forward into his embrace. "I know you will."

Over her shoulder, she met her father's sad gaze.

"I'm sorry, Randy," he said. "I'll do whatever I can to help you."

She had no doubt which of her parents had driven the decision to hide the truth, and someday she'd make her mother see how wrong that was.

"Will Lucy help?" she asked Adrien.

"Absolutely. I'm certain she'll dispatch someone to finish the list I was working on, and Jack is going after the Whitaker baby from Rebecca's paper."

"Then let's get back on that plane and get to South Carolina. Maybe hearing my voice will wake Eileen Stafford up. Maybe she has more to tell us." She drew back and gave him a smile. "I know it's kind of impulsive, but it feels right."

"I know the feeling, and I like it." He tipped her chin and kissed her forehead.

CHAPTER
TWENTY-FIVE

THE SUNSHINE SEEMED unnaturally bright, shining on stark gray cement buildings surrounded by a deadly barbed-wire fence. It warmed the backseat of the sedan, where Miranda sat listening to Jack Culver's New York accent volley with Adrien's gentle Australian clip as they discussed the botched trial of Eileen Stafford.

The whole trip had been surreal, from the moment they'd arrived in Columbia and met the tall, disheveled former cop who had once saved Adrien's life. He'd moved mountains to get them cleared to visit the Camille Griffin Graham state penitentiary the next day, where, deep in the bowels of the health-care facility, Miranda would meet the woman who gave her life.

Correction: the woman who gave triplet babies life, then let them be taken from her. A woman who, eight months after she gave birth, was arrested for the murder of another legal secretary at the Charleston County Courthouse. She'd been in that alley—her fingerprints were found on the gate. The murder weapon was in her car. She had no alibi and had been seen arguing with the victim the day before the shooting.

Yet Jack was convinced she'd been framed.

In the front passenger seat, Adrien combed through Jack's notes, asking questions and making comments. "What's your theory on why she had the murder weapon?"

Jack stabbed his hand into thick black hair that fell over his collar against cheeks that hadn't been shaved for at least two days. His stubble was less refined than Adrien's, more a function of a man who simply forgot the basics. "Someone planted it."

"Do I look like her?" Miranda suddenly asked, not even embarrassed by the non sequitur that revealed her thoughts.

Jack threw her a look in the rearview mirror. "Hard to tell. Her hair's gone, and her face is worn. Her eyes are blue but lighter than yours."

"Would you like to see a picture, Miranda?" Adrien asked. "There's one here, from the trial."

She reached for the glossy picture he held, their hands touching.

"You okay, luv?" he asked, rubbing his thumb over hers.

She nodded. "I'm fine. I'm ready."

They'd spent the night in a hotel on the outskirts of Columbia, awake until nearly dawn. They'd made love, then spent the last few hours sleeping in each other's arms. When she woke that morning, a sense of peace and purpose had settled over her. She wouldn't make this journey with anyone else but him. And that might be the most surreal sensation of all.

She was falling in love with him.

She took the picture and angled it into the sunshine, ready to scrutinize every feature for something, anything, that connected them.

But instead of a reflection of herself, she saw . . . strength. Strength like Miranda had never known. An inner fortitude that was so powerful it leaped off the picture.

She saw it in the set of her jaw, in the hold of her shoulders, in her smoldering stare at the cameramen. After listening to Jack describe the way her case was brutally mishandled, the unreasonable leeway the judge gave to the prosecution, and the spineless defense, the very last thing Miranda expected to see was *inner fortitude.*

Yet Eileen Stafford had it in spades. Along with cheekbones that reminded Miranda very much of her own.

Jack pulled the car up to a heavily armed guard, who demanded identification for all of them.

"Keep your wallet out," Jack said after they'd been through the first gate. "They're nothing if not thorough at Camp Camille."

He wasn't kidding. By the time the three of them were reunited at a two-story windowless building called the Medical Eval Unit, Miranda had been searched, fingerprinted, and subjected to so many indignities that she almost forgot why she was there. But when her escort walked her up to join Adrien and Jack, her limbs tingled in nervous anticipation of meeting Eileen.

Inside, a nurse behind a desk greeted Jack with a friendly, familiar smile. Another came down the hall, an officious-looking black woman with a clipboard, who also acknowledged Jack as though she knew him well.

"How is she, Risa?" he asked.

Risa shook her head, and the smile disappeared. "Her vitals are normal, Mr. Culver, but she simply isn't responding to anything. She's been sound asleep since you were last here." She glanced at Adrien and Miranda. "You can go in, but don't expect a response."

Jack thanked her and they started down the hall, but Risa kept talking.

"I told that man yesterday the same thing, but he waited and waited until we had to call a guard to make him leave."

"She had a visitor?" Jack asked with incredulity. "Who was he?"

Risa shut down. "I'm not allowed to tell you that, Mr. Culver. I shouldn't have said anything." He eyed her for a minute, and she responded with a turned-down mouth. "Don't try to get it out of me, 'cause I'll get fired."

"Strange," he said to Miranda, guiding her forward. "Eileen hasn't had a visitor in years. Maybe ever."

Near the end of the hall, a door stood open.

Miranda slipped her hand into Adrien's but looked at Jack. "Is this it?" she asked him.

"This is it."

She took one slow step, then another. First, an empty bed. Then, a few feet away, a bald woman in a blue and white hospital gown, her arm connected to softly beeping monitors, a clear inhaler sending oxygen up her nostrils.

She could have been a hundred years old, and if she'd ever had the inner strength Miranda had seen in the picture, thirty years in jail and a battle with cancer had sucked it all out of her. She looked old, beaten, and seconds from death.

Miranda walked to her bedside and closed her hand over the metal bed rail, studying the grim turn of her mouth, the vein pulsing on her head, the closed eyes, with lashes and eyebrows sacrificed to chemotherapy.

This sick, sad, dying woman was her mother.

She closed her fingers over the narrow wrist. Her skin was cool, dry, old.

"Eileen," she whispered, leaning closer. "My name is Miranda Lang. I'm your daughter."

Nothing. Not a flicker of response, not a roll of her eye under her eyelid.

Miranda looked up at Jack, who stood on the other side of the bed. "Do you think she can hear me?"

Jack shrugged. "Can't hurt to assume she does."

Adrien came up behind her, easing a chair for her. "Here, luv. Sit with her. Talk to her."

She did, maintaining contact with her hand on the soft, old skin.

"I live in California, Eileen," she said, feeling awkward. "I'm a professor at Berkeley, of anthropology.

I . . ." She glanced at Adrien, who stood next to her, his hand on her shoulder. "I wrote a book," she finished, and for the first time, a tear stung her eyes. She paused for a minute, and he squeezed her shoulder and nodded encouragingly.

"I grew up in Atlanta," she continued, her voice tightening. "My . . . parents are really great. They . . ." Her voice cracked, and she fought a sob. "They love me."

The first tear trickled, and she swiped it, gently squeezing Eileen's arm as the wave of emotion washed over her.

"I know about . . . my sisters. I have a friend." She smiled up at Adrien. "He's more than a friend, really. He works for a company who can help me find them. I'm going to find them both, and we're going to come back here, and surely one of us can give you what you need to live."

She sniffed and took a breath. "And then," she whispered, her voice hoarse, "we're going to find out who killed Wanda Sloane."

Eileen's eyelids moved, and Miranda sat closer, excited.

"She heard me. Don't you think? She heard me?"

"Maybe," Adrien agreed.

No maybe. She'd *heard*. Miranda stood and leaned over the railing, wanting to get closer, to smell her and connect to her. She bent all the way over and put her lips on her mother's dry cheek.

"I'm glad you looked for me," she whispered, tears rolling from her cheek to Eileen's.

She stood and turned to Adrien, who closed his

arms around her, holding her so long and hard it felt like he was trying to give her all his power, all his bravery . . . all his love.

She took it, hugging him close and sobbing into his shoulder. "I want to take the blood test as soon as possible. Can I do that?"

"It looks to me, luv, like you can do anything you want."

Dropping her head onto his shoulder, she closed her eyes. She *could* do anything she wanted. And she knew exactly what that was.

"I want to meet my sisters. I want our mother to live. And I want to clear her name."

"Then you will." He kissed her hair. "I have no doubt about that at all."

Nearly a hundred people crammed into the back half of the Vero Beach Book Center, most of them holding copies of *Cataclysn't* to be signed after Miranda's brief reading. Standing outside in the humid Florida air, Fletch watched the crowd through the large front window as he listened to Lucy's message on his cell phone.

Miranda would be thrilled with the news. At least, she'd be hopeful. They'd finally narrowed down the list to the last name, a woman living in New York named Vanessa Porter.

Jack hadn't found the right Whitaker yet, but he was working on it. Lucy had kept her promise and, in true Lucy fashion, extended it to include providing resources to search for Miranda's sisters. She said it was because they could be in danger, as that mysterious phone call to Jack had implied, not because her former employee was involved. Either way, there was a full-field press, and Miranda was optimistic.

She needed that optimism after the frustrating news that although she carried Eileen's DNA, she wasn't a match for a bone-marrow donation, intensifying her determination to find her sisters. Eileen hung on but remained, a month later, in a coma.

Fletch watched the bookstore manager speak to the crowd, knowing the introduction wouldn't be much different from the half-dozen he'd witnessed in the past month. A snappy overview of her credentials, some glowing reviews for her book, and a teaser for a possible follow-up on the great ruins at Palenque.

Introductions that, in Adrien's opinion, didn't even begin to scratch the surface of what made Miranda Lang extraordinary and exceptional. Such as the way she fought for what she wanted, never giving in. And the way she laughed and listened and loved. He'd never known such love.

"And I have more news." Lucy's message pulled him out of his reverie and back to the present. He knew what was coming next. The diamond drop in Antwerp. *Please, Lucy. Take pity. Don't send me to Belgium.* He wanted more time with Miranda. Bloody hell, he wanted *all* time with Miranda.

"Victor Blake is apparently willing to turn over the entire estate and the property of Canopy to the state of California as part of his plea for a lesser sentence. As you and I discussed, I put in a call to my friend, who has arranged for Miranda to meet with the Governor's

Arts Council. They are extremely interested in her proposal to transform Canopy into a revenue-generating
museum and education center for Maya studies."

Yes! Now all he needed was to be based in Santa
Barbara, and life might be close to perfect.

He turned back to the window to see Miranda
perched comfortably on the table, having ditched the
podium several signings ago. She read from her book,
then set it aside to walk around the crowd as he imagined
she did in a college classroom, making each point with a
sparkle in her eye and the confident tilt of her head.

He'd heard it many times by now. He knew all
about what the newspapers and television interview-
ers called "twenty-twelve-ology" and how they'd used
Cataclysn't as proof that there was no need for a mass,
worldwide panic. But he never tired of listening to her
bring her world to life.

He tugged open the glass door and walked inside
the crowded beachside bookstore, snagging the last
copy of her book. When she caught his eyes, she
smiled the secret smile she saved for him. A few in the
audience turned to look at him, but soon they were
riveted by the presenter.

Two hours later, he tucked her hand under his arm
and led her out of the bookstore into the clear, warm
night.

"I sold out," she exclaimed with a little bounce in
her step. "Can you believe it?"

"Of course. And I've been waiting to give you some
wonderful news I just learned from Lucy Sharpe."

She froze. "They found someone."

"Close. We have an ID on the last woman on the list. Vanessa Porter, from New York—but it seems she's just left for a Caribbean vacation. Lucy's planning to send a man down to talk to her."

"That will put a damper on her vacation," Miranda said. "And the Whitaker lead?"

"Jack is searching every Whitaker in the state of Virginia," he said.

She hugged his waist. "We'll find them. I know we will."

"But listen, luv, there's more," he said, turning them onto a side street next to the little bookstore. "Blake said yes to donating Canopy to the state, and Lucy got you a meeting with the Arts Council to present your proposal."

Her eyes flashed with joy, and she gave a victorious laugh. "Fantastic! I guess it helps that she's on a first-name basis with the governor. Perfect timing, too. We can stop in California on the way to Australia."

He rolled his eyes. "Teach a woman how to fly, and the next thing you know she's a one-person travel agency."

"You're not going to change your mind, are you? We had a deal."

"No," he assured her, leaning her against the brick wall of one of a store. "If you can fly over the Pacific Ocean, I can attempt peace with my parents."

She smiled. "Good onya, mate."

"And there's one more thing." He dipped his head closer to her mouth.

"You want to remind me that you're a helluva good

kisser?" She closed her eyes and lifted her mouth, but he didn't kiss her. Instead, he slipped the book between them.

"Sign this."

Her eyes widened in surprise as she flipped open the cover and saw the note inside. "I . . ."

"I know you're a linguist, Dr. Lang, but those three words are fairly common. And in this case, quite true."

She touched his lower lip and dipped her finger into his soul patch. "I love you, too. Now will you show me what a good kisser you are?"

Not quite yet. "Pretty smooth move, don't you think, the note in the book?"

She stood on her toes and kissed him lightly. "Very smooth."

He backed away. "Miranda, do you remember what Taliña said? That I wanted to steal your soul?"

She nodded, tunneling her fingers into his hair and caressing his neck. "No one can steal another person's soul, Adrien."

"I know." He cupped her chin in his hand and lifted her face. "But I wouldn't mind having a pass at your heart."

"Aww." A slow smile lit her face. "You've had that for a while now."

"Excellent." He took a moment to enjoy the sensation of being loved by this strong, smart, beautiful woman. And to build to his grand finale. "Because I'd like to keep it. For a long time."

She nibbled at his jaw line. "Mmm. Good. Kiss me?"

But he didn't. "Turn the note over."

She finally did, taking in a tiny breath as she read what he'd written.

"There are two more common words for you to decipher, Dr. Lang."

She was very still. His heart pounded, and he could feel hers beating in the same rapid rhythm. Was that a yes?

She finally looked up, her eyes filled with tears and love. "No question mark, I see."

"It's not actually a question, luv. It's a rash suggestion for how we spend the rest of our days on this earth." He waited a beat. "Unless, of course, the idea terrifies you."

"Nothing terrifies me." She laid her head on his shoulder. "Except maybe life without you."

"No worries, then. I'm in it until the end of time." He tipped her chin. "Which I happen to have on good authority is *not* in the near future."

"Right," she said in a perfect strine accent, then winked. *"Now* will you finally kiss me?"

He did, long and tender, tasting the sweet mouth that he loved. He closed his eyes and waited for the warning, that menacing, nasty hiss . . . *this is a mistake.*

But that little bunyip in his head was stone-cold silent. In fact, the monster seemed to have disappeared for good.

Turn the page for a preview of the next
exciting book in the Bullet Catchers trilogy

Then You Hide

by Roxanne St. Claire

Available from Pocket Star Books
in July 2008

CHAPTER
FOUR

TRIPLETS. *TRIPLETS?* For the second time in one day—hell, in one hour—Vanessa was dumbfounded. "Nobody even *had* triplets thirty years ago, did they?"

Wade laughed softly. "They had them, it was just a surprise on delivery day."

"How could I not know this?" After all the research she and her father had done, it didn't seem possible that a fact as monumental as *there are two sisters* slipped by some of the best adoption investigators Daddy's money could buy.

"Very few people do know about this," he said.

"No shit, Sherlock. Where are we going?"

"You look like you're going to faint," Wade said as he ushered her to the same patio restaurant she'd been at less than two hours ago.

"I don't *faint*," she shot back. "It's a thousand degrees out and you shocked me and I—I'm *reacting*."

"Gotcha. Well, you look like you're about to react, so let's sit down in the shade here, under this umbrella, and have a cold drink and talk about it, okay?"

His patronizing drawl infuriated her, but the suggestion had definite appeal. She needed something cold—and potent—to make sense of everything that had happened since she got off that boat.

"Two iced mineral waters," he said to the waitress.

"And a vodka tonic," Vanessa added. "But skip the tonic. And no lime."

One side of his mouth lifted in a half smile. "You drink like you talk and walk. Tough."

"I hate limes. And tonic." *And you.* She crossed her arms. "You'd better have proof."

"There's no actual paperwork."

She slammed her hands on the tabletop and pushed back in the chair. "I knew this was totally bogus."

"But I have a picture." He placed a photograph on the table between them.

Wasn't that a fine twist? For the first time in three days, *she* was being shown a picture instead of the other way around. Though she wanted to be a complete brat and refuse to look at it, curiosity won out. She squinted at the photograph, half expecting—and half dreading—to see a reflection of herself.

"Oh." The word was a note of pure wonder, matching the sensation that rocked her. "She's beautiful." Then she shoved the picture back at him. "And she doesn't look a thing like me."

"You're beautiful." He slid it forward.

"Thanks, but I'm blonde—natural, by the way—

and my face is longer, my mouth is wider, my eyes are shaped differently." Unable to resist, she took one more look. "She's really . . . delicate looking." Willow-thin and fragile. No glasses. No boobs. No cleft.

No dice.

"We don't even look related." She gave the picture a good shove.

"Triplets aren't always identical," he said. "Sometimes two are, and one is from a different egg. That might explain the difference in your looks, and makes it possible that you're a match for the marrow, when she's not."

"She's not?" That hit her hard. If this alleged sister had been a match, would Eileen Stafford have dispatched an investigator to find *her*? Or would she have let Vanessa go to her grave without ever initiating contact? Of course she would have. God, she despised the woman right down to her last bad cell.

She turned toward the bar, lifting her hair with one hand to get a nonexistent breeze on her neck. "Where is that drink?" This was so ugly, so complicated, and so *not* what she wanted to be doing with her time in St. Kitts. Or anywhere, for that matter.

With impossible purpose, Wade inched the picture back across the table, like a gambler willing to risk a decent card for the remote possibility of a better one.

"Her name is Dr. Miranda Lang."

Something slipped inside Vanessa. *Miranda.*

She didn't care what her name was. She didn't *care.* Didn't he get that?

"What kind of doctor?" she asked, so casually it couldn't be interpreted as anything but small talk.

"An anthropologist. She has a book out that's been getting some media coverage, about the Maya calendar and the myth that the world is going to end in 2012. Have you heard about it?"

She lifted an indifferent shoulder. "Unless it moves money, changes the Dow Jones Industrial Average, or otherwise generates cash with at least seven, preferably eight, figures involved, no." She fanned her sticky neck, the heat pressing hard on her chest. At least, she thought it was the heat.

Finally, a drink tray landed on their table.

"Thank Christ," Vanessa mumbled, her gaze sliding over the much-needed vodka only to land on the much-hated picture.

Wavy auburn hair. Wide smile. Pretty. An anthropologist.

She grabbed the ice-cold glass and plucked out the damned lime. "There's obviously been a mistake. I'm sorry she's going to be disappointed. But my father and I did exhaustive research and there were no sisters."

She put the cold glass to her lips.

"I have another picture."

She didn't drink. She couldn't. She watched as he slowly reached back into his billfold, methodically drawing out another picture. Part of her wanted to kick him into faster action and get this hell over with. But it was easier just to watch his stunningly masculine hands as they moved to find something she just knew she didn't want to see. Nice hands. Sexy fingers. Bad, bad news.

"I think you'll be real interested in this one." He burned her with a look that might have been a warning, or might have been something else. It was hard to read this man, hard to get past the eyes and the body and the face.

Was that a calculated move by Eileen? *Send an irresistible hottie to sway her. I need bone marrow.* Her stomach tightened and she pressed the cold glass on her cheek.

"This picture," he said, his voice as measured as him movements, "is actually of the back of Miranda's neck."

Her choke sent vodka splashing over the rim of her glass. Oh, no. *No.*

"Right here." He reached a hand around her head, making a tiny circle with his fingertip, right above the nape, a million little hairs rising up at his touch and sending shivers down her back.

"She has a tattoo right here, and all three babies were marked with them. You have one, don't you?"

The drink slipped out of her grasp and clunked on the wooden table, drenching her shorts and legs with ice and vodka.

She pushed back from the table and swiped at the spill much harder than necessary. "Screw you."

He instantly grabbed a napkin and started swabbing her soaked thighs. His hand was hot on her leg and she jumped back, standing up.

He looked up at her. "I'm gonna take that as a yes on the tattoo."

"Then you'd be mistaken." She whipped the napkin from his hand, despising the crack in her voice. Crack? That was a bona fide sob. "I hate this. I hate that you're making me . . ." *Feel.* She flicked the napkin at the picture, a clinical looking thing showing a close-up of a woman's head, her long hair pulled away to show a tiny dark mark. "Oh my God." She leaned down closer, pushing her glasses up her nose. "Does that say 'hi'?"

"Miranda thinks it might be the numbers one and four. Which upside down look like hi." He straightened the picture. "So did you say you don't have a mark like this?"

"No, I don't." Not since her laser tattoo removal. "And I'm glad. I don't want any connection to a killer."

"I understand that. However . . ." He sat back in his chair. "Some people believe her trial might have been unfair, and that she's serving time for a crime she didn't commit."

Not a chance. "I read enough about it to know she didn't take the witness stand, she had the gun in her possession, and she was jealous of the woman she shot. Pretty incriminating stuff."

He shrugged a shoulder. "Two sides to every story. So, do you have the tattoo?"

"No." Damn him. Damn that evil woman. Damn this whole situation.

"Are you certain?" he asked. "It's kind of a hard place to see yourself."

"I'm certain." Certain she had a faint red scar that

he could see in this sunshine. Certain the scar didn't look anything like the design in the picture. And definitely certain that she just couldn't handle this right now.

She wanted to find Clive, get back to the familiarity of New York and the cool, controlled comfort of her office at Razor Partners. Maybe then, in the vault of protection she'd built around herself since her mother flew the coop and her father was killed, maybe she could figure out what to do. But not here, beaten down by a blistering sun and an equally blistering man on his own mission, with his own agenda, and his own pictures.

Vodka dribbled down her thigh like a tear.

"Could you excuse me?" she said, as calmly as she would to an enemy attorney in the middle of a merger negotiation when she needed to change the direction from give to take. "I'd like to go wash this off."

"Certainly. I'll order you another."

"Thanks," she said, grabbing the shoulder strap of her bag.

He stood, gesturing toward the back of the restaurant. "I'll wait for you."

He didn't sit as she walked away. A Southern gentleman. Great looking, polite as hell, and carrying a wallet full of news she didn't want.

She rounded the bar and gave a questioning look to the bartender. "Ladies room?"

He pointed his thumb to a hallway that led into the building behind the bar. It was much cooler in the dimly lit passageway. As she reached for the doorknob a clammy hand seized her upper arm and made her spin with a gasp.

She half expected to see crystal blue eyes, but the ones she met were dark, bloodshot, and sunken inside the face of a thin, Hispanic young man.

"What do you want?" she asked, wrenching from his weak grip.

"For you." He stuffed a piece of paper, folded into a square, in her palm. "From a friend of Clive's."

He disappeared out into the sunlight, leaving the scent of pot in his wake.

Her heart stuttering, she turned over the note. A friend of Clive's?

She shouldered the door open into a dingy bathroom with a yellowed toilet and a cheap vanity, lit only by sunlight filtering through a window over the sink. As soon as she locked the door, she unfolded the note.

The man you want is in Nevis.

Nevis? Clive was in Nevis? That was what, just seven miles away? A bunch of the passengers on board the cruise were taking a ferry from St. Kitts to that island today.

Who had sent her this message?

And more important, should she act on it? Did she have time to go to another island and get back before the ship set sail?

Who cared? She couldn't give a rat's ass about the cruise. She not only wanted to find Clive, now she *needed* to. He'd jump all over this; he was great at stuff like this. When he took his Zoloft, anyway.

Once she found Clive, she could get him out of whatever life crisis or love affair he was caught in, and then he'd help her. He'd know whether she should take this new, twisted road in her life.

Her brain raced, planning the steps.

She could run back to the ship, grab just one bag, and go to Nevis. After she found Clive she could have her stuff sent back to New York, or, if it was in a day or two, they could catch up to wherever the ship was docked.

Oh, yeah. This was totally doable. Nevis was a small island, and the gay community was tight-knit everywhere. She'd find him in no time.

She fingered the note. *The man you want is in Nevis.*

Two cryptic messages in one day. This and *watch ur back.*

Which should she believe? The one from Clive's cell phone or the one that came from out of nowhere? And what about the complete stranger sitting fifty feet away who delivered the worst message of all?

If she spent too much time with Wade Cordell, he'd wear her down with those insanely blue eyes and those masculine hands and all that Southern comfort. Slow and gentlemanlike, he'd polish her down until she said *yes.*

Because, in her heart, isn't that what she wanted?

No. *No.* She owed far more to Clive than to Eileen Stafford.

She eyed the dingy countertop around the sink. Kneeling on it, she pushed the window higher, checking out the alley through the sizeable opening. One quick hop and she'd be gone. Wade would probably wait another ten minutes before looking for her, and she'd be on her way to the ship before he figured it out.

Flipping her bag over her shoulder, she climbed through the opening, dropped to the ground, and ran all the way to Port Zante without stopping.